Nameless

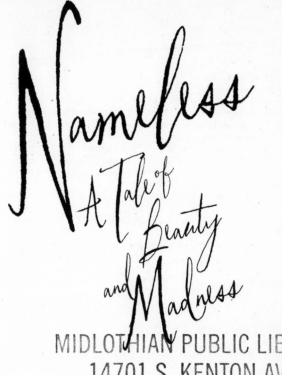

Nameless
A Tale of Beauty and Madness

LILI ST. CROW

razor
bill

An Imprint of Penguin Group (USA) Inc.

Nameless: A Tale of Beauty and Madness

RAZORBILL

Published by the Penguin Group
Penguin Young Readers Group
345 Hudson Street, New York, New York 10014, U.S.A.
Penguin Group (USA) Inc., 375 Hudson Street, New York, New York 10014, U.S.A.
Penguin Group (Canada), 90 Eglinton Avenue East, Suite 700, Toronto, Ontario, Canada M4P
2Y3 (a division of Pearson Penguin Canada Inc.)
Penguin Books Ltd, 80 Strand, London WC2R 0RL, England
Penguin Ireland, 25 St Stephen's Green, Dublin 2, Ireland (a division of Penguin Books Ltd)
Penguin Group (Australia), 250 Camberwell Road, Camberwell, Victoria 3124, Australia (a
division of Pearson Australia Group Pty Ltd)
Penguin Books India Pvt Ltd, 11 Community Centre, Panchsheel Park, New Delhi – 110
017, India
Penguin Group (NZ), 67 Apollo Drive, Rosedale, Auckland 0632, New Zealand (a division of
Pearson New Zealand Ltd)
Penguin Books (South Africa) (Pty) Ltd, 24 Sturdee Avenue, Rosebank, Johannesburg 2196,
South Africa

Penguin Books Ltd, Registered Offices: 80 Strand, London WC2R 0RL, England

10 9 8 7 6 5 4 3 2 1

Copyright © 2013 Lili St. Crow

ISBN 978-1-59514-357-0

Library of Congress Cataloging-in-Publication Data is available

Printed in the United States of America

For all of us.

OF ALL THE CARS IN NEW HAVEN TO FALL BEFORE, *I chose Enrico Vultusino's long black limousine.*

The Dead Harvest had been dry for once, but Mithrus Eve had brought a cargo of snow, a white Mithrusmas for New Haven after all. There was the alley, close and dark and foul. The reason that I ran, I know, was a rat with a loathsome plated tail and beady little eyes. For years I remembered nothing before the rat, which was probably a mercy.

Fierce fiery cold, and the car's tires squeaking as they crushed the swiftly-thickening carpet of white. The headlamps made everything a blare of blank cold brilliance, like the light dying people are supposed to see at the end of a stone tunnel. The brakes were grabby that night—I've been told the story so many times I can repeat it almost word for word.

If you don't mind waiting while my tongue stumbles over it, I guess.

Chauncey was driving Papa Vultusino home from the

traditional Seven and Elders meeting, watching the snow clot the wipers on the bulletproof windshield, thinking of nothing more than staying on the road and getting everyone home safe. He saw a flicker; the instinct of two decades of driving in New Haven rose under his skin and he jammed on the brakes, hoping the tire treads were deep and the snow thin enough to give him some traction. The limo slewed sideways and the small shape toppled, lay curled in a ball under an awkward slice of headlamp glow.

There was a splash—Vultusino had dropped a glass of whiskey and calf. Thankfully, it hadn't broken. "Chauncey?" His voice floated from the backseat through the open pane of more bulletproof glass, down because Chauncey liked the smell of Papa's cigars.

Chauncey blinked, restrained the urge to rub his eyes like a waking dreamer. "There's a kid in the road. Not smoking, so it's not a faust. Doesn't look like a Twist either."

Another sound—a click. Trigger Vane, sitting next to his employer, had pulled a nine-millimeter Stryker from its holster. His other hand touched the hilt of a wood-bladed dagger—good against fausts and some Twists, but not against minotaurs.

Nothing but running is good against minotaurs. And even that may not work.

Taut and ready, Trig's chin tilted up. "Sir?"

Papa's salt-and-pepper mane nodded. "Take a look."

So it was Trigger, his lean lanky frame in a violently plaid, orange-yellow sportcoat and baggy chinos, the gun in his hand, who bore down on me, each step squeak-crunching in the snow. He glanced around—it wasn't unheard of for an ambush to happen, even on such a hallowed day as this—but saw nothing. He stood for a few moments, gazing down on a child, her hair a messy tangle of deep blackness.

She appeared fully human. So thin bones were working out of her pallid skin, and she shivered like a trapped rabbit. Bright red striped her trembling legs, wasted muscles twitching as if she thought she was still running.

Around him, the town remained Mithrus Eve silent, snow whirling down. This was the industrial section, slumping buildings full of heavy machinery and poverty, slaughterhouses, Twisthouses, and desperation. A train newly arrived from the Waste chugged in the distance, its lonely whistle struggling through the deadness of falling flakes.

And somewhere, there were dogs, muffled as they bayed with frantic excitement.

It was the child's bare feet, filthy and bleeding, that convinced Trigger this was no decoy, no ambush. Not many would attack the Family, and their internecine rivalries were not redhot-smoking as they had been in some other years. All was calm, the Seven were in accord, and New Haven was tranquil enough.

He stood, stolid, for what seemed a long time. Thinking quickly wasn't Trig's strong suit unless there were bullets involved, or violence. He preferred to chew anything else over thoroughly before he made up his mind.

The child wore a thin faded-white cotton dress far too small for her; her legs were covered with welts and burns, fresh slices welling with hot blood. She was so bruised and thin, he often remarked, that he wondered if she'd just dropped dead in the road. But her breath made a small frosty cloud over her face. Panting lightly, and likely to be dead of cold or shock before long.

He paced back to the car. "It's human," he murmured through the back window, dropping the words into Papa Vultusino's waiting silence. "Barefoot. Beat up pretty bad." He paused. "A little girl."

Papa blinked. What he was thinking in that moment nobody has ever ventured to explain or guess. "Bring." His accent, the ghost of another language that haunts Family wherever they settle, thickened the word.

So Trigger returned to the little girl in the snow. He bent to pick her up, and she nestled limp in his arms. He carried her to the limousine and managed to fold himself up inside the warmth of the car. His large capable hands could have held the girl still if she'd struggled, but she didn't.

They might have taken me to the hospital immediately; a police report could have been filed. But none of them liked the police, though the Seven owned the law in New Haven. The Family remembers other countries where the police were the enemy; they don't ever forget an enemy.

That's one thing "Family" means.

Papa Vultusino examined the shivering little girl, who stared wildly, blank-faced and trembling. Eyes as blue as her hair was black, and her skin so cold and oddly translucent, as if she had never seen the sun. The wounds on her legs were vicious, some of them still seeping thin crimson and others oozing.

Even that trace of red was dangerous. Another of the Family might have wanted it, fresh and hot even if its vessel was weak and perhaps infected.

But Enrico Vultusino did not Borrow from children. Not like some of the Stregare, whose favorite vessels are those smallest and most fragile. No, he was the Vultusino, the head of a proud Family, and weak prey did not interest him.

Or perhaps it was something else, moving through his old, canny, labyrinthine brain.

Finally, Papa stirred. "What's your name, little girl?"

I remember leather and spilled liquor and copper, whiskey-calf if the story is told correctly. For almost as long as I can remember that has been the aroma of safety for me. That, and Papa's bay-rum aftershave, as he peered at me through his wire-rim reading glasses. "Little girl, piccola, what is your name?"

I began to cry. Why isn't exactly clear to me, unless it was the stinging of heat in my hands and feet and the throb of cuts and welts returning to shivering life. Big tears splashed on my refuse-caked dress, but I made no sound. I had learned to cry quietly, wherever I'd been, and years later someone told me that Papa Vultusino's mortal wife had wept like that before she died, tears and silence and nothing else.

"Pour her a drink?" Trigger suggested. It was not sarcasm— he simply didn't know what else to do. A jolt of liquor to fix shock was the best idea he could come up with.

Papa made a small snorting sound. He withdrew inside himself, his stillness becoming a living thing in the limo's interior.

Trigger waited. The little girl smelled of rubbish and abuse, but underneath, Trig once said, there was a heavy spice. Like incense, clove-caramel smoke, a drugging aroma.

He did not recognize it until much later.

"Stevens." The name was also softly accented, and Papa's mouth moved slightly. His consigliere would be standing, stiff and tall, in the house on Haven Hill's quiet dimness, hearing the Vultusino's voice. "Meet me at Harborview. We'll be there soon."

Chauncey, however, waited until Papa returned fully to himself. He knew better than to anticipate.

Papa lapsed into silence, staring at the girl shivering on Trigger's lap. The snow came down in thumb-sized flakes, spinning lazily in thick curtains. The dogs bayed and yapped, their voices muffled but still urgent, knifing the blanket of soft white.

He finally spoke again, the tone of a man accustomed to command. "What's your name, bambina? Where do you live? Where is your momma, your papa?"

The little girl shook her head. When she tried to speak, she only made a small sound, like a bird caught in a net. And the tears welling in her blue eyes kept splashing onto her dress, dewing the thin material. Her knees were knobs, crusted with scabs. Some of the marks were cigarette burns, raw and ugly.

Outside the window, snow fell over the empty warehouses. This was not a part of town for children. Now that it was dusk the smoking, demon-infested fausts and Twisted hulks of minotaurs would be creeping forth to hunt. The regular Twists, too—those of them who lived by violence, anyway. There might even be Family hunting tonight, those who preferred their Borrowing hot and from a struggling victim.

The little girl raised a trembling, tiny hand as she flinched to ward off an invisible blow—even her fingers were bruised—and Papa saw something else. Trigger saw it too, and hissed out through his teeth.

Familiar deep marks on the child's wrists, red and weeping. Handcuffs.

The train sounded its long lonely whistle again, perhaps in relief at having crossed the Waste safely, and the girl shivered, blanching. The dogs' full-throated cries faded in the distance.

They had found other prey, perhaps. A minotaur—but who would be so foolish as to hunt one of those after dark?

"How old are you, bambina? Do you know?" Papa's tone was carefully, softly kind, and her shivering eased a little.

Gravely, the child held up one hand, wincing as if it hurt. She spread her fingers wide, concentrating, her face a mask of effort. Then she lifted the other hand, one finger up.

"Six years old. Well, bambina, we will take care of you." Papa nodded. "Chauncey?"

"Yessir?"

"Turn around; take us to Harborview." Papa turned inward again, into whatever dark thoughts occupied the freshly voted leader of the Seven. "Stevens will let Evelyn know."

"Yessir." Chauncey knew better than to think his wife would take offense. It was Mithrus Eve—but working for Papa meant that no day was safe from a favor called in, or a sudden emergency. The little girl lay in Trigger's lap, something hard digging into her side—the butt of the wooden dagger, smooth and dark. If it was uncomfortable to have a filthy, wet child shivering on him, Trigger's lined gaunt face gave no indication.

Enrico Vultusino, a fresh whiskey and calf in hand, watched the child as she fell into a light sleep, or shock. Eventually he moved as Chauncey turned the car up Harbor Hill. He set the drink carefully in a holder, and freed a few buttons. His suit jacket rustled as he leaned forward and tucked it around the girl, so she lay wrapped in cologne and expensive tailoring.

There was no human child reported missing in the wilderness of New Haven that night. While I lay in a private hospital room, fed by tubes and monitored by beeping machines and crackling watch-charms, under a steady glow of healcharming, Trigger stood guard in a chair by my bedside. Stevens and Papa conferred in low tones. Once it became apparent I was feral, things became easier. A human magistrate was rousted, papers signed, and I'm sure money changed hands, as it always does in New Haven. By the time the sun rose, I was legally if not the property then at least under the protection of Enrico Vultusino, who left early that morning with Stevens and Chauncey. Trigger Vane stayed, and when I was brought to the house on the hill two weeks later, it was Trig who rode beside me in the big black car, staring out the window. I still had not spoken.

Whatever had happened to me before the alley I could not or would not remember, and I seemed to have forgotten how to talk— if I had ever learned. A hired psychologist came while I was in the hospital, a human woman with long blonde hair—and I cowered away from her into the bed, making a small whimpering sound.

I never saw her again.

The snow lasted two months, shrouding New Haven in white and making traffic difficult. But the snowplows and the drags ran night and day, and by the time winter raised its icy back higher and New Haven crouched submissive under its grip, I was safely in the house on the Hill, settled into my new life.

Papa named me Camille. It was his dead mortal wife's name. And so I was rescued from the snow, on Mithrus Eve, by the man they called "the Vulture," one of the living Seven of the Families.

PART I: A Princess

ONE

ST. JUNO'S WIDE GRANITE STEPS COULD CRACK YOUR head like an egg. Which was maybe why Cami always slowed down, dragging her glossy black maryjanes over the white and black linoleum squares, when they hit the wide, high-ceilinged main hall, minnows in a sea of girls set free for the afternoon.

And it was definitely why Ruby always sped up, tugging Cami's arm, her candygloss lips going a mile a minute. Ellie ambled alongside, always gliding at the same clip. Lockers slammed, and the surf-roar of girlchatter was a comforting blur punctuated by squeals, catcalls, laughter, and groans.

In the middle, Ruby's running narration, a bright thread as she batted her eyelashes, heavily mascara'd in defiance of both St. Juno's archaic rules and her grandmother's iron old-fashionedness. But everyone forgave her. "And so I thought, oh my *God*, if you're going to do this you might as well do it right, and of course Hunt was there—"

You just *had* to forgive Ruby. She would cock her head and smile at you, the grin that lit up the world, and that was that. Cami's long heavy braid swung; she tugged at her skirt with her free hand, getting it to fall right, and juggled her notebook. There were never enough hands for what you needed to get done at the end of a school day.

"Hunt's always there," Ellie threw in, tucking a bit of sleek blonde hair behind her ear. "And of course Thorne didn't like it. You'd think they were best friends or something."

Ruby tossed her auburn curls, tugging at Cami's arm. "Who's telling this story? Anyway. Come on, we're going to be late."

For what? But Cami grinned. Ruby was on her own clock, and it was at variance with the rest of the world more often than not.

She finished wedging her notebook safely into her bag and got the strap settled. As long as Ruby was on one side and Ellie on the other, she didn't have to think about where she was going, and she didn't have to talk. They would take care of it for her.

What else were friends for?

The hall was awash with white blouses, rounded turndown collars, the traditional ugly Juno blazers with their itchy blue wool and embroidered crests, the blue and green tartan skirts swinging. This autumn the white wool socks were all the way up to the knee, and little silver luckcharms were attached to maryjane buckles, chiming sometimes. They didn't work inside, but you still had to wear them if you wanted to be *in*. Head-bands were *in*, too—the thin ones, you could only find them in certain stores. Ruby, of course, knew exactly where. And Cami would make sure to buy far too many, and Ellie would later find them in her bag and might as well wear them because well, they were there, right?

That was the way the cookie crumbled, so to speak. The way it always had, the way it always would. Or if not always, then as long as the three of them lasted.

"*So.*" Ruby found her stride again. The doors were choked, as usual, but their last class of the day was High Charm Calculus, math and charm working together, and Ruby had declared that if she *had* to stay inside *one more minute* she would *die*. So instead of their usual stop at their lockers near the main stairwell to preen, they were heading for the front door when everyone else was, even the bobs and the ghoulgirls. "Hunt says, 'I was here first' and Thorne says, 'It's a free country' and I say, 'You two are *soooo* immature,' and I ended up leaving with a guy from Berch Prep—"

"Who had sweaty hands," Ellie mock-whispered. "They *all* do."

"*And* a hip flask!" Ruby crowed triumphantly. "I

didn't get slammed, though. You'd be proud of me, Miss Stick-In-The-Mud."

"Oh, she *only* got a little bit hazy." Ellie's eyeroll was a wonder of nature. "Why aren't we skipping to get a charm to keep you from spawning?"

"Because, and this is what I'm trying to *tell* you, prepboy lost his starch."

Breathless silence. Then Ellie and Cami both exploded into bright bird-laughter, and Ruby grinned, white teeth behind crimson-glossed lips.

"Get *out!*" Ellie crowed, and manhandled the door open. They tumbled out into rich golden fall sunshine, the sudden slice of a crisp breeze against bare knees, lifting Ellie's sleek blonde hair and wringing hot water from Cami's furiously-blinking eyes.

"*Seriously!*" Rube had the bit in her teeth now. Cami checked the stairs.

They were still there. Still granite, still with sharp edges, and still too steep.

St. Juno's was a pure-human charmschool; it only took in girls with rich families and unTwisted Potential. The Family sent all their daughters to Martinfield, but Cami wasn't pure-blood. So it was St. Juno's for her, along with the young girls of New Haven's aristocracy of money, magic, and social standing.

The stairs were . . . troubling. Sometimes she thought the

hedge of defenses that kept anything non-human or Twisted out of the buildings would smell the Family on her and rise, veils of flickering Potential ready to rip her into bits. And then there were the dreams, of stairs and a tall draped figure shimmering-pale.

Don't think about that. The dreams didn't belong in the day-light, so she just shivered. They left quietly, this time. "N-no w-way!" she managed, very carefully.

"*Way!*" Ruby almost wriggled with delight. "So things are looking good, right? Things are looking flat out *great* in the front seat of the Cimarro—did I tell you? He had a Cimarro, positively *antique*, cherry too."

Considering Cimarros had been popular when Papa was a boy—there was a yellow one in the capacious Vultusino garage, lovingly tended by Chauncey—it gave new meaning to the word "antique."

The first few steps went by in a rush, and Cami let out a half-whistle of relief. Ruby knew she hated the stairs, but she was always of the opinion that if you hated something, you just had to run right through it. Ellie was more of the sneak-up-and-hit-it-with-a-shovel persuasion.

Cami didn't want to take the time to stammer through an explanation of her own philosophy, which was more "live to fight another day" than Charge of the Twist Brigade. But that was a Personal Choice, and her Personal Choices not to speak were okay, or so the speech therapist she'd seen for four years—before the woman's Potential Twisted—had said. *Your choice to speak or not is your own. Let's try it very slowly, if you feel like it.*

Cami had liked Miss Amanda. But once the Twisting had struck, there was no way Papa would let her go back. The risk of the Twist spreading was just too high, and plus, Twists sometimes . . . snapped. Miss Amanda's hands had trembled, the bones sprouting claw-spurs through the skin, her Potential eaten up either by an anger she had never given voice to or just plain ill-luck, or maybe a bad charming. She'd had just enough Potential to qualify as a charmer, not good as a Sigiled or anything but able to heat a kettle of water to boiling with a snapped word or two, or make colored light dance in the air to form letter-shapes her struggling students could read. When the proper sound was made, the letters would glow and change to other shapes.

It was dangerous to have a lot of Potential, but it was less likely to Twist you than just a little was. Still, Cami'd gotten more from four years of weekly meetings with Miss Amanda than she had from plenty of other teachers.

But that was in the past, and the past was never helpful. So she just nodded as Ruby plunged into the story again and dragged them all down the steps, her hair a bright copper flame.

They arrived at the bottom breathless, in a wider crush of girls waiting for buses and cars crowding the curb. This year bigger utility vehicles from overseas and overWaste were popular, hunkering on shiny black tires with charm-spinning, gleaming hubcaps, the glass darkened and crawling with Potential. Watchwards, defense-charms, charms to keep dust and rain from smearing the glass—pickup time at St. Juno's was like an exercise in conspicuous charm-viewing.

"And so Berch Prep Boy says, 'I don't think I'm gonna make it,'" Ruby confided. "And *sploosh*, there it goes. All over the seat." The giggles were shaking all three of them now, and hard. Cami's midriff ached.

Fortunately, laughing didn't stutter.

Ruby jolted to a halt between one word and the next. "Hel-*lo*. Cami, sweetheart, why didn't you tell me?"

"T-T-Tell you wha—" But as soon as she followed the line of Ruby's glance, she figured it out.

The sleek black '70 Ivrielle—another antique, though not as old as a Cimarro—crouched, in lazy defiance of the yellow Bus Zone paint. And leaning against its front was a tall, rangy young man with slicked dark hair and the indefinable stamp of *other* on him all the Family displayed. Their cheekbones were arched oddly, their eyes spaced just a fraction differently, the line of the jaw too sharp and the musculature visible in shoulders or arms or legs, even the girls', was . . . unusual.

"*Nico!*" Cami shrieked, and the fact that she didn't stutter over his name was lost in the wave of muttering schoolgirl envy. Ellie caught Cami's dropped schoolbag, Ruby rolled her eyes, but Cami pounded across the pavement and flung herself into Nico's arms.

"Mithrus *Christ*," he managed, "watch it! Break my ribs, kid!"

"You d–d–didn't—"

"Tell you I was coming." He smelled of fresh air, a faint breath of cigarette smoke, and bay rum—Papa Vultusino's aftershave. Though Nico would probably just get That Look if she tried asking him about it. "Wanted to surprise you. Hey, Rube. Ellen."

"Vultusino." Ruby showed her teeth. "Look at you, parking in the fire lane."

"It's bus parking, not fire lane. Gonna give me a ticket? Cite me for being Family on school grounds, too?" His smile didn't change, and Cami hugged him tighter, reading the tension in his shoulders. *Not now,* she told him silently. *She's my friend.*

"You wish. Guess we know who's driving her home today." Ruby's baring of teeth was more of a smile now, Potential-haze like heat over pavement crackling on her shoulders. Her Potential was vivid, not soft like Ellie's or invisible, like Cami's. "Come on, Ellie. Buzz you later, Cami."

She let go of Nico once she was sure he wasn't going to say anything else. "Y-yeah. B–b–babchat."

"But of *course,* my dear." Ruby pecked her on the cheek. "Still have to tell you how the night turned out," she whispered, a hot wash of Juicy Charm gum from her teeth and chocolate-salt smell from her skin.

Cami choked on a laugh, and Ellie handed her schoolbag over. "Babchat," she said, softly. "Nine-thirty? High Calc's gonna kill me." Gray eyes wide, her blonde hair pulled sleekly back, the faint dusting of freckles on Ellie's nose turned gold in the light. This close you could see her collar fraying, and the shiny patches worn into her blazer.

I'm going to have to do something about that. But the words wouldn't come.

So Cami just nodded, and her two best friends in the world other than Nico linked arms and were away. Ruby would drive Ellie home, stopping at the gate and making the usual cheerfully obscene gesture safely behind the smoked glass of the windshield so Ellie's nasty-tempered stepmother didn't see her, and later when the Evil Strepmother was occupied, Ellie would use her Babbage-net connection—St. Juno's required one and logged student times, and the principal Mother Heloise knew some about the Strep so the Strep couldn't take the Babbage set away—to confer about the homework.

Cami hitched her bag higher on her shoulder and looked up at Nico.

He was just the same. A little taller, like he grew every time he went off to Hannibal College up-Province on the ribbon of safely-reclaimed highway, green and gray kolkhozes lurking on either side behind electrified fences.

His dark hair combed back, the moss-green eyes, the wide cheekbones. You could see Papa in him, just a little. He'd had time to change out of uniform too—Hannibal was a Family school, and it kept to old ways. So it was jeans and a black T-shirt, his heavy watch glittering silver, the old leather jacket with all its scrapes and wrinkles. "See something green, schweetheart?" He waggled his eyebrows, an oddly childish expression. "Get in. I've got places to be."

Still, she waited, watching his face. Watching the shadow of anger, dull rage that never completely receded. She dug one polished maryjane into the pavement, biting her lower lip, and didn't give up until he broke and grinned at her, his shoulders relaxing and the anger draining away until it was just a shadow.

"Jeez, you just never quit, do you? Come on. I hurried back to see you, babygirl." He opened the door for her, as usual, and Cami tried not to notice the envious glances. The girls dawdled, and the ones who knew whispered to the bobs—the new girls, still finding their way around St. Juno's hedge of restrictions—about it. The ghoulgirls, playing at being black charmers with teased-out hair and long dagger-shaped earrings, hissed and jabbed their fingers at him and his shiny black car, muttering to each other.

Nico Vultusino. He's supposed to be her brother, but he's one of those on the Hill. Shows up every once in a while to pick her up.

They didn't know anything. They *couldn't* know, and even if she could talk without her tongue twisting on her, Cami wouldn't tell them. Nico was *hers*, and he had been since the moment he stamped into the library years ago and announced he hated her and would never like her, because she wasn't pure-blood like him.

He dropped into the driver's seat. "I'm not gonna do this when you get to college, you know." Twisted the key savagely, and music blared—Gothika's driving beat, Shelley Wynter singing over the top of it about a minotaur in snow and the bass line popping like a runner's pulse. He grimaced, spun the volume down, and tossed a battered pack of Gitanelles into her lap. "Light me up."

"C-College. Long time away." If she spoke slowly, she didn't stutter too much with Nico. He was patient, though.

He *listened*.

"Not so long," he said, as he popped the parking brake and she tapped a Gitanelle out, pushing the cigarette lighter in. "You're growing up fast, babygirl. Want to have some fun?"

She didn't think she could speak, so she just nodded, and lit the first of what would probably be a *lot* of cigarettes. She stuck it in his mouth as he turned the wheel, the tires chirped, and Nico spun them away from St. Juno's like he was playing a roulette wheel.

TWO

"RACK 'EM, KID." NICO DRAGGED ON HIS GITANELLE. Smoke wreathed his head as if he was a perpetual-burning scarecrow; but a faust wouldn't be out during the day. Besides, fausts and Family made each other very nervous. It used to be Family sport to hunt them, back in the days before the Reeve.

It probably still was, in some places.

Cami leaned over the table, made sure the rack was tight, and lifted the triangle off with a ceremonial flourish. The pool balls gleamed, each one a different jewel against worn green felt. Her job done, she retreated to the booth and dropped down and took a sip of expensive imported-through-the-Waste Coke. The only way through the Waste was sealed in a train; the iron in the tracks kept the blight, the random Twisting, and the nasty creatures that lived outside the order of the cities and kolkhozes mostly at bay. The collective farms were full of jacks and Twists, but someone had to grow the food, right? And you couldn't farm the Waste without reclamation to drain off the blight and channel the wild magic into systematic forms.

Thinking about the Waste was always bad, too. Cami heaved a sigh, returned to the essay she was supposed to be outlining.

Lou's was full—but then, it almost always was. A long low pool hall, the bar at the front a reef in a sea of cigarette smoke, its mirror a giant cloudy eye behind racks of bottles. The tables marched in orderly ranks, just enough space around them for the players. Older men with open collars and cigars, young whip-thin hungry men working on their shots, the cracks of good clean breaks and the serious murmur as money changed hands all familiar and soothing. Green glass shades hung from long cords, the electric bulbs over some tables blinking a little as the dampers wedded to the shades suppressed Potential. Not the free-floating stuff the entire world was soaking in, but the kind that would tell a ball to roll a certain way, or whisper some English-spin onto it.

Lou's was straight gaming. Anyone caught charming, consciously or not, was thrown out. Cami had only seen that once or twice, and the thought still made her a little sick. All the yelling, and the blood.

You had to be careful with blood in a Family place.

The booths were empty. Nobody really sat there, but Cami had a favorite one near Nico's usual table; it was kept dusted and ready. Whenever he was home from Hannibal, Nico played here, and Lou never made a peep about little sis bending over her homework while Vultusino's son ran games. At least Nico didn't play for money.

Well, not often.

And he didn't tell Cami not to tell when he did, but he would often give her that considering look. Just one more secret for them to share.

My little consigliere, he used to call her, back when he was twelve. Not anymore, but she didn't miss it. That was one job she could do without.

Cami tapped her pencil against her teeth. She should be at home typing this stupid essay, or even working on French or practicing the short list of safe charms to be mastered this year. Instead it was this stupid essay about the First Industrial Expansion, 1750–1850, machines and factories replacing cottage industry and cities turning into sooty hellholes.

Not like they were much different nowadays, but at least they were safer than the Waste. The Waste used to be just empty land, or small farms—*country* was the term they'd used back in the day.

Cami shifted again, uncomfortably. History was boring as *shit*.

Who cared about the Industrial Expansions *now*, for God's sake? Especially after the Reeve (for *maaaaaaa*-gic *Reeeeeee*-volution, Ruby would say, rolling her eyes). Post-Reeve studies weren't until next year, along with serious charmwork and the settling of Potential.

Even the Reeve wasn't that interesting. It was just *there*, like fausts and Family and minotaurs, charms and griffs, and all those other things that had been hiding during the short Age of Iron.

They had been hiding only to burst out when the World War ended, 1918, the last Year of Blood. Something about the War—the blood, the trenches, the masses of death—shook everything loose, and when it all settled in 1920, the Reeve had exploded and everything was different. The Deprescence had hit, and the ones that didn't die as the country turned to Waste ended up Twisted, the first jacks—Potential-mutated babies, horns and feathers and fur—were born, and even being rich wouldn't save you from starving to death. Or worse, being eaten by something nasty.

The Family didn't talk much about the Reeve or the Desprescence.

Population movement from rural to urban, she wrote, and circled it as Nico muttered something and the rack was cracked. His opponent, a weedy man in a shiny blue jacket with a tooth-brush-thin fair moustache clinging to his thin upper lip, lit a cigarette. A puff of harsh smoke, not silky like the Gitanelles—he was smoking cheap, and Cami suspected the guy was new and thought Nico was a pigeon.

Oh well. He'll find out. She hunched further down, pencil

scraping. *Effects on rural society. One, wages down. Two, breaking of social bonds. Three, the encroachment of the Waste and the Wild.*

Ruby was great at bullshit essays. She was good at bullshit in general, but she had a special *genius* for packing an assignment full of enough vocab to dizzy one of Juno's Mithraic Sister teachers. She joked that it was her Potential, as if the teachers weren't full-settled, their own Potential respectable and staid, and immune to schoolgirl pranks.

Cami sighed, scratched at an itch on the side of her neck. She'd undone her braid, her hair fell over her shoulder. True black, deep black, sometimes with blue highlights under strong light. She didn't look like Nico; the darkness in his hair was underlaid with red. She didn't look like *anyone*, really.

Some days she didn't mind. Today was one of them.

Her neck still itched, and she glanced up to find the guy with the toothbrush moustache looking at her.

She dropped her gaze, hurriedly.

"Pay attention to the game." Nico sounded pleasant enough. Nobody else, maybe, would hear the danger in his tone.

"Ain't she a bit young to be in here?" Moustache Man had a surprisingly deep, harsh voice for such a skinny guy. Cami restrained the urge to roll her eyes. The door thudded open and everyone paused, but it was just a man in a long tan overcoat headed for the bar. He slumped a little, shuffling as if he was tired. He couldn't be visibly drunk, smoked, or Twisted, though, or Lou would send him right out.

"You gonna check her ID?" Nico's laugh now *definitely* had an edge. He stalked around the side of the table, sighted, and sent the yellow and the red careening into separate holes with one shattering crack. "What are you, a cop?"

Oh, no. Cami very carefully kept her head down, as if she was studying intently. But her pencil had halted, and she had both of them in her peripheral vision.

Moustache Man laughed. "Hell no. Just wondering."

"That's my girl." Nico sighted again, and sent the solid green thudding home. "Don't wonder."

My girl. A warm flush went through her. Nobody else would know what he meant by that, they could take it or leave it. Just like pretty much everything he said.

They settled into serious playing, and Cami relaxed a little. Maybe she could just put the damn thing down for a bit; it wasn't due until next week. It wasn't like she was going to *fail*, even if her Potential was invisible. Especially not with Papa making donations to St. Juno's like he did. Still, she worried.

Having anything half-done nagged at her. She chewed at her lower lip while she scribbled, grateful that her fingers, at least, didn't stutter.

"Hey." Nico leaned over her, setting down his empty, red-streaked glass and reaching for a fresh ashtray. "Get me another one, huh?"

Not a good idea. "Y-y-you're—"

"Driving. Yeah." He nodded, a vertical line between his dark eyebrows. "Don't *worry*. Get me another one."

Fine. But if you get pulled over it's not going to be pleasant. "K-kay." Her stupid mouth wouldn't work right. She blinked, the smoke suddenly stinging, and Nico squeezed her shoulder before turning away.

He scooped up his cue and settled the cut-glass ashtray; he gave Moustache Man a brilliant smile, his eyes lightening a shade or two. "Ready to play for real?"

Uh-oh. Nico was about to fleece him. Great. Cami sighed and hauled herself up, brushing at her skirt. The vinyl, even though it was washed and dusted, was still sticky, and she probably had red marks on the backs of her thighs. They would match all the other scars, and make some of the ones on the backs of her legs more vivid. The knee-high socks in fashion this year helped, not that many people said anything about her legs. She wore long sleeves as much as possible, and the uniform made people's eyes slide right over her.

Mostly.

The floor was tacky-sticky too, and she kept her head down as she passed, acutely aware of the looks. The regulars knew, yeah—but sometimes there were guys who didn't. She wished she hadn't taken her blazer off; the scars on her arms and wrists would show up if she got warm or blushy.

I wish he wouldn't come here. But Nico was in a mood, and she had to let him run for a bit before he'd tell her what was wrong. It was probably Papa, again.

Sooner or later, if you scratched Nico hard enough, you got down to Papa.

"Well hello, Cami." Lou, broad, bald, and mahogany-colored, ran a hand over his shaved, oiled dome of a head and grinned. Nicotine stained his teeth and his blunt fingers, and he was probably scary if you didn't know he had a huge gooshy soft spot under his big ribs. His Potential was like a brick wall, though, and it crackled and fizzed whenever the mood inside the pool hall got dangerous. "What'll it be?"

She managed a smile in return, setting the glass carefully on the bar's mellow polish. The guy in the overcoat down at the end hunched, a gleam from under the bill of his baseball cap oddly big for eyes. He looked like a hobo, kind of, the coat was ragged and torn, and she was glad she didn't have to stand closer. "O-one m-more. F-f-f-for N-n-n—" Frustration boiled up inside her. "*Nico*," she finished, finally, and peeked up to find Lou didn't look upset in the least.

He never did, but she couldn't shake the habit of checking.

"Sure thing. He should be careful; that kid he's playing has a nasty temper." Lou read her shrug accurately. "I know, so does Nico. Eh, well. Small-time sharks playing in a Family yard have it comin'. Here ya go, sweetness. Give me another one of those smiles?" His broad dark face split in a wide yellow grin that wasn't scary at all. At least, not once you got to know him. She ducked her head slightly, unable to stop grinning back. "There it is. Go on back and—"

"Little girl," someone rasped.

It was the man with the tan trench coat and the stained red baseball cap. He was gaunt, unshaven, and his dark hair was matted into grizzled dreadlocks. A pair of feverish dark gleams for eyes and a scar-stubbled jaw; his hand bit her upper arm, fingers clamping with surprising, scary strength. Cami flinched.

"I *know* you, little girl." He slurred as if his tongue was too big for his mouth. He inhaled sharply, his breath whistling.

She had time to be surprised that he didn't smell bad—he reeked, in fact, only of fresh lumber, sap and sawdust—before he leaned close to her face and yelled, the whiskey on his breath burning her nose. "*I know you! You were dead!*"

THREE

I⊤ HAPPENED SO *FAST*.

One moment Cami was trying to back up, her shoes scuffing the peeling blue-flecked linoleum, the man's skin hard-callused and fever-hot against her arm where the short-sleeved white button-down didn't cover. A cloud of whiskey fumed around his lean desperate face, and she realized the gleam over his eyes was a pair of small round lenses—sunglasses, even in the dimness of Lou's Pool. There was a wet resinous slickness on his cheeks too, and not only did he smell like sawdust, but he *looked* like he was made of wood—weathered skin carved with deep lines, a long nose, his hard thin lips pulled back from yellowed gleaming teeth.

Her heart gave a huge shattering leap. *What IS he? Please don't let him be a Twist—*

The next moment, Nico arrived, his fingers just as bruising-hard as he peeled the man's grasp from Cami's arm. A cracking groan, like wood splintering, and Nico's eyes were ablaze with a low red glow. His lips had skinned back and his canines came to sharp points, a pearly glitter as the whiskey and calf on the bar spilled, a drench of coppery red and alcohol.

The sound coming from Nico's chest was a deep thrumming. He twisted the wooden man's hand aside, and Cami hit the bar because he had shouldered her aside.

"You were *dead*!" the brown man screamed again. "*Dead dead dead! She ate the heart! She ate theeeeeee heaaaaaart!*"

Cami lost her footing, hitting a barstool and tumbling into a heap. Oddly, stupidly, her skirt flipping up and showing her unmentionables was the thing she worried about most as her knee scraped along the footrail on the bottom of the bar. She scooted crabwise, her hands burning as she scrabbled to get *away*. Glass rained down, shimmering, as Nico half-turned and threw the wooden man onto the bar. Empty glasses went flying, and Lou let out a yell that almost drowned the wooden man's high whistling scream. A lick of fire pierced Cami's palm, and the scream ended on a rending crack.

"Mithrus *Christ*!" Lou finished yelling. The baseball bat held high in his beefy paws didn't get a chance to flash down; brick-red sparks of Potential crackled defensively on his bare skin. Nico glanced at him, and the deep thrum from his chest faded bit by bit. The wooden man's head tipped aside, his sunglasses falling with a clatter, one lens cracked clear through. He blinked, slowly, and stared *through* her.

Cami's ribs heaved. She just sat there for a moment, clutching her left fist to her chest. Liquor dripped, broken glass glittered, and she figured out her skirt hadn't rucked up too far.

Well, thank God for that. Her throat was dry as summer pavement. She gathered herself enough to look down, her left hand opening, a red flower in its palm. *Oh, shit. Is it deep?*

"NGGGAAAAH!" The man on the bar thrashed into life again. Nico hauled him down, the tan trench coat flapping like a flag in a high wind, and was suddenly at the door. It opened, and he flung the man into the street outside.

At least he didn't toss the limp form dangling from his fists *through* the door. And at least he hadn't killed him.

That would be Very Bad, even if he was Family. Papa would—

"Oh, Christ," someone said, very low and clear. "She's bleeding."

Cami found her voice. "I-i-i-it's n-n-not—" *It's not bad,* she wanted to say, because Lou looked horrified. He was already backing up, his meaty hip hitting something behind the bar and another glass falling, crashing into splinters.

Nico whirled away from the door. There a breath against her face—bay rum, cigarettes, whiskey and calf—and he was kneeling in front of her, his gaze flat, dark, and terribly empty. The red glow had gone.

"Don't—" Lou swallowed whatever he'd intended to say when Nico Vultusino glanced up at him. Nico's canines were fully distended, and there was a ripple through the rest of the hall as every Family member tensed. They were daywalkers, true, and young ones, not yet burning with the Kiss of immortal undeath after years of service. But they were still Family.

Family meant Borrowing. And Borrowing meant *blood*.

Nico's gaze swung back down to Cami. She swallowed, hard, and cupped her left hand. Slowly, she extended her fingers toward him, uncurling her arm. Blood dripped, a tiny *plink* sound in the utter stillness. At least she hadn't smeared any on her shirt. Marya would scold her to no end if she had.

A river of shudders worked down Nico's body. His hand shot out, closed around her wrist. Another rustling ripple of tension, as the non-Family drew back, hardly even daring to breathe. Moustache Man was holding his pool cue up like it was some sort of weapon.

Cami licked her dry lips. Her own Potential was a barely-seen shimmer hanging an inch from her skin, like the air over scorching blacktop. Fear, or anger, or any high emotion could make it visible even before it settled. Everyone would see it, and know she was . . . afraid?

Not of him. She concentrated, fiercely, and hoped she could speak without mush for once. "S-s-sorry, N-Nico." *He won't bite me. He never has before, even when we were little.*

At least, *she* had been little. He hadn't. Even the few years' worth of age he had on her was different, because you matured early when you were Family.

And she wasn't.

He blinked. The shudders vanished. His canines retracted with a slight familiar crackling sound. He coughed, dryly, and looked up at Lou. "'Nother drink." Sandpaper in his tone. "And the first-aid kit. Mithrus, how'd that happen?"

I was trying to get out of your way. She shrugged. A silent sigh of relief filled the pool hall. If he was talking, he wasn't about to go crazy. Well, craz*ier*.

He straightened, slowly, bracing her, brushing her off. "You okay? Hurt anywhere other than this?" Trying to be gentle, but his hand shook just the slightest bit. Her blood dripped again, and he could smell it.

They all could. *Like sharks*, Nico said. *It only takes a little.*

Her ribs ached from where he'd careened into her, and her shoulder had somehow bonked something and would be bruised. She shook her head, half her hair falling in her face, strings of jet-black, not curly like Red's or sleek and behaving like Ellie's. Lou banged the first-aid kit on the bar—there was a dent in the wood's shiny polish.

A man-sized dent.

"Another drink, comin' up," Lou announced. "Billy, get your ass over here and help me clean this up. What the hell *was* that guy, anyway?"

In New Haven, you could ask that question, but you probably wouldn't get much of an answer. The man could have been a jack born with weird skin, or a fey fresh from the Waste where they had their own strange ways of traveling, or anything else. Who knew?

Life and motion returned. They went back to their games, the Family members unfazed and the others maybe a little rattled. Moustache Man was nowhere to be seen, and after Cami's hand was bandaged Nico found out the bastard had left with the cash sitting on the pool table. Gone while the getting was good.

Which meant Nico was pissed off pretty much all afternoon, even though he made it up in no time, skinning double from table to table.

Cami didn't blame him. He fussed at her constantly, too, and she wished he wouldn't. Because she kept thinking about the wooden man's eyes, staring through her.

His blue, blue eyes. Like hers.

FOUR

IT WAS DUSK BY THE TIME NICO SHOT THE IVRIELLE through the slowly opening iron gates, barely avoiding taking off his side mirror. The pavement, shiny black and freshly sealed every summer, rippling with almost-visible defenses, was a ribbon between torch-burning trees, their leaves on fire with fall. Cami stared at the bandage—so white, Nico had done a good job wrapping it up. Then he'd taken down three shots of whiskey and calf and played for money the remainder of the afternoon, getting more and more worked up.

He locked the brakes, skidding to a stop, and Cami heaved an internal sigh. There was Mr. Stevens on the front steps, a thin stick in a dusty black suit, his slicked-down gray hair glinting a little as the sunset died.

"Just in time." Nico kept the engine idling, his foot on the brake. "And look who's here to greet us. My, my."

Awkwardly, she grabbed at his shoulder with her bandaged

hand. He checked, caught in the act of reaching for the door handle. His profile, with its proud nose and sullen mouth, didn't change.

"Nico." It was a miracle, something came out right. "P-please."

"He's gonna have my ass for taking you out." His chin set. "I'll—"

"Yeah, you'll work on him. I know. It's okay."

It's not okay, the way you look is not okay. "He l-l-loves—"

"I'm *disappointing.* We've had this conversation. The ghoul's waiting, you'd better go on in."

Stevens can't be a ghoul. He's not even dead. She got the string of words together inside her head, let them out. "P-papa wants you t-to have a ch-childhood." Why couldn't he *understand*?

"I don't know if you noticed, babygirl, but I'm not a kid." He sighed, heavily, and some of the tension left him. "You go in. Have Marya take a look at that hand, too. I'll see you later."

"Nico—"

He cut her off. "Go *in*, Cami. I'll deal with Papa. It was my fault anyway."

Oh, for Chrissake. But there was no arguing with him when he was like this, so she shrugged, leaned over, and gave him a peck on the cheek—at least he looked happy with that—before she popped the lock and the car door.

Stevens looked a bit green—of course he would be worried,

it was dusk. The sun was actually touching the horizon, and of course Nico would feel it. He probably had judged their arrival time within seconds. Just to get close to that edge.

Stevens would feel it too, Papa's attention becoming heavier as the sun sank.

Her schoolbag slipped, and she hitched it higher on her shoulder. Nico carefully waited until she was clear before he gunned the engine and peeled toward the garages.

Cami sighed.

The steps were wide and low enough that they gave her little trouble, and this close you could see the surface of the front door shimmering a little, like the haze above hot pavement. "Hi, S-s-stevens." She dredged up a smile—one she hoped wasn't as tired as she felt.

"Good evening, Miss Camille." The sticklike consigliere bent at the waist, and his seamed face under its skullcap of oiled hair held no glimmer of expression.

Nico was just being nasty. Stevens wasn't like a ghoul; he was just . . . closed off. He was a blank door to everyone. Except probably Papa, who called Stevens the perfect well. You could drop secrets in and hear the ripple, but then they vanished.

I never want to find out. "Nico p-picked me up f-from sch-school," she offered tentatively, as he turned and preceded her to the massive doors. "W-we g-g-got—"

"Mr. Vultusino requested your presence." Stevens touched

the door, running his spidery fingers over it. The house's defensive haze shimmered, and the *chuk*ing sounds of locks and bolts sliding free fell out toward the circular driveway. "Mr. Nico was instructed to bring you directly home."

Oh, no. Cami stifled a sigh. *Why does he have to do this?* She dug for some kind of excuse to offer, but Stevens didn't pause, simply bowed again and indicated the door. Hitching her schoolbag up higher, she trudged in to face the music.

She was still no closer to figuring out how to smooth the waters as she climbed the carpeted stairs—these gave her no trouble either, their edges weren't so sharp—to the red hall. Trigger was at Papa's door, of course, and he tipped her a lazy salute. Against the rich crimson of the carpet and the heavy velvet of the muffling drapes, his baggy chinos and blue and red plaid jacket were just shabby enough to be familiar and comforting. "How was school, Miss Cami?"

Pretty boring. We did icecharms in Potentials class and some of the beakers shattered, that was about it. It would have been nice to talk, but her tongue was a knot of anxiety by now. She shrugged, ducking her head and spreading her hands. Then she mimed inquisitiveness—pointing at the door, raising her eyebrows.

"Nico's in for it," Trigger said shortly, and stepped aside. "He was supposed to bring you straight home. Sir wanted to see you."

Well, I'm here now. Another shrug, this one with a helpless motion.

"I know." Trig patted her shoulder, awkwardly. "God only knows what Nic was thinking. If he *was* thinking. Go on, sweetie. He's tired today."

He's always tired. I wish . . . But she knocked, softly, on the carved-oak door. The knob was red crystal; she turned it gently and stepped in.

The windowless room was lit only by a single candle on the nightstand. It smelled of copper, bay rum and leather, and the faint everpresent tang of illness and age. For a moment her throat closed to a pinhole, the air dead-still and the dark wainscoting and heavy maroon brocade wallpaper threatening to fall in until they crushed all her breath out.

It passed, and she inhaled deeply. The closeness was scary at first, but then it was comforting. Like a heavy coat on a cold day.

Nothing bad could happen to her here.

Papa Vultusino, close to the culmination of the Kiss, lay on the massive four-poster bed. His barrel chest rose and fell steadily, and his breathing wasn't a wheeze today. The candle flickered as she approached, and he opened his eyes.

Propped on the snowy pillows, he didn't *look* very ill until you got close. Then the red spark in his pupils, strengthening daily, became apparent. So did the papery thinness of his skin, and the deep-scored wrinkles as well as the fine dry lines.

The Kiss took its own time, and it was burning away his mortality. When it finished he'd be one of the immortal Unbreathing, an Elder instead of a daywalker, and his only son would take his place as the living Vultusino of the Seven.

If Nico could just stay out of trouble long enough.

The chair pulled up to the bedside had a thick pink cushion and a straight back. The fireplace was empty, so he wasn't cold today. That was a good sign. A large leatherbound book with yellowing pages lay open on the red silk comforter, and Papa's wide capable hands—bony and spotted now, but still hard and solid—lay discarded on either side of it.

Those hands held all the gentleness in the world. She remembered Papa bandaging a scrape on her knee as Marya fluttered in the background. *Little girl sometimes need Papa to bind up the wound, Marya. Let me.*

Cami lowered herself down, gently. Her left hand was awkward with the bandage, but she scooped it gently under one of Papa's, closed her other one over it. His skin was cooler than hers, and dry, calluses rasping.

The rasp reminded her of the wooden man, but she didn't want to think about that. So she just patted Papa's hand, watching his face as it shifted and the red spark dimmed a little.

He came back, bit by bit. Wet his lips with a paper-leaf tongue, and she glanced at the cut-crystal water pitcher on the nightstand next to the candle, rainbows shimmering in its angles. His hand squeezed a fraction—no, he wasn't thirsty. His left eyebrow lifted a tiny bit, and he squeezed again. Very, very gently, with the strength of the Family that could injure or crush running in his bones, especially as he lay so close to the Kiss.

He could feel the bandaging.

Cami patted his hand once more, very gingerly. "It's a-all r-right," she whispered. Her stupid tongue wasn't too bad in here. Papa had never told her to hurry up. He had always waited, with no trace of impatience. "J-just a scratch." She decided to plunge right in. "N-nico b-b-bandaged it. D-don't be m-m-mad—"

Papa's eyebrows drew together, a faint thundercloud. Cami stopped. Listened to the dry hiss of the candle burning, to his breathing, to the absolute stillness.

She decided to risk a little more. "He w-w-wants you t-to be p-proud of him, Papa."

Papa sighed. *If he only knew,* that sigh said, and Cami nodded in agreement.

Should I tell him about the wooden man? Maybe not. It'll upset him, and he'll be even madder at Nico.

So instead she told him about Potentials class and the shattering beakers, how Ruby's of course had broken with a terrific crack and Cami's own had crumbled into fine crystalline dust—proof that she had Potential, and further proof that it hadn't settled yet. You could never tell where someone's ability to charm would end up. Air, water, earth, sometimes fire, metal, wood, crystals and light, Affinities showed up generally about the end of puberty. Always assuming, of course, that you didn't Twist.

Ellen's beaker had turned into a solid jewel of water and glass, scintillating, and Sister Frederick's Sainthood had nodded with warm approval, her apple-cheeks glistening.

Papa listened, breathing steadily, and she plunged onward, into the stupid paper she had to do. His expression lightened as she spoke, slow and halting, the stutter receding as she relaxed and he began to look a little less gray. His hand warmed too, and when she talked about the Reeve a different gleam entered his gaze. After a little while his hand loosened, and Cami picked up the bone comb on the nightstand. She set his salt and pepper mane right again with careful, gentle strokes, leaning over the bed and smiling every time she glanced at him.

It was just like crouching under his desk, in the long-ago. She would hide there, playing with his mirror-polished wing-tips or just half asleep and listening as he made phone calls and attended to paperwork, Stevens murmuring advice or giving information in a monotone. Marya had turned the house upside down a few times looking for Cami until she started checking under Papa's desk first; Nico had sometimes tried hiding there with her but was always summarily dragged out into the hall and sent back to his practices with Trigger.

A Vultusino man must fight, Papa would say. *Go learn how.*

Well, Nico had. Now Cami wondered if he would ever learn how to *stop*.

When she'd set his mane to rights and talked about Ruby and Ellie some more, and explained the current crop of High Charm Calculus problems, she took his hand again. Lifted it gently, and pressed it against her cheek. "I'm s-sorry I w-was late," she whispered.

Papa was still for a long moment. His other hand lifted, slowly, and he patted her hair, very gently. Once, twice. She smiled, and his thin lips twitched in his still, pale face. The red sparks strengthened, and he gently took his hands away.

She rose, slowly, lit a fresh candle from the old one. Left both burning, and gave his hand one last squeeze before padding quietly to the door.

The hall was bright and oddly loud after the hush of the Room. She blinked, pulling the door shut, and found not just Trigger but Stevens too, standing poker-straight and staring unblinking at the mirror at the end of the hall, and Nico, who had changed into a light woolen suit, cloud-gray, and a maroon tie. His hair was slicked back, and his shoulders slouched just a little. He looked miserable, his chin set defiantly and the bloodring gleaming on his left middle finger.

The Heir's ring, worn for formal occasions.

Uh-oh. She brushed her hair back, tugged at her skirt, and basically stalled for a second or two. "H-h-he's—"

"Expecting us," Stevens said. The flat tone took on a richness, and the gaunt man's dark face slackened a little.

Which meant Papa was inside him, looking out.

"Marya's got your dinner, sweetheart." Trig had folded his arms, and was staring at Nico. "Run along."

There was nothing else she could do. But she dragged her feet, lingering a little so she could brush by Nico, hoping he could tell she'd done all she could. Before she was halfway down the hall the door had opened and closed behind Vultusino's wayward son and his consigliere, and Cami flinched at the little snick of the lock echoing all the way to the stairs.

Outside the windows, dusk had finished falling into night, and a chill soaking rain pressed against the panes. The red-tiled kitchen was a relief, warm and full of the smell of tomatoes and fresh bread. "*There* she is!" Marya cried, spidery six-fingered hands on her ample hips and her hair floating fine around her head. Her ears came to high points through the dandelion-burst, and if that didn't give it away you could tell she was fey by her eyes, black from lid to lid. "Naughty little girl out until dusk. Worrying us all to death, yes!"

For the first time that day, Cami's shoulders relaxed completely. She stood still as the housekeeper enfolded her in a hug redolent of heat, clean cotton, and the peculiar muskiness that was just plain and simply *Marya*. Fey always smelled of the earth, at least the low ones did. High fey didn't come out of the Waste, or if they did, it was only to make mischief or steal babies and leave changelings.

Passing from Waste to city was a fey trick, and one they never shared the secret of.

The feywoman clicked her tongue, brushing at Cami's hair, examined the bandage critically. "And what is this? Trouble? Ah, Nico." A long theatrical sigh. She could give Ruby lessons in the sigh department.

"W-w-wasn't his f-fault," she began, but Marya waved her hands.

"He *knows* better. Wild, that boy, just like a Twist." Her eyes—no iris, no pupil, just sheer glossy darkness—briefly swirled with opalescence, oil on black water. Her blue silken dress fluttered, a sure sign of agitation. "And he probably took you to horrible place, and you—what *is* that, little thistledown? What did he do?"

"He was p-p-p-*prot-tecting* me." But she was saved from explaining further by Marya's sudden flurry, her skirts swishing and her nut-brown face wrinkling against itself like she tasted something awful.

"If he not *take* you to horrible place, you not *need* protecting. Here, sit, sit, dinner. Growing girl needs good food." She snapped a single word, and a pot on the stove ceased bubbling over and subsided. Fey lived and breathed Potential, and they didn't Twist. They were just . . . *different*, and even with the low ones you had to be careful around their prickly notions of politeness—and their fickle, fluid notions of "truth."

Marya was certainly the most stable fey Cami had ever met. Most of them had attention spans no longer than a humming-bird's, and they flitter-fluttered around selling charms, or working at odds and ends for as long as the wind blew from a certain quarter.

On the other hand, anything outside Papa Vultusino's walls did not interest Marya very much, if at all. Her concerns were immediate—the woodwork that needed waxing, the feeding of those in her domain, the scouring of the copper-bottom pots that hung, shining suns, in the russet-tiled kitchen. A brick hearth and a fire for pizzas and other things—*can't cook without smoke*, Marya was fond of muttering—gave a comforting crackling; the gas range held bubbling pots, and the dishwasher chuckled. In the warm womb of the kitchen, Cami let Marya fuss over her, and by the time dinner was over she had almost forgotten about the wooden man.

But not quite.

FIVE

THE NIGHTMARE WRAPS ITS FLABBY, TOO-LARGE
fingers around my entire body, and will not let me go.

*The beautiful woman smelling of cloves and perfumed smoke,
her golden hair a fountain of clean light, leans down. Her red lips
are set in a slight smile, just the barest hint of amusement that will
not wrinkle her soft white face. Winged eyebrows, high cheekbones,
everything about her is so lovely. The heavy velvet of her indigo
dress drags in the soft ankle-high dust. Her hands are broad and
white and soft as well, oddly large for such a delicate frame, and
her eyes are blue as summer sky. They are darkening, those lovely
blue eyes, and when they are indigo to match her dress, it will be
my time.*

She whispers, as the frantic barking of the dogs grows nearer.
You are nobody. You are nothing.

*I know it is true, but still, I struggle. She strokes my dirty face
with those big cold soft hands, rings glinting on her fingers, and my*

head snaps aside. The rest of me is held down, throbbing with nips and crunches of pain from the last beating.

My teeth sink in. I worry at that hand like a rat with a bone, and she jerks back, shrieking with fury. The shape behind her is a man, and as I thrash against the handcuffs his expression twists. It is familiar, a lean dark face; he is in a leather jerkin and breeches, a collage of brown and green muted by the dimness of my cell.

Her shriek ends, and her contorted face smoothes itself. She hisses between her teeth, a long catlike sigh, as the silver medallion at her breast, its spot of bleeding crimson in the center, runs with diseased pale light.

This one's heart is fiery.

They leave, the cell door swinging shut, and I am alone. No, not alone. There is a strange lipless voice throbbing all through me, and my head feels funny from the smoke. Empty and too-big, as if I am in a place I cannot remember, not this small concrete cell. The voice always says the same thing.

You are nobody. You are nothing.

And I know it is true, but I pull against the handcuffs. I twist them back and forth, and I am making a sound like a bird's thin cry, because my throat is crushed.

"Shhh." Nico's hand at her mouth. "It's me."

Cami sat bolt-upright, pale sheets and blankets caught to her chest, her sides heaving and sweat dewing her forehead.

Nightmare. It was familiar, and she had felt it coming as she lay stiff as a poker, waiting to fall asleep.

The white bedroom was full of shifting shadow. The curtains were drawn over the huge bay windows, but the glimmer of the parchment walls, the creamy carpet, the pale wood and white-painted furniture made it brighter than night should be—only by a shade or two.

She let out a garbled sound, the high piping of a bird, and Nico's hand eased. "Shhh," he whispered, again. "It's just a dream, I'm here."

You are nobody. You are nothing. "N-n-n-ni—" Even *his* name wouldn't come.

"Cami." He caught her hands. His skin was warm, solid, real. "Book."

The same old charm. "B-b-book."

"Candle." He was kneeling on her bed, and she saw the mess his hair had become. How late was it?

"C-candle." Her breathing evened out. Her heart still hammered, but it wouldn't explode. She could tell, now, that it would calm down. If she just gave it a little time.

He smelled of cigarette smoke, copper, the tang of whiskey. So he'd been at the decanters again. "Nico," he whispered.

"Nico," she whispered back. Relaxed all at once, a loosened string.

"There it is." He relaxed a little too, but stiffened when she moved to hug him. "Easy, babygirl."

"What h-h-happened?" But she knew. The cuts on him would be closing, the weals healing themselves slowly. By morning he would be good as new, not even a scar left to mark the punishment.

Family healed fast. And it used to be that this sort of punishment made an impression on Nico.

Now, though . . . nothing much did.

"I deserve it. Move over." He lowered himself gingerly, hissing as his bare back met the sheet. "Mithrus, move *over*."

"I *am*." Irritable now, she scooted, freeing the topsheet. She'd thrown her pillows somewhere, but he rescued them, and in a little while they were safe together, her head on his bare shoulder, her nightgown caught on his pajama-clad knee. She tried not to hug him too hard, but he tightened his arm and pulled her closer, only tensing a little as it hurt. "Why d-did y-y-you—?" *Why did you take me out? It's like you wanted to get punished on your first night home.*

"Shhh. Listen."

She did. The wind was up, trees making an ocean noise, branches creaking, and the house's corners whistling to themselves. How many nights had they spent like this?

She used to scream when the nightmares came. Now, not so much—but it was easier when he was there, warm and close and safe. Nobody had ever caught him—Papa had once or twice given her a penetrating look at the breakfast table, asking how she had slept, and Cami had blushed without knowing why.

I don't like it, Nico had said the first time he'd appeared in the darkness, whispering fiercely. *Tell me what it is. I'll hurt it. I'll kill* it *for you.*

As if she could. The words wouldn't come. The dreams faded as soon as she jolted into waking. There was only the feel of the soft, large hands, and the directionless voice in the darkness.

You are nobody. You are nothing.

She shivered, and Nico rubbed his chin against her head. It scratched a little. In prep school he'd liked the stubbled look until she complained that it was scratchy and made him look dirty. The next day he'd shaved, and grumbled when he nicked himself. As if it didn't heal immediately.

"Winter's coming." He let out a sigh. "Go to sleep."

The heat all through her was different now. She'd noticed it before, her hands shaking a little and her heart in her throat, a pleasant excitement like when he drove too fast. A curious safety, but the nervousness in her itching all over, and she couldn't figure out why. "How b-bad d-d-does it h-hurt?"

He made a slight movement, as if tossing away the question. "Not bad." But his voice broke, and he lay stiff and unbending while the tears trickled down his temples and vanished into their hair—his and hers, mingled together on the white pillow. When they were done he relaxed, slowly, bit by bit. Cami fell asleep after his breathing evened out, and as usual, he kept the bad dreams away.

And, as usual, when she woke up in the morning there was only the dent on the pillow next to hers, and a deep tingling on her cheek, as if he had kissed it before ghosting out her door.

SIX

THE POOL, A LAZY BLUE EYE, THREW BACK uncharacteristically fierce autumn sunlight with a vengeance. Cami drew her knees up under the umbrella's shade; Ruby, applying crimson lacquer to her nails, made a clicking sound with her tongue. "It's just *sunshine*, it's not going to *kill* you."

"CANNONBALL!" Thorne yelled, barreling past them, a lean brown streak with a shock of wheat-gold hair and orange trunks. Hunter was right after him, dark-haired and sleek in bright yellow. They hit the water with a shattering double splash, and Ruby made a little *eww* sound and leaned back.

"J-just water." Cami settled back in the chair, adjusting her sunglasses a little. "N-not g-gonna—"

Ruby pointed with the nail brush. "You just watch yourself, missy."

Cami pursed her lips and made a raspberry, and shared laughter rose.

You didn't get leftover summer like this in New Haven very often, but when you did it was to be seized with both hands. Which explained why Marya had been chattered into providing notes for the three girls; Thorne and Hunter—Woodsdowne cousins, and warring for Ruby's attention, like always—were on their own for track-covering. But Marya had long ago become adept at counterfeiting parental scrawls on St. Juno-charmed paper, and Papa turned a blind eye as long as Cami didn't skip more than once a month.

I was young once too, Papa had said long ago, patting Cami on the head. *Be reasonable, eh, bambina?*

He never let Nico skip, though. The Vultusino-in-waiting couldn't afford to.

Ellie emerged from the changing room in a bright blue bikini that hugged her lovingly. The bruises on her arms were fading and yellowgreen, and the one on her thigh wasn't bad.

Ruby whistled. "Look at that. Fits you like a chaaaarm!" She giggled as Thorne heaved himself up out of the pool, shaking his head, bright droplets splashing. He went right back in with another gigantic splash, graceful as an otter.

"I am not even gonna *ask* why you have a bikini in my size," Ellie said darkly, settling on the lounge chair next to Cami's shade.

Because I know what the Strep does to all your clothes, and then she tells your dad you did it. And you get it from both sides, so this is just easier, right? "G-good." Cami snagged the cocoanut-oil sunscreen. She passed it over, pulling her hand back quickly.

"White girl thinks she'll explode if she catches a ray or two." Ruby's eyeroll was so pronounced you could hear its mutter in the mountains.

"She just wants to avoid skin cancer." Ellie began the process of slathering on sunscreen. "As do we all. What time is it?"

Red sighed again. "Not even *eleven*, worrywart. Chill. The Strep won't find out."

"She knows things," Ellie muttered darkly. Of course, the Strep was a charmer strong enough to have a Sigil of her own— the two high-heeled shoes, a symbol of her work and talent. She was the best couturier in New Haven, and her work was sent over Waste, too. No doubt Ellie's dad, reeling from the loss of his first wife, had thought the Strep quite a catch.

Even Ellie had been cautiously happy to have a mom again. Until the Strep showed her true colors, that was. It was a wonder the woman hadn't Twisted yet, she was so full of spiteful rage directed right at Ellie.

Rube snorted. "What, like how to be the biggest bitch in Haven County? Gran could eat her for lunch."

Ruby's Gran lived in a tiny cottage in the Woodsdowne area, full of the smell of baking good things, the scorch of an active charmer at work, and pretty small for a woman who controlled a good chunk of the import traffic through the Waste or the port. The de Varres were an old clan, almost as old as the

Family and allied to the Seven in New Haven.

In some other provinces, though, Ruby and Nico wouldn't just snarl at each other. There might have been actual blood. But here in New Haven, a treaty held, and Gran's house was the closest to absolute safety you could find outside a Family home.

At least, if she liked you.

Ellie's laugh was laced with hard bright bitterness. "I wish she would. But that would poison your dear sweet Grannie."

"Good luck." Ruby critically examined her pinkie, drew another stripe of polish down it. "Hel-*lo*. What's that?"

Cami glanced up. Across the pool, something moved in the greenery. Her heartbeat thundered in her ears for a moment, and she hugged her knees even tighter. "N-new g-garden b-b-boy." The head groundskeeper had just hired four more since some of the old ones were off to college; Trig and the security team had cleared the applicants and Marya had given her approval. They were like all the rest—silent plain-normal humans, young men without any Twist to them, low Potential and low prospects too, probably from the fringes of New Haven's crumbling inner core where the minotaurs walked, the dead-eyed hapsters hawked their drugs and gave the Family a percentage, and the gunfire echoed. Working for the Families was one way to get out and away from the coreblight—and Papa Vultusino gave college scholarships in return for loyalty and discretion.

Some of the other Seven weren't so kind. But the boys from

the fringes kept coming. They didn't have many other chances.

This particular garden boy was tall and lanky, with messy coal-black hair. He kept it shaken down over his eyes, and something about him made Cami uneasy. If she said anything, he'd be sent back to the core; once, there had been an under-groundskeeper who had told her she was such a *pretty* girl while he tried to touch her scarred left arm. She'd flinched just as Nico came around the corner to call her for lunch.

That had been awful.

"Nice shoulders." Ruby capped the polish, deftly. "Cami, dearie, I could get accustomed to this summer stuff."

Cami silently agreed. Even if she hated the naked way her scars flushed in this kind of weather.

"Too bad tomorrow's going to rain." Ellie finished her anointing and wiggled her toes, luxuriously. The garden boy started trimming something on the far side of the pool, while Thorne and Hunter did their best to duck each other. They must have been hoping Ruby was watching.

Cami relaxed a little. It was just the right temperature under the umbrella, a breeze redolent of mown grass and autumn spice moving over her. Her one-piece cream swimsuit and the matching sari-skirt covered up just about everything. There were the dimpled burn scars on her arms, and there were her wrists. But if she stayed out of the sun they wouldn't show much, and the long thin white marks from cuts didn't show too badly anyway.

Nobody ever said anything about it. Nobody but Nico did, anyway. And he only wanted to know if they hurt anymore. Or if she remembered anything before being found in the snow.

He didn't like things he couldn't fix.

"God *damn* it." Ruby sighed. "Can't you ever be wrong about the goddamn weather?"

Ellie shrugged, picking up a thick battered copy of *Sigmindson's Charms*. She'd tested ultra-high on Potential. It was a good thing—it kept the Strep from being *too* awful, because of the risk of Twisting Ellie with hate and rage. But still. "Wish I could, Rube. It would be nice."

"Lottery numbers," Ruby muttered darkly. "Minotaur races. Even something at the Avalon Casino."

"Improper use of Potential." Ellie began flipping. The conversation was so familiar, they could have had it in their sleep. Cami watched the new garden boy trimming, his shoulders broad-muscled under a white T-shirt. He moved a little oddly, but she couldn't figure out just how. "The risk of Twist increases with each—"

"—use of unsanctioned or unsafe charm," Ruby finished. "Being responsible is so *boring*."

"Being responsible doesn't bite you in the ass like being irresponsible does." There it was, Ellie's Words To Live By boiled down to a single sentence.

"What if you like your ass bitten?" Ruby arched her eyebrows, her oiled skin brushed with gold.

"Hey, what?" Hunter heaved himself up on the edge of the pool, water-jewels on his skin sparkling in bright sunshine. "I can help with that."

Right on cue. Cami suppressed a sigh. Rube seemed genuinely oblivious to the way the two cousins kept showing off for her.

"Ha." Ruby waved a languid crimson-tipped hand. "Ask Thorne. I hear he likes that sort of thing."

"What are you getting me into?" Thorne rose from the pool, sleek and lean. Cami looked away. "You guys are in *swimsuits*. Why don't you ever *swim*?"

"Maybe because you're all spazzy and scare them," Hunter sniffed, and it was on. Thorne grabbed him and they thrashed in a roil of brown limbs and crystalline water. The garden boy moved to another shrub.

It didn't look like they needed trimming, but what did she know about bushes? His hair was really black, with odd undertones. Blue glimmers, like hers. You didn't see that color a lot.

"You're staring," Ruby mock-whispered, not opening her eyes. "Are you actually showing interest in something male? Other than you-know-who?"

Cami dropped her face into her skirt-covered knees. Her cheeks burned.

"You *are*. Wow." Ruby sounded genuinely amazed. "Is he cute?"

"Can't tell at this distance." Ellie continued flipping through the charm-book. "Oh, look. Here's one to save someone from drowning."

Ruby's aggravation was a long, drawn-out sigh, rippling the air with a ruffle of Potential. "Oh, Mithrus."

"I'm just being *cautious*."

"You are not going to die by drowning, Ell. Not while I still find you amusing."

"Your arrogance is almost as large as your ass."

"Come closer and say that, my dearest." Ruby chuckled, a low throaty sound. "Cami, you can *look*, you know. It's actually a good sign if you do. Remember Puberty Ed?"

Cami almost flinched. Now *that* had been uncomfortable. Sister Eunice Grace-Atoning was the oldest, dottiest teacher at Juno, and listening to her mumbling explanations of how to keep from getting pregnant or diseased—or worse—in a classroom full of blushing, giggling girls while outside spring sunshine drenched the world with gold . . . if there was anything more deadly boring and stupid, she hadn't come across it yet.

Ruby had, quickly and frankly, told Cami everything she needed to know in sixth grade, during one of their many sleepovers. The blush had been hot enough to still feel—*they do what? Ewww, gross.*

Shhh! Ruby had looked very serious. *They say you can catch Twisting that way too, so you've got to be careful.*

I'm never *doing that.*

Gran says, Ruby had nodded sharply, in unconscious imitation of Gran de Varre, *some day you might change your mind, so it's best to be prepared.*

"Leave her *alone.*" Ellie sighed dramatically. "Thorne! Go see if you can talk Marya into getting us some beers!"

Cami peeked up from her knees. The garden boy had stopped, his handheld clippers paused. The scissor blades gleamed in the sun, and sweat darkened his white shirt. He had lifted his chin, and he stared back at her.

"He's looking." Ruby whispered for real this time. "I can tell he's looking. Cami, are you looking?"

"N-n-no." But she was. The heat was all through her, a rose stain like some of the windows in the long shaded hall near the library where all the paintings hung, and the scars would all turn white against that flush. It felt as if she was near Nico, charm-voltage all through her, and she shifted uncomfortably.

"You're *lying.* How soon they grow up." Archly amused, Ruby snuggled down on her lounger. It had to be her russet-golden length the garden boy was staring at. "*Thorne!* Fetch us some booze, we're thirsty!"

"I'll get—" Hunter was half out of the pool already. Thorne tackled him. Par for the course. As if being the first to bring

Ruby a beer would make her settle, once and for all, on one of them.

"Oh, Lord." Ellie sighed again.

"I'll g-g-get it." Cami was up off her lounger in a heartbeat, and she retreated from the sunny poolside. Marya would scold, but she could be persuaded to part with some honeywine coolers—the fey had funny ideas about alcohol. Ruby would bitch, of course, but the list of things Ruby would bitch at was so long there was no point in letting it run your life.

Past the changing-house, down a leaf-shaded pathway, the slate pavers gritty and warm underfoot, she was almost clear when she heard a rustle.

It was the garden boy. He must have cut around the back of the changing-house, even though it was a tangle of thorny-wild rosebushes. Cami flinched, stared at the pavers, and hunched her shoulders.

"Hey."

He was actually *speaking to her*. Mithrus, what was she supposed to *do*? She pulled further into herself, hunching more, and he'd somehow stepped right in her path.

"Hey," he repeated, very low. Confidentially. "Princess girl. Can I talk to you?"

Oh, God. She weighed her options. Walking through him was one, but he might try to touch her. Retreating was a better option, but then Ruby would ask her what the hell and Ellie would probably guess what had happened and sooner or later Nico would find out—

Caught between several unappetizing alternatives, she had a wild idea of diving into the rosebushes pressing against the side of the path and the changing-house. There was no good reason for him to be talking to her, and if someone found out there would be trouble. Not just trouble but Trouble, underlined and in neon.

"*Shit*," he muttered, just as Thorne and Hunter bailed around the corner.

"Hey, Cami, take us with you!" Bursting with energy and a haze of warm water, they splattered up to her, Thorne halting and shaking his head. Cami flinched from the spray of droplets, and the garden boy had vanished.

It wasn't until later, pleasantly buzzed on honeywine and watching as Ruby leveled herself effortlessly into a clean skimming dive, that she realized she was almost disappointed about that.

SEVEN

Two days later, Nico was finally willing to talk about why he was home from Hannibal. "There was some trouble. Fighting." He lounged on paint-splattered carpet, the cut-crystal ashtray balanced on his stomach. "It's just a couple weeks, Cami. It's already smoothed over. And Papa wanted me home anyway. Something about . . . well, he's worried about something in the city."

She might have asked him about that, except she knew Nico wouldn't tell her about anything upsetting or dangerous. She knew things, of course, picked up around the edges, heard in corners. You would have to be blind, deaf, *and* terminally stupe-Twisted not to overhear . . . things . . . in a Family house.

Right now, though, that wasn't her problem. *You keep picking fights and the Family might do something big to you.* "I w-wish you'd b-be c-careful." Rain swept the window, restlessly, false summer fled as if it had never been. Ellie was grounded again, the Strep using some bullshit something-or-another; Ruby's grandmother had caught her sneaking out of her window at midnight so *she* was grounded too, and Nico was . . . Nico.

"Your tang's all tungled again." Nico propped his head up on a pillow dragged from his hacked-up bed and waggled his eyebrows. His suite had been in dark green, a Family Heir's traditional color. Nico, however, had taken black spray paint and an edge to pretty much everything, and after a while Papa had told Marya not to repair or redecorate.

Marya obeyed, of course. But she also tried sneaking pillows and pretty things up to make Nico happy. Cami could have told her it was useless. When he was determined to be an ass, there was just nothing to be done about it.

"You're *mean*." At least she didn't stutter over *that*. It was all she could say.

He ground out the Gitanelle and curled up to sit cross-legged, his eyes dark. "I'm sorry."

It was the same conversation, started so many years ago. *You'll never be a pureblood! I hate you!*

You're m-mean, she'd yelled back, shocked at her own daring but on fire with the injustice. They were the first words she'd spoken since coming to live in the house on Haven Hill, and Nico had balled up his small fists. Coming home from yet another expensive boarding school for the winter holidays and finding everything suddenly arranged around another child hadn't been high on his list of favorite things, and he'd even shown his baby fangs.

But Cami had flinched, her eyes widening, and Nico had immediately dropped his hands. He had stared, horrified, as she shrank back, his mouth falling open and his fangs retracting. *Don't . . . hey. Oh, hey. Don't cry.* Drawing himself up, little-boy proud. *You don't have to cry. I don't hate you.*

Marya had found them an hour and a half later, curled up together in a faded-rose, velvet-curtained window seat in the dim whisper-haunted library, Nico stroking Cami's long black hair soothingly, both of them sleepy-eyed. Cami had blinked, slowly, and said *M-m-Marya,* pointing like a toddler.

That's right, Nico had replied. *Marya. Book. Candle. Nico.*

M-Marya. B-book. C-c-c-candle. Nico.

"I'm sorry," he repeated. "Mithrus. I don't mean to be. Not to you."

Everyone else, but not me? "I kn-know." She was curled in the one leather chair he hadn't taken a straight razor to, her special chair in his room. Big and wide, and deep enough for both of them as children, it was a smaller ship to sail rougher seas now.

Thunder muttered in the distance. The storm was sweeping in. Nico sighed, hauled himself up, and turned out the electric lights. He moved around, lighting candles and sticking them anyhow in a collection of holders or just in built-up wax charm-softened with a muttered curse.

Family didn't Twist, like fey. There were other dangers— the sickness of too much Borrowing, the Kiss finding one of them unworthy, a faust's terrible fire-breath doing what the sun couldn't to daywalkers and Unbreathing alike. Also like fey, their Potential was a part of what made them . . . different, and they swam in it without worrying about anything toxic.

Except the Waste. They were human enough to have to worry about that, at least.

He knocked a chunk of wax down from his scarred wooden dresser, kicked it skittering across the room. *Why shouldn't I ruin things?* he'd said, bitterly, once. *None of it matters. It's just stuff.*

It m-matters, she'd replied. *It's b-b-beautiful.*

Not to me. And there they had left it.

When he had enough candles lit to suit him, he crouched in front of the chair, watching her, mossy eyes dark. They played the game, holding eye contact for as long as possible, until their breathing melted together. When he shifted his weight she shifted too, and in a little bit he let out a long sigh and settled down on his knees. He leaned into the chair, and Cami stroked his hair, pushing her fingers through the dark waves. The candleflames danced like charmer's foxfire, and when she shivered he did too.

"Book." His tone was soft, thoughtful.

"B-book."

"Candle."

"C-c-candle."

"Nico."

"Nico."

"See? All better."

Even if it wasn't a real charm, it worked. "You're so angry."

"Born that way."

Maybe you were. "We l-love you."

"*You* do. Them? I'm just another piece to shove into the Seven."

"They may not. If you . . . " Her throat refused to fill with the words. She couldn't imagine what they would do to him, but it would be dire. The "punishments" administered when he incurred Papa's displeasure were bad enough.

"So what? They fire me from the Seven. From being the Heir. We go to the Island."

Another childhood game. So he wanted to be kids again tonight. She gave him the next line, gently. "And h-how will w-we eat?"

"You'll pick fruit. I'll hunt. At night we'll share, and you'll be Family."

I can't be Family. I wasn't born in. But she still smiled. "How?"

"I'll find a Waste-witch to make you. Or we'll get my heart-stone and make you into a leman; I'll hunt for you, and you can Borrow from me. Then we'll live until the Kiss comes, and we'll be Elders together on our very own island. Move it." He clambered up, and they squeezed together in the chair. Rain poured down the windows. His breath was hot on her neck, and she closed her eyes. This was part of the game too, relaxing until they were one heartbeat, and the flutter inside her skull was the silent brush of his strange dark fiery thoughts. He shifted so she wasn't hitting anything sensitive in his lap, and she fought back a hot blush.

"Where will we l-live?" she whispered.

"We'll build a hut from palm stuff. Like in *Crusoe the Man-eater*. We won't need it, though. It's warm on the Island."

She could almost pretend to be nine again, small and safe. "Trop-pical r-rains."

"The jungle's thick. We'll be okay." He paused. "You really are upset."

Now she could tell him. He wasn't likely to go flying out to find the wooden man and do something awful. "The w-wooden m-man. At L-l-lou's."

"Wooden . . . oh, *that*? He was probably just a drunk jack. I was there, right?"

Do you think I would go there alone? "His eyes. B-blue."

"Lots of people have blue eyes, babygirl."

"*R-r-really* b-blue. L-l-like m-m-m-m—"

"You're not a jack. *Or* a Twist. You'd be one by now, if you were going to."

That's not what I mean. He recognized me from somewhere. She made a helpless movement.

But he just forged on ahead, as usual. "I don't care where you came from. You're with me. That's all."

"S-something's h-happening." *It's not just the wooden man. It was his eyes. And something else. Everything's wrong.* She'd felt this when Papa first took to bed in the Red Room months ago, a strange shifting sensation like the ground crumbling beneath her.

And it was getting worse.

"It's Papa." For once, he didn't sound bitter. "He's really close. And you think without him . . . Christ, Cami. Don't worry so much. Family doesn't give up what's theirs."

"I-i-if you k-keep d-doing things, they'll maybe get a-another S-s-seventh." *There's plenty of youngbloods, even if they're not Lineage.*

"I won't let that happen. Every boy's Wild before he steps into the Seven, Cami. I'm just doing what they want, still." He sighed. "I can't get away from it."

She squirmed until she could put her arms around him, and the sound of rain filled the silence with its deep silvery mutter.

"You've been having more bad dreams, too." He was taller than her, but he still managed to curl up and rest his head on her shoulder. It was uncomfortable, but neither of them wanted to admit they were too big for the chair. "You always do before your birthday."

She was hard-put to stifle a groan. *We don't know my birthday.* But Papa had suggested Octovus, because it was Dead Harvest season, and because that way she would have presents twice in a year, not just near Mithrusmas. It was nice ... but still, sometimes, she wondered when her birthday *really* was.

And if she would ever really know.

"Sweet sixteen, and a big party all planned," Nico teased. "Wait until you see what I got you." And he wouldn't tell, no matter how Cami poked him. For the rest of the evening she forgot the world-tilting feeling, and everything was all right again.

EIGHT

The shops in Haven South—the old city—were mostly run by jacks. You could, if the wind was right, hear the sirens from the blighted urban core, and sometimes on the news there was footage of a stray minotaur stamping through smoke and dusk up the center of zigzagging Southking Street. It would shrug through canvas awnings, jacks and humans scattering, gaining what safety they could as the shifting bullheaded thing made of mutating Potential and pain ran itself into nothingness, away from the core-chaos that gave it birth.

Sometimes minotaurs happened in the suburbs too, but not often. It took a huge irruption of hate- or rage-fueled Potential before they were even viable, let alone heavy enough to coalesce onto a person and spin them past jack, past Twist even, into the shadow-realm of cannibal monster with hulking shoulders and wide-horned, bone-shielded head.

Following Ruby down Southking Street deserved its own

athletic badge. Usually Ellie was there to steer Cami through the crowd and track Ruby down after she got excited and zoomed away to look at *oh my God this cute little thing!* But Ell was still in what Rube called Strep Durance Vile, and Cami glanced away from Ruby's copperbright hair for just a moment, when a jack with warty gray skin held up a fistful of thin silver bangles and shook them, cawing her sellsong.

"*Pret*-ty things for a *pret*-ty girl, come buy some sweetsilver miss?" The jack's mouth split open, showing broad yellow teeth, and the edge of Potential between her and Cami flashed into visibility for a moment. It crackled with hexagram flashes, a shiver spilling down Cami's spine as she backed away, almost tripping, and looked wildly around for Ruby.

No luck.

The lunchtime crowd was thick and she should have been in French class, bored out of her mind and droning along with Sister Mary Brefoil as verbs were conjugated and sleepy slants of thin autumn sunshine pierced Juno's high narrow windows. But Ruby had cajoled, Ruby had wheedled, Ruby had said, *You're only young once and I need to shop* . . . and Cami had given in.

Stay calm. You'll find her. She might even go back to Ruby's car—they had parked on Highclere, and Cami could go back and wait. If all else failed she could find a public shell and call the house. If Marya picked up, Nico would come get her. But it was Thursday—Market Day for most of New Haven—and

Marya might be a-marketing in the Arbor to the north, where the servants for the upper crust and the powerful and Sig-iled charmers did their shopping for organics and Twist-free produce from certified kolkhozes, and other essentials. So the phone might ring, Chauncey or Stevens might pick up, and she'd have to explain why she was skipping—and why on earth she was on Southking, of all places.

And *that* would not be pleasant. She'd never gotten in trouble before, but what if Papa's patience snapped, so close to his transition? The unsteadiness was under Cami's feet all the time now, and she didn't want to take any chances.

She set off through the crowd, her schoolbag hitched high on her shoulder and her blazer welcome warmth, a chill wind, threading between jacks and humans, cold lipless breath touching her bare knees. She shivered, scanning for Ruby's bright hair, and saw only backs and legs, jacks and humans hurrying in the frosty sunshine. Her breath came fast in a thin white cloud. False summer was long, long gone.

Smoking peanut oil from the foodcarts, signs proclaiming *Real Meat*, spices, the dusty scent of imported cloth, the hawkers crying their sellsongs. Cheap jewelry, more expensive jewelry, tailor stalls, a ringing clatter from a blacksmith shaping anti-Twist charms, the forge a blare of heat and a young jack working the bellows, his clawed hands oddly graceful. He blinked one cat-pupiled yellow eye, then the other as Cami stood and watched for a moment.

If she'd been born jack, with feathers or fur, or if her Potential had turned that way when the hormone-and-charm crisis of puberty first hit, would Papa have taken her in? Or kept her for this long? Or would she have been abandoned, maybe sent to a boarding school far away? There were jack-only schools in the cold North, past the Province border and over Waste, and the stories about them were terrible. Accidents happened around jacks.

Bad accidents.

Don't think about things like that.

A stray dog barked as it ran between two canvas tents. She flinched, turning away. A bookseller—a normal, with an iron anti-Twist pendant at his neck on a leather thong—eyed her curiously. Cami blushed, looked around for Ruby again. Scarves fluttered, a fortuneteller's tent stood tall, purple, and motheaten, spangled with tarnished gilt; a knifemartin stood behind his table of bright blades and watched the flow of foot traffic with narrowed eyes. Some of the darker tents were accorded plenty of space—one had the serpent-sign of a poisonmaker, and everyone hurried past *that* awning. People would wait for dusk and go in through the back.

New Haven was a hub, with both the port and the sealed over Waste trains bringing goods in and exporting charmwork and finished products. The de Varres took their percentages, and the Family took theirs, and everyone else crowded around the rest like grinmarches around a pile of husks and clippings, getting their fair share and making credits any way they could.

The trouble with wondering about where she'd be now if Papa hadn't kept her was that it made the unsteadiness under her feet so much worse. Windchimes tinkled and good-luck bells chattered uneasily as the wind picked up, and her stomach turned over, hard.

Screw this. Cami spun on her heel and set off, her head down, with a purposeful step. If she went up two blocks she could cut over to Highclere, find Ruby's Semprena, and sit on the hood until Rube noticed she wasn't around and—

"It's Camille, right?"

She almost ran into him. White shirt, tan leather jacket, faded jeans, a glitter of silver at his throat. She mumbled an apology, moved aside, but he stepped to the side too, as if they were dancing.

So she *had* to look up.

The garden boy, his messy black hair actually pushed back from his forehead, had an odd face. He was tanned—of course, he worked outside. Strong jaw, too-strong cheekbones, like he hadn't quite grown into them yet. His eyes matched his hair, pupil and iris blending together to make a dark hole. Bad-luck eyes, but he couldn't be Twist, not if Marya had given him the okay. Cami dropped her gaze, confused, and the silver at his throat was a small medallion, some kind of star engraved on it.

Her head filled with rushing noise.

"Whoa, there." He actually caught her arm as she swayed. "Mithrus, what are you doing *here*?"

The dogs bayed and she scrabbled, desperately, the Queen's rising scream filling whirling snow. The rats ran after her in a swelling tide, their sleek-oiled coats gleaming, and the cracking, rending sound of glass breaking tore the universe apart . . .

Cami came back to herself with a jolt. She was sitting down, and the garden boy had a straw to her lips. "It's just fruit juice," he was saying. "It's okay, it's not—"

Is it charmed? She pushed the cup aside. Swayed again, almost falling off the stool. A striped awning flapped overhead, and Southking Street throbbed like a bad tooth. She blinked as something liquid splashed, and the garden boy backed off.

"I'm sorry." He had a nice voice, at least. It reminded her of Nico's, but without the sharp-edge anger. "You looked like you were gonna faint."

The foodcart had a shiny chrome counter, and the burly female jack in a red plaid shirt behind it was studiously ignoring them as she messed with a hissing-hot grill, the scales on her wrists and the back of her neck bright green and glowing. The garden boy lifted the cup and sipped, carefully, the clear straw holding red liquid.

"Strawberry juice," he said after swallowing. "Fixes everything, and I've taken some so you know it's not charmed. Plus I know I'm not supposed to even talk to you. Believe me, I know."

What the hell just happened? She'd lost Ruby, and then . . . something. Like a bad dream, but during daylight. She swallowed hard, realized she still had her schoolbag, clutched to her chest like a drowning girl would hold driftwood. "I l-l-lost R-ruby." The words tripped over each other. "I'm s-s-s-sorry."

He actually leaned back, gazing at her like she'd just produced a Twist charm, or started to sprout jackfeathers. She would have flinched, except it was impossible to hunch her shoulders any further. One of these days she was going to get over the effect her stutter had on people.

But not today.

"So you do talk." He nodded, once, like he was surprised she could make words. So was she, right now. "I thought you just, you know, didn't bother. Because you're beautiful."

What? "I s-s-s-st-st—"

Another nod, just like Nico. The jacket was butter-soft leather, but scuffed and scarred. "Stutter. Yeah. So? Hey, Danna. Something nice for the lady."

The jack cast one disdainful glance over her meaty shoulder. The scales spread up her cheek, a fanlike pattern that was actually beautiful, if you looked close enough. "You payin'?"

Nameless

The garden boy tossed a couple crumpled paper credits on the counter, their woven surfaces alive with heavy-duty anti-charm ink. "I can take my business elsewhere."

It *was* kind of like being with Nico. Cami found her hands working again, and her brain too. She dug in her schoolbag, coming up with a crisp five-cred note. "H-here."

"My treat." The garden boy grinned. "I'm Torin Beale. Tor, for short."

"C-c-cami." She wished she could add more, but she could just *tell* her tongue was knotting up. But she did offer her hand, and he shook, gravely, his jacket creaking a little. His skin was warm, and not hard but firm. You could tell he worked hard every day.

"I know." But his smile took the sting out of it. The jack banged an unopened bottle of limon down on the counter, sweeping up Tor's creds and making them disappear.

Cami took it, cautious; the tingle in her fingers told her the bottling-seal was unbroken, and therefore safe enough. She cracked the top. "Thanks." It was a miracle, the word came out whole.

"No problem. Hey, what are you doing on Southking? Shouldn't you be at that school? What is it—that's right, you're a Juno."

"S-sk-k-kipp-ping." Of course it was too good to last. She made a face, sipping at tart cool fizzing limon, and the garden

81

boy—Tor, a short hard sound of a name—actually laughed.

"Me too. Were you, you know, here with someone?" He took a long draft of strawberry juice, and Cami glanced at the crowd again. No sign of Ruby. Her head felt strange, stuffed with cotton wool. When she looked back at him, something seemed different. It took her a moment to figure it out.

His necklace was gone. Or had she imagined the silver gleam? The thought made her queasy, so she swept it away. It went quietly. "Y-yeah. Sh-she g-g-ot d-d-istracted, though. I g-g-guess."

"Lots to be distracted by here. You want to look for her? Or you want me to take you home? Because really, you shouldn't be wandering around alone."

The jack behind the counter found this suddenly interesting, turning away from the grill. The scales on her cheeks flushed and popped with Potential, just like the grill behind her popped with heat. They crawled over her skin, and the red tint between them swelled, destroying the beauty of the pattern. "What, like you're some sort of knight in shining, orphan boy? Please."

"Did I *ask* you?" His black eyes sparked, and Cami didn't even think about it. Her hand shot out, closed around his wrist. The strawberry juice in its wax-paper cup splashed, and she pulled a little, just as if he was Nico and ready to go ballistic.

The jack laughed, a nasty bitter little sound of jacktemper.

"Oh, cute. Yeah, you hold him back, Juno bitch."

"Come on." Tor slid off his stool. "Danna's in a mood today. She's all *jealous*."

The jack paled, and licked her thin lips. It was funny—she had such a small mouth and the rest of her was so hard, corded with muscle. It looked like she could knock the cart over without half trying, and the scales on her cheeks actually lifted a little, tiny muscles underneath swelling with anger. Cami slid off her seat, schoolbag awkward under her arm and the limon almost fizzing free of the bottle. Tor steadied her, and his hand was oddly gentle. "Fucking jacks," he said, just loud enough to be heard. "We don't want to stay around. It might be *catching*."

Why did boys always have to be so nasty? Cami pulled him away. "D-d-don't. P-p-please."

He shrugged, his jaw set sullen. It was amazing how eyes so dark could be so scorching. "Fine. But just 'cause *you* say so."

Well, great. I'm a hero. "She c-c-can't h-h-help it. J-j-jacks—" Jacks usually had temper problems—not enough Potential to really charm, and they most probably wouldn't end up Twisting, but still. They weren't awfully employable, and had to live on the edges of the core. Almost-Twisted, just like they were almost-charmers. In-between and always angry. Or maybe they were scared of becoming Twists and being pushed even further down the chain.

Sometimes, *angry* just meant *scared*.

Ellie would be a strong charmer, maybe even Sigiled. So would Ruby, it was obvious. Cami wasn't so sure. Her Potential tested high, sure, but you could never tell until it quit being invisible and started settling. Ruby always told her not to worry.

Where was Ruby now?

Tor's grin lost some of its hurtfulness. He stripped his hair back from his face with stiff fingers, and for a moment he looked almost . . . vulnerable. "Yeah, a jack's a powder keg. I know. So, you want to look for your friend? Or should I take you home?"

Well, wasn't he just taking charge of everything. Cami shrugged, dropped his wrist and took another pull off the limon. "I d–d–don't want t–t–trouble."

"That's a shame." He cocked his head, tossing the leftover strawberry juice at a chained, dozing trashulk, hunched pluglike on a patch of verdant charmgrass in the midst of concrete and metal. The hunched gray green lichen-starred bulk snapped, catching the cup out of the air and munching, the collar at its throat flushing dull-red with pleasure. Its almost-snarl, vibrating just below the surface of the audible, sent a shiver up Cami's spine.

Or maybe it was the way Tor was looking at her. Serious and intent, his eyebrows coming together and his mouth relaxed. "Seems to me you could use a little trouble. The right kind, I mean."

Did he really just say that? Heat rose up her neck, as if she was the jack's sizzling grill. "R–r–right k–kind?" *As in, is there a right kind of trouble?*

Oh, my God, I'm actually flirting. Ruby would be thrilled.

The thought of Ruby jolted her, and she looked around again. The crowd had thickened for lunchtime. The sun was high enough to pierce the lowering gray that was autumn sky in New Haven, but it looked like rain soon.

"Yeah." Tor's smile was like sunrise, all the anger gone. His teeth were very white. "Maybe not today. And I can understand, if you don't want to be seen with me. You're Family, right?"

Not really. She contented herself with a shrug. He kept changing on her, she couldn't keep up. "I th–think I sh–should—"

"*There* you are!" Ruby chirped, her lacquered nails digging into Cami's shoulder. "What the hell are you doing?"

When Cami turned back, he had vanished into the crowd. Just evaporated, and good luck getting Rube to slow down enough for Cami to explain. So she just held the sweating-cold bottle of limon to her hot-throbbing forehead while Ruby, glowing with excitement, scolded her and dragged her along, telling her all about this *fabulous* shop where they could get earrings and hair ribbons nobody else had, and Ellie was just going to *expire* of joy.

NINE

THAT FRIDAY NIGHT SHE TYPED OUT THE STORY, hesitated, and punched the send key.

There was a long pause, and Cami was seriously considering chewing her nails as she watched the Babbage's flat glowing screen. Rain fingered the window, heavier than a mist but not heavy enough to be a downpour. The Dead Harvest was probably going to be cold and wet this year. All the costumed revelers would be buying turnaside charms to keep dry, and even the lure of free candy and tiny cheap flash-loud charmpoppers dropped into bags like party favors wouldn't bring so many of them to the door to scream their traditional *Trick's-treating!*

On the other hand, the house parties would be spectacular this year. If Nico was home still, he might even drive her to a few. She would go as the Moon, of course, just like every year. The costume was simple, it covered everything, and even had a veil. Maybe Nico would go as Hellequin again, prodding sinners and Twists toward the underworld as fausts leapt to obey his every bidding. Last year he'd been Gaston Wolfhunter, complete with ax and staff, and it had been a job keeping Ruby distracted enough not to snap at him. He hadn't made it easier by poking at her while driving between parties, and Rube had announced flatly that she would *never* be in a car with Nico Vultusino again.

Cami heaved a sigh. The white room sighed around her too, smelling of beeswax and lemon polish.

Finally the cursor blinked, and the *BlueEllen is typing* message showed up, faint and sparkling. They were supposed to be babchatting about Calc homework, but Cami had hijacked the conversation, for once.

At least Ellie let her get it all out, and fingers on keyboards didn't stutter. One of these days someone was going to figure out how to shrink a Babbage so Cami could stick it in her pocket and have it talk *for* her.

Wouldn't that be a dream. Of course, they'd have to discover how to ground it so a stray burst of Potential didn't fry everything. Once they did that, electronics were going to get a lot better. If the Great Tesla hadn't Twisted in 1919 when the Reeve hit, maybe he would have figured it out. There were legends of him heading into the Waste instead of waiting to be hunted down as a Twist, and the blue Potential-lightning out in the dangerous wilderness was called Tesla's Folly.

Ellie finished typing.

BlueEllen: *So you're going to see him again, right?*
CV528491: *I dunno. Should I?*
BlueEllen: *Was he cute?*
CV528491: *I guess.*
BlueEllen: *What EXACTLY did he say?*
CV528491: *He asked me if I wanted the right kind of trouble.*
BlueEllen: *THEN HELL YES.*

Well, that was as unequivocal as it got. Especially from Ellie.

CV528491: *I dunno. What did you get for #4?*
BlueEllen: *Do NOT change the subject. When you gonna see him?*
CV528491: *He works here. I guess he'll be around.*
BlueEllen: *You need a plan.*
CV528491: *I have a million plans. Unfortunately none of them are applicable.*
BlueEllen: *I can bring a quart of charmsauce and a couple grenades.*
CV528491: *You have grenades?*
BlueEllen: *I could always use one of the Strep's tantrum tampons.*

Cami grinned. "Tantrum tampon" had been one of the few

times she hadn't stuttered, and it had made Ellie laugh instead of crying. There weren't many jokes just the two of them shared, without Ruby being in on it . . . but that was one of them. And she had hugged Ellie so tightly that evening, the first time the Strep went all jack-mad on her.

> **BlueEllen:** *But seriously. You need a plan for this. It involves a boy.*
> **CV528491:** *What I NEED is to finish that stupid Hist paper. #4?*
> **BlueEllen:** *Let me check.*

Ellie took the hint, then, and kept it to Calculus. She also suggested Cami trash the outline and just get Ruby to write the goddamn thing. *She's already doing mine,* Ellie pointed out, and just then **RubyRedHood** popped up in the Juno intrachat and Ellie, being mod for this turn, hit the "accept" button.

> **RubyRedHood:** *What did I miss?*

Ellen, thank God, didn't tell her. By the end of the chat, the HC Calc homework was done and Ruby had decided she was going to do all *three* papers, because she liked it. Cami would take the French homework, and that was that. For someone with a tongue that tripped over itself, she was remarkably okay at French. It helped that it was all in the back of the throat, instead of in front where said tongue would mess it up.

She leaned back in her chair. It was a gray, raw afternoon, and in a little bit she would go visit Papa. He had been closeted with Stevens and Nico since she got home from school, and that was probably bad. Maybe Nico had been acting up. Again.

Well, I can't watch him all the time. He doesn't listen like he used to, either.

She chewed at her lower lip. Of course she knew what they were talking about.

The disappearances. Her shudder made the chair squeak.

The newscasts and tabloids were full of them, three children with high Potential vanishing from their houses in the last two weeks. Sometimes, when things happened, the Family would quietly step forward and help the cops figure things out. If it turned out to be a ring of fausts or a mad Twist taking kids, the Family would . . . arrange . . . things, and Nico would tell her just enough so that she knew, without having to worry.

As if he didn't know she would worry no matter what he told her.

Vanishing children were bad for business, some of the Family would say. Cami personally thought it was bad for *anyone*. And not every kid who disappeared had it as lucky as the Vultusino foundling.

She leaned back in her chair, tilting her head.

White walls, silky blond ashwood furniture, thin gauzy white curtains under the thicker cream-brocade ones. The carpet was cream instead of snow. It was like the surface of an egg, and Marya had moaned about putting a child in such a room. But Cami's disorderliness had been entirely confined to the kitchen and the playroom on the first floor, with its bright primary colors, blocks and toys and every variety of messmaking a little girl could want. Wherever she'd been before Papa found her, she had learned not to mar a blank white surface.

A flash of noise filled her head, and she smelled fresh-cut apples. Maybe Marya was baking and Potential, or just the heating duct, was carrying the aroma up here. Cami pushed away from the Babbage, wandered to the wide south-facing window. Her schoolbag was a dimple of darkness on the bed and the closet was ajar, showing clean Juno uniforms, white shirts, sweaters. She'd draped a long gauzy blue scarf—originally bought for Ellie, but torn now—over the full-length mirror, and she avoided looking through the gauze with the ease of long habit.

Mirrors weren't quite . . . safe. For one thing, Potential behaved a little oddly around any reflective surface. *They were called soulcatchers for a reason,* Ellie had remarked once. *There's all sorts of stories. Didn't you know?*

Cami just didn't like them, that was all. Meeting her own eyes was never a comfortable experience, and sometimes she wondered that Nico and her friends had such an easy time with it.

The window seat was white watered silk, and she braced a knee on it, her breath touching the glass with flowering mist. Below, some of the garden boys were working at the margins of the pond and the rose garden, in the hedge maze dewed with rain. Even in the cold months there was plenty for them to do. Nico didn't even notice them, the way he didn't notice the army of maids Marya fussed at to keep the whole house shining.

That's the difference. He can't see, I can't look away.

A sharp unpleasant shudder raced down her back with small prickling feet. One of the garden boys had messy black hair. He wore a white T-shirt even in the chill, steam lifting from his skin as he worked at trimming a hedge with what looked like a giant pair of scissors. He tossed his hair back with a flick of his head, a habitual movement, and Cami recoiled as if scalded. She was on the third floor; they couldn't see up here in the afternoon, even with the golden electric light shining behind her.

Here she was, barefoot in a pair of jeans that probably cost more than the garden boy made in a week, her pale-pink long-sleeved silk T-shirt barely meeting Ruby's standards of fashionable—expensive, yes, but not nearly eye-catching enough—but also probably worth more than a day's wages for him. He'd be sent to college, sure, and maybe end up a kolkhoz smallcharmer or low-level industrial tech.

But right now he was out in the rain, while she was warm, and dry, and moaning about homework. Not to mention

looking forward to a party and presents and all the accoutre-
ments of a cushioned life on the Hill.

Why would he say *anything* to her? Some guys thought the
scars made her easy, or that she could introduce them to Family. And all the Family boys were never good enough for Nico's
approval. *I know what they're thinking*, he would say darkly, and
scowl. Asking just how he knew what they were thinking was
guaranteed to make him stamp and be difficult. And God forbid
she actually asked what *exactly* he thought they were thinking.

She kept breathing on the glass. Maybe a pattern would
show itself in the condensation, something that would solve the
problem.

What problem?

Her fingertip rested on the glass. It wasn't quite a star, she
decided. Star-shaped, but not a star. And there were little things,
like seeds. She traced it, rapt concentration taking over as her
finger followed an invisible thread. The window-glass shivered.

Below, in the hedge maze, a dark head paused. Tor looked
up, and black eyes flashed.

Cami snatched her hand back, guiltily. She ducked as if he
could see her, three stories above in her eggshell bower. The
vapor on the window vanished, leaving the pattern unfinished.
What had she been thinking of?

The design on his necklace. A star. Only not a star.

Cami slid off the window seat. Her legs were trembling

slightly. For some reason, the image of a round, juicy, ripe red apple had filled her head. Was Marya baking? It was silly, but this *particular* apple loosened her knees and made the rest of her cold all over, as if she was outside in the rain too.

Not rain. Snow. Lots of snow. Her wrists ached, the old scars twinging.

She shook her head. There was a soft respectful tap at the door. "Miss Cami?" It was a servant, a cheerful brunette girl who was often in the hallways dusting in a black uniform and a starched white cap. "Miss Cami, Sir is asking for you."

Cami let out a long shaky breath. Papa was done with Nico and Stevens. It was time to go comb his hair and talk to him. She could talk to him about Ellie and Ruby, maybe. That was a safe subject.

Southking Street, Torin Beale, and apples were definitely *not* safe. Who *could* she tell? What did she have to talk about, other than a persistent feeling of cold sinking dread?

Her hand was on the colorless crystal doorknob. Something splatted against her window.

Cami jumped, but there was nothing. Not even a mark on the rain-soaked glass.

"Miss Cami?" Another soft tap.

"Y-yes." Her throat was dry. Her head ached, suddenly, and her wrists gave another flare of pain, as if sharp metal was tightening around them. She managed to twist the knob and summoned up a pale smile for the worried-looking maid. "Th-thank y-you. Y-Y-Y-Yol-landa, right?"

The brunette beamed, her round face splitting with delight. "Yesmum. Thank you." Blushing fiercely, she retreated, and Cami hurried in her wake, padding barefoot and trembling toward the Red Room and an old man's labored breathing.

TEN

THE BIG, SOFT FINGERTIPS ARE AT MY THROAT.
LONG broad hands, the fingers slightly swollen and manicured, and Her face is a white moon with golden hair fountaining over it. She traces my windpipe, the thin skin and ridges of cartilage underneath. The buzzing in my head is full of that funny smell—apples and heavy incense, a drugging smoke that makes my entire body a slow, lumbering mass. I am so small, and I am being spread out, too thin, butter scraped over too much bread. That cannot be right, for I am curled forward, my head on Her pillow, our hair mingling as She settles next to me. Dust rises, each speck of it glowing with Her presence, and under the drugging incense is a hint of sharpish rot.

But I do not care. It is soft here, but so cold. She is the only heat, and it is a chill that burns.

This one's heart, She whispers, Her red lips shaping the words so slowly. You love Me, don't you? My Nameless.

Oh, I do. I cannot help myself. We are wound together, Her palm against my tiny chest, everything in me rising to meet Her. She is gravity, She is dim light and life and love, and I make small piping sounds as She caresses me. This pleases Her, and Her nails scrape lightly, sliding through layers of pinhole-eaten velvet brought from Above. Only the big ones go Above, the littles are not allowed. The bigs bring back food and cloth, shinies to please Her and refuse for the littles to eat after the dogs are done.

Always after the dogs are done.

Sometimes, often enough, there is a new big one, to shave and to bring to Her for the oblivion She promises. A refugee from Above, where everything is too bright, too loud, too sharp, too deadly.

There is a steady persistent drip-drip-dripping, water on stone, and the badness is coming. Suddenly I am even smaller and a flood of chill ink is rising, its surface glittering with flecks of dusty phosphorescence, and as it creeps up my legs and reaches for my hips I hear the chanting. They worship Her, and She laughs, and the gleam is a glass knife, wicked and sharp. It flashes down, held in a muscled, tanned hand, a child's scream is cut short, and Her laughter, Her laughter, it is bells and cruel beauty—

"Shhh." Nico was on the bed, bare-shouldered, red sparks in his pupils. A wedge of golden electric light spilled in from the hall, and there was Marya, blue silk and her fey-woven shawl fluttering as she made helpless little movements with her hands.

"Shh, Cami. It's just a dream. You're all right."

"Nightmares again?" Trigger, a scarecrow with a mop of messy hair, an unusual shape because he wasn't in a baggy, beaten sports jacket. His white T-shirt glowed, and he kept his right hand low, because there was a gun's gleam clasped in it.

"S-s-s-s-so-sor-r—" The word wouldn't come, it was a stone of panic in her throat, and the white bedroom shivered around her, trembling like oil on the surface of a puddle. Underneath that thin screen the bad blackness lived, it was rising, and as the dream shredded, Cami's cheeks were slick and hot with tears.

"She's okay," Nico said over his shoulder. "You can go on back to bed."

Marya was having none of it. "Little *sidhe*. Screaming so loud. Is it *them*? Are they here?"

Who? But Cami was shaking so hard, the question wouldn't stay in her head.

"Shhh. Don't." Trigger had the feywoman's arm. Marya's eyes glowed with bluish foxfire over the smooth black from lid to lid—*she must be upset*, Cami thought, and another apology was caught and murdered by her stupid, treacherous, stuttering tongue.

Why can't I TALK?

"Stop saying sorry." Nico snapped his fingers sharply under her nose. "Book. Say *book*."

It won't work. This will be the time it stops working.

Marya resisted Trigger's trying to hurry her out of the room. "If it's them, little *sidhe*—they take the littles, and the hounds—"

Cami sobbed in a breath. Two.

"Get out," Nico said quietly, but his tone rattled with menace. "Marya. Go on. Let Trigger take you back to the kitchen. All's well here."

"Cold iron," Marya muttered. Her shawl moved on its own, the fringe slithering with cold sullen sounds. "Naughty little things."

"Come on, Marya." Trigger cast Nico a significant look over the feywoman's drooping head, and there were other voices in the hallway. "She's fine, it's all right. Little girls have bad dreams sometimes."

"Book." Nico's face was in front of hers, familiar in the darkness but strange with the red in his pupils, his canines touching his lower lip. "Come on, babygirl. Take a few breaths. No hurry."

"S-s-sorry," she managed, relieved that she could at least get *that* word out. Her hair was a sticky weight against her back; she had sweated and thrashed. Her arms hurt, a fierce dull ache centering on her wrists. Nico's fingers were warm; he had her shoulders. Crouching on her bed as lightly as a cat, and his head made a small sideways sound, inquiring.

He could hear things she couldn't, being Family.

The door swept closed, Trig saying something to whoever

was out in the hall. Was the whole house awake? How loud had she screamed? Did Papa hear it, down in the Red Room? Was he now lying propped on pillows and staring, with the Kiss burning in his familiar-strange face? You could see he and Nico were related, closer even than the similarity between every Family member.

Except Cami. She didn't look like *anyone*.

"Book," Nico said, patiently. His pajama pants were worn at the knees, battered blue-striped ones she'd bought for him two Mithrusmases ago. The tang of cologne—or Papa's aftershave—mixed with the healthy heat-haze of Nico, but overlaying it was a scrim of cigarette smoke and a copper breath. Either he'd Borrowed, or he'd been downing something with calf. "Don't worry, Cami. We've got all night."

I have school tomorrow. So she struggled with her breathing, and the gasps evened out. Her pulse continued to pound, but Nico relaxed a just a little. "B-b-b—" She coughed, swallowed, tried again. "*B-book.*"

The red was fading from his pupils. His shoulders lowered a bit as his canines shrank, tiny crackling sounds as the bones shifted lost under her shivering. "Good girl. Candle. Take your time."

"C-c-candle." Sweat cooled on her back, and her pajamas were all rucked around. The tank top was soaked through, and her sheets were probably gummy. "*C-candle.*"

"Marya."

"M-mar-y-y-ya." Her teeth threatened to chatter. She realized she still had her hands up, as if to ward off a blow, and dropped them. Nico relaxed even more, his knee wringing a creak from the springs. She blinked several times, and the white room stopped twitching as if it would shatter around her.

"Ruby."

Oh, Mithrus. "Y-you h-h-hate—"

His laugh was sharp and short, freighted with the copperiness of calf. "We don't like each other. You can still say her name. Come on, babygirl. Play the game."

"R-ruby." Her tongue was beginning to unknot itself.

"Ellen."

"Ell-l-l-lie."

"Good. Now take a deep breath."

She beat him to it. "*Nico.*" Once more, the charm worked.

Another laugh, this one more genuine. "Good. Move over."

The covers were a mess. And the cloth sticking to her skin was clammy, like the touch of cold fingers. Cami shook, stripping her sodden tank top off while he was punching the pillows into submission. When he settled with a sigh onto his back and she slid close enough to put her head on his shoulder, he stiffened.

"Whoa." But his arm didn't pause, he hugged her close, and she realized they weren't kids anymore just as her entire body turned into one of Marya's crackling fires.

"S-sor-r-r—" *Oh, damn it.*

"It's okay. Shush." He relaxed all at once. "Nothing I haven't seen before, jeez. Marya used to put us in the tub together."

Well, yeah. But that was years ago. "Th-they kn-know y-you're u-u-u-up h-here." The stutter got worse when she tried to whisper, now. Stupid thing, her tongue in revolt.

"What, you think I'm bad for your reputation?" But there wasn't any bite to the words. He sounded, of all things, amused. "Better get used to it."

"N-Nico." She tried to put all the aggravation she could into it, and poked him in the ribs. His skin was rougher than hers, and the heat of him was cleaner than nightmare-sweat. When she moved, her chest bumped against his side, and he swallowed hard, very quickly.

"Do me a favor and settle down, okay? I'm being a *gentleman.*"

Oh really? The scalding flush subsided, bit by bit. When she let out a long shaky sigh, every muscle suddenly deciding to unstring itself, he murmured quietly.

"You remember this one?" Very careful, very soft, as if by asking gently he could bring the dream out into the light.

Nothing but whiteness, choking softness, and the cold. *This one's heart.* She shook her head, carefully, trying not to move anything else.

"Someday you will," he said, into the darkness. "And I'll fix it. I promise."

"Y-you d-don't have t-to." *If I could remember, I might not want to tell you. Because you'd do something, maybe something the Family couldn't cover up, and Papa would get mad. I should distract you.* "Wh-what w-was M-Marya saying? *Th-th-them.*"

"Nothing." Slightly irritated now. "Family stuff. It's being taken care of."

She said nothing. Her chest hurt, but she didn't dare move. The rock in her throat was dry, but getting up to get a glass of water suddenly seemed like a bad idea, since she'd tossed her tank top over the side.

Nico's arm tensed. He squeezed her, very carefully. The crackling tension and strength under his skin suddenly made sense—it wasn't just whiskey and calf he'd been at.

He'd Borrowed. *Family business.* The ache under her ribs was a sharp spike.

"It's nothing you should worry about," he said, finally. "There's some . . . problems. In town. And Papa's close to transition. So some things creep out of the cracks and think that the Seven are distracted."

"Th-the k-kids? The m-missing ones?"

"Like I said, nothing for you to worry about. Think about your party instead."

Oh, yeah, that makes it tons better. "R-ruby has a d-dress for me."

"Can't wait. And no, I won't tell you what I got you. You're gonna have to wait and see."

Cami turned her head a little. Her lips met the hollow between his shoulder and chest, muscle and skin fever-hot against her cheek. His hand had slid down, cupping the curve of her hip through her own flannel pajama bottoms. He had gone so still she wondered if he'd transitioned right there, and she almost winced. Just another reminder of what would eventually happen to him. Papa's dead mortal wife hadn't been Family; but once you had some of the blood, you were part of the chain. Did Nico ever wonder why Papa had given Camille that name? Did it bother him?

I wish I knew my born name. "I w-w-wish I b-belonged," she whispered against his shoulder.

"You do," he whispered back. "With me. Now go to sleep, before I get the urge to do something I shouldn't."

Would that make it better? Do you really want to? She held herself stiff and silent, afraid of moving, until the rhythm of his breathing lengthened and his head tipped back. Huddled against him, Cami stared over his chest at the curtains over her window moving slightly, maybe in a breeze from the heat register in the floor, and tried not to think about apples until sleep finally found her.

ELEVEN

OCTOVUS BLEW IN WITH SOAKING STORMS FULL OF Waste-lightning, but the week of Cami's birthday was only cloudy and cold. The house throbbed and whispered, the manicured grounds were starred with charmed lanterns, bright dots of golden light, gleaming now that dusk was falling and the party was about to start.

"Oh, wow." Ruby touched one of the shoulder straps, pushing it up a quarter-inch. She also brushed at a stray strand of Cami's hair, her quick fingers tucking it behind a bobby pin and magically making the mess artful instead of silly. "Almost perfect. Where are the pearls?"

"Here." Ellie blinked, biting at her lip a little. The single strand of irregular, pinkish pearls, red silk thread knotted between each one, nestled against Cami's collarbone; Ellie fastened the clasp. "Yeah. Wow is right."

Cami shut her eyes. Next would come the mirror. "H-how

b-b-bad is it?"

"Don't be ridiculous." Ruby actually bounced on her toes, a movement Cami could *feel*. "You're gorgeous. Let me get my heels. Ellie, make her look."

"She has to get her own shoes on, too." Ellie patted Cami's silk-clad shoulder. "Cami, sweets, it's not bad at all. You're gonna knock 'em dead. Cheer up, it's your birthday."

Not really. But they didn't know that.

"J-j-just a-n-n-nother F-f-f-family p-party." Things were getting more tangled by the minute. *Oh, God, I probably look ridiculous in this thing. Why did I let Ruby talk me into it?*

It was traditional for the daughter of a Seven to wear red on her sixteenth. Not just any red, either, but heartsblood, the red so dark it could only come from the last wringing of that deep organ. The straps would have worried Cami, but they were wide enough—and Ruby had come up with a pair of long white opera gloves to cover most of the scars. The others wouldn't show much unless she blushed, so all Cami had to do was stay away from anything embarrassing.

This is so *not going to work.*

"Cami, honey." Ellie patted her bare shoulder again. "You're going to have to see to step into your shoes."

The V waistline of the dress had looked okay while it was on the hanger, and the skirt skimmed her hips and flared enough that she could walk without tripping herself. Ruby had also found a pair of pumps in exactly the right shade; Cami didn't have a clue just *how*.

Doesn't matter, Ruby had said, cheerfully. *If it exists, I find it. I'm a hunter, baby. Rawr!*

Ellie and Ruby had fussed over her hair, torturing it with flatirons and pins with holding charms, and Ruby had painted the makeup on with a steady hand. *Don't make me look Twisted!* Cami had wailed, only it took her three times as long to say it.

The reply was classic Rube: *Relax, bitch. I wouldn't Twist you up.*

"I c-c-can't. They'll all b-b-b-be l-l-l-looking."

Ellie's fingers were warm and gentle. "If it makes you feel better, they'll be looking at Ruby looking slutty more than either of us. You're not showing enough skin to be a Magdalen, even."

"I do not look *slutty*," Ruby piped up. "You're just *overly modest*. Or, to put it another way, boring."

"I am comfortable with my boringness, thank you." Ellie snorted. "Come on, Cami. One foot in front of the other."

Sometimes she wished she'd met Ellie before Ruby. When Ruby arrived in third grade at the Hallows School, one of her first acts at recess was decking one of the girls teasing Cami about her stutter. Cami had simply put her head down and shrank into herself, but Ruby, afire with indignation, took on all comers. *It's not FAIR,* she would yell, before leaping on someone in a flurry of fists and feet. From that moment, they'd been friends—and Ellie had come along later, in middle school at Havenvale. Private schools in New Haven had their own language, one Ellie hadn't known since she and her dad had moved from another city, over Waste in a charm-sealed train—but again, Ruby had ridden in to save Ellie from getting picked on, and now they were a troika.

Or more like Ruby and Ellie were best friends, and Cami was the third wheel that made the thing stable.

She opened her eyes. Ellie was grinning, the faint freckles on her nose almost invisible under a light coat of translucent powder. She had great skin. "That's good. She's breathing and has her eyes open."

"Check her for a pulse. Maybe she's transitioned." Ruby snorted, leaning over the vanity and touching up her eye makeup. The little black dress sheathing her was almost indecent, but with her glory of coppery hair and the expertly applied eyeliner she somehow looked fresh instead of whorish.

"Wow, even more tasteless than usual, Rube." Ellie was in black too, a halter-topped satiny number that made her into a sleek old-timey film star, her pale hair slicked down and her lack of jewelry classic instead of poor. *It weighs me down*, she said, twisting at the ring on her finger—a charmed star sapphire, the only thing left from her *real* mother. The Evil Strep had been talked into letting Ellie stay the night, probably because

Stevens had taken care of sending a formal invitation to one Ellen Sinder, with the Vultusino crest impressed on the wax seal and a heavy scent of money wafting up from the pressed-linen paper. *She looked just about green when she got it, too*, Ellie had whispered gleefully.

Even a famous charmer with a Sigil like the Strep feared Family.

"I can't help it. I'm nervous. If Cami faints I might turn into a puddle of tears." Ruby turned away from the vanity mirror and batted her eyelashes, making little kissy noises.

"F-f-f-fuck *you!*" Cami burst out.

They all dissolved into laughter, and Cami stepped into the pumps. They were okay, she guessed. Heels always made her unsteady, no matter how many Family functions she attended.

Ellie took her elbow, and they approached the full-length mirror in its heavy frame, the scarf over it fluttering from a stray breath, probably from the heater registers. Ruby arrived on a wafting breeze of chocolate perfume, whisking the gauzy material aside. "*Voila*. Gaze upon fair princesses, better than mortal man deserves."

"Amen to that," Ellie muttered.

Cami peeked at herself.

Oh.

The slim, red-wrapped girl in the mirror hanging on Ellie's arm had a shy disbelieving smile. Her gloves were spotless white, her lips carmine, her black hair an artful mass of charmed curls, a single charmstick thrust through it and dangling a string of crystalline red beads. The kohl smudged around her blue eyes made them huge, and she looked tall, elegant, and completely unlike the regular, everyday stuttering Cami.

This once, the mirror didn't frighten her. It was a miracle. "Wow," she breathed.

"Amen *again*." Ellie grinned. She tugged at her skirt, removing an imaginary wrinkle. "There. I think she appreciates our efforts, Rube."

"She'd goddamn better." Ruby tossed her curls. "Come on. We're fashionably late, ladies. Let's go Make An Entrance."

Every house of the Seven had a ballroom. The Vultusino's was a long wood-floored expanse, spindly wrought-iron chairs and tables along the walls and several smaller chambers opening away—the ladies' resting room, the smoking room, the two supper rooms, the solarium, two private audience chambers for Family business, the playroom for children too young to participate in the dancing, and a private room for members of the Family hosting the event to retreat to. The licensed and charm-bonded caterers were already at work, threading through guests with silver trays bearing fluted crystal glasses of champagne, champagne-and-calf, and fruit juices, as well as tiny, exquisite canapés. The mirrored bar was two deep already, the massive crystal-draped chandelier blazed, and the portly moustachioed herald at the door—another traditional feature—gave a signal. The music halted, turned on a dime, and became a tinkling fanfare.

"The Lady Camille Vultusino has arrived!" The herald's bass voice cut the hush, and Cami stepped through with her head high. Her knees almost buckled, and she heard very little of the herald announcing Ruby and Ellie.

Well, Ruby would be thrilled with *that*.

There were Family everywhere. The others of the Seven were represented—a contingent from the Cinghiale, and the Canisari their traditional opposing force, the Vipariane the balance to the Vultusino, the Stregare who were balance to no one, with their distinctive long tapering fingers and gold jewelry. The two branches of the Diablie, the Destra and Sinistra, mingling and indistinguishable except for their Unbreathing Elders, who stood stiffly, gleams of coal-red or foxfire-blue in their clouded pupils.

There were so many Unbreathing here, probably because Papa was close to transition. So still, only the gleam of their eyes moved as their gazes combed the crowd of breathing life. They stood tall, thin, and motionless, somehow avoided even in the heaviest crush of bodies.

You never wanted to crowd the Unbreathing. They didn't see things the way the mortal living did, and sometimes they . . . did things.

Nico appeared. She threaded her arm through his and tilted her head, accepting the polite applause. "Finally," he muttered without moving his lips. "You're beautiful."

The flush was all through her. Everyone could probably see the thin white scars on her upper shoulders. The music began, and he was heading straight for the dance floor, where the crowd was pulling back and away.

"N-no." She tried to tug on his arm. "Y-you're c-c-cra—"

"Relax." With his dark hair slicked back and his eyes blazing, he looked more Family than ever. Next to his impeccably crisp tuxedo and the Heir's bloodring glimmering on his finger, she already felt a little rumpled and wilting. "It's just a waltz. Tradition, kid."

It's always tradition in a Family. Why was this tradition okay with him, and other ones not?

The empty floor looked *very* large, and Cami caught a flash of russet hair. Ruby was already heading for the bar; Ellie had a glass of plain champagne half drained, and both of them looked inordinately smug. Trouble was on its way. For once, though, she didn't have to worry about derailing it.

Or, she could worry, but she couldn't exactly *do* anything about it.

Nico halted, the music began, and her body obeyed woodenly. She'd liked dance classes well enough; every girl of New Haven's upper crust had them at the Vole Academy. Madame

Vole never made fun of Cami's stutter—in fact, she understood Camille Vultusino would prefer not to speak at all, and Cami never got into trouble for giggling in class.

Her feet didn't stutter, either.

Nico paused, catching the rhythm. Her hand on his shoulder, his secure and warm at her waist, and all of a sudden they were nine and thirteen again, sneaking into the shuttered ballroom and pretending to be grown-ups. Waltzes and foxtrots, a scratchy tango played on an ancient Victrola from just after the Reeve, and she found herself moving with him, the flush fading as the world dropped away. He gazed steadily over her shoulder, and she could just let him do the directing.

"I mean it," he said, finally. "You're beautiful."

She nodded. *Thank you.* She could feel the words knotting up. So could he. "Book."

"B-b-book." Automatically.

"Candle."

"C-candle."

"Nico."

"Nico." Her smile caught her unawares; she watched his face.

Serious, intent, a sharp line between his eyebrows. His eyes were darker than usual, too. "I want to tell you something."

"Okay." As long as they kept dancing, she could handle this.

"But not until later, okay? Just . . . relax. This is your night. And there's a surprise."

"Surprise?" *Another one?*

"Yep." And he whirled her to a halt amid a swirl of polite applause. A shadow loomed in her peripheral vision, and Cami almost flinched.

But it was only Papa, straight as a poker in his own tuxedo, mane of graying hair combed neatly and the Vultusino signet on his left hand glowing with its own sullen crimson spark. He moved stiffly, and the ruddiness in his graven cheeks told her he had Borrowed.

Stevens would be upstairs in the Red Room, probably with Chauncey transfusing him from canisters—breathing Family couldn't take transfusion, it had to be straight from the living. It was dangerous for Papa to Borrow so close to the Kiss, and Cami gasped as a murmur swelled through the crowd.

Nico handed her over, and the music came back on a tide of strings. Papa's smell—bay rum, leather, and copper—enfolded her. The world righted itself once again. She laid her head below his shoulder carefully, so she didn't disarrange the charms in her hair *or* throw him off balance.

She shouldn't have worried. He was strong, especially so near the Kiss, and his iron grip was carefully gentle; she could feel the restraint quivering in his hard hands.

"Bambina," he whispered, his lips moving slightly. "My little girl."

It wasn't like dancing with Nico. She could *let* Nico do the steering. Papa wasn't being *let*. He just did it, like a tidal wave or a minotaur. There was no stopping him.

That was an even greater relief.

"You are Family," Papa said, in that same stilted whisper. "Nico knows."

If Papa says it, it has to be true. She kept dancing. A nod, letting him know she heard, her cheek moving against his chest. His tuxedo smelled of fresh air and starch, and somehow it was subtly wrong. The humanity in him was burning out, and what was left was dry clove-and-copper, a mix of crusted blood and the ancient spice of the Unbreathing.

Already, Papa's great barrel chest was thinning. "When I am gone—"

"No." She had never in her life dared to interrupt him. "No, P-papa." Unbreathing wasn't *gone*, it was just *changed*. But things looked different on the other side of the Kiss, and the Unbreathing retreated from the world. At least, they didn't keep charge of Family affairs, unless there was an inter-Seven dispute. Then they moved, swiftly, to punish—or simply to *appear*, their mere presence often solved any number of . . . problems.

Papa's hand tightened a fraction on her waist. "When I am gone, bambina, Nico protects you, eh? It is arranged."

It is arranged. Those three little words, the seal of finality. How many times had she heard him say it, deciding some detail, from a business deal to other, darker things? Things she wasn't supposed to know or think about. The lump in Cami's throat didn't go away, and the water in her eyes was going to ruin Ruby's careful work.

It was arranged. Well, okay. Great. Except she didn't want Papa to transition. There. She'd admitted it, at least to herself.

Because once he was gone, the others with their flaming eyes and their cruel mouths would maybe not keep their disapproval whispered behind ring-jeweled hands. Nico wouldn't notice, or if he did, it would only make him furious. There would be Trouble, capitalized and underlined, and there was no way she could head that trouble off without Papa's breathing presence keeping the worst of it at bay.

His certainty of her belonging was the only anchor she had, really.

The music finally came to a close, and there was more applause as Papa handed her back to Nico. She tried to look happy. Papa patted her cheek, his hand feverscorching and dry. At least *he* looked pleased, an infinitely small smile creasing his coppery face, thinning as the Kiss hollowed him out.

Trig was suddenly there, angular, scrubbed and slightly ill-at-ease in a black jacket instead of his usual violent plaid, his bowtie just a little askew. Papa took his proffered left arm, and the respectful murmur hushed even further.

Nico was very still, watching.

Something's wrong.

The wrongness crested. Papa stopped, Trig at his elbow, and his gray head lowered. A sigh went through the assembled Family—bright-eyed, clothed in expensive dark fabrics, their faces all slightly similar in some way outsiders could never quite articulate, broad high cheekbones and their foreheads all curved to the same degree, a similarity more instinctively felt than actually *seen*. Ruby and Ellie stood out in that sea of sameness, Ellie's face very pale as she stood rigid next to Ruby's bright flame. Rube had her fingers around Ellie's arm, digging in.

What's wrong?

The black-clad servants began to notice the hush. One of them was the garden boy. Tor stood by the door to the smoking room, and he was the only person not staring at motionless Papa Vultusino.

Instead, his black eyes burning, his hair messily declaring war on whatever he'd tried to plaster it down with, he gazed directly at Camille. His lips moved slightly, as if he was mumbling a message, or singing to himself. There was a glitter at his throat—a silver chain, the necklace tucked below the black button-down shirt with its starched and ironed creases. Roaring filled Cami's ears. She swayed on her heels, and Nico steadied her absently. High flags of feverish color stood out on Nico's shaved cheeks, and the tips of his canines touched his lower lip.

Enrico Vultusino collapsed, his rigidity crumbling and the rest of mortality sloughing from him as the tuxedo flapped on his suddenly slimming frame. Trig caught him; several other living Family moved forward to help. They halted, however, as a sound like a hot wind through a wet cornfield echoed in the ballroom. The living Family parted, and the Unbreathing came forward, moving like eerie graceful clockwork, their motionless bone-dry faces merely settings for the bright jewels of their eyes. They closed around Papa and bore him away, leaving Trig adrift-alone in the middle of the dance floor.

The Kiss had claimed Enrico Vultusino, after long years of service to the Family. It was an honor to be allowed to see the Unbreathing, an honor to see them claim one of their own. The older Family daywalkers clustered about, clasping Cami's hand and murmuring how they were proud to be part of the occasion, how lovely she looked, how Papa was an Elder now. The younger stared, some of the girls with frank envy, the boys getting close whenever the crowd took Nico away, one or two of them bending over her hand and pressing their lips to her gloved knuckles while she smiled and tried to look pleased.

It was like seeing everyone celebrate because the sun wasn't going to come up again. There was a Papa-shaped hole in the world now, and she just felt cold.

For the rest of the evening, as the Family celebrated both a daughter's birthday and the ascension of another of the Seven to the Unbreathing, Cami could not shake the image of Trig with his hands loose and empty, suddenly old as he watched the man he would have died for taken away into strange heatless immortality.

Trig was mere-human too.

Just like Camille.

Even Ruby was yawning. She and Ellie leaned together at the bar, giggling, as a few Family bravos complimented them and did shots of vodka-lamb instead of calf. The charms on the girls' hair glowed as the lights sank, the house preparing for dawn. Outside in the cold rain, small golden flames guttered out one by one in a randomness not even a Sigiled adept could discern a pattern behind.

Camille leaned into Nico, his the only heat in the chill surrounding her. They swayed together in a private corner of the dance floor, near a bank of small tables littered with napkins, empty glasses, twists of paper from the canapés and jack-d'oeuvres. The crowd was thinning. The music, drifting from speakers hidden in the ancient moldings, had turned sleepy, but Nico was still bright-eyed and tense.

"Hey," he whispered into her hair. "You awake, babygirl?"

Not really. But she nodded slightly. Her hair had held up wonderfully, though a single charmed curl had fallen free over her face. *Leave it,* Ruby had said in the ladies' dressing room a few hours ago. *Looks smashing.*

Smashing hell, Ellen had replied. *You're the one smashed.* She was one to talk, getting another gin and tonic down with a practiced bolt. *The blond's mine.*

D-d-don't, Cami had told her. The champagne had been fizzing in her head, loosening the knot in her tongue. She'd blinked, nodding sagely. *He's m-mean, and he has a d-disease. N-n-nico told me.*

For some reason, that had cracked both of them up—but Ellie had given the blond boy from the Cinghiale Family short shrift after that, and he'd left with a group of youngbloods for some club or another close to the core. Something about a minotaur cage, and Cami didn't want to know.

Family girls didn't go out after dark. They were taken home in private cars, put to bed and fussed over. Some of them sneaked out and ran with the boys—but they were Wild, and even they had stringent rules to obey. They never went out alone, and *absolutely* never without a Family boy or two. Even Cami knew *those* rules.

"Having a good birthday?" He didn't sound angry, just thoughtful. But he was so tense, humming electricity going through him. She rubbed her cheek against his shoulder, trying to soothe.

"Y-yeah." The word was hollow. Papa was gone. *Really* gone. Not just up in the Red Room, listening to whatever seashore song the Kiss brought close. She would never comb his hair again. Or sit between his feet in the mothering dark below his desk, hearing the reassuring thunder of his voice from above. Never sit on his lap and play with his tie, while he patiently explained things to her or listened to her halting little-girl babble.

Maybe if she'd been born Family she wouldn't feel this hollowness.

"Good deal." He stopped moving, and the champagne made her head spin. He was digging in his trouser pocket, destroying the line of his jacket. It was a wonder he'd made it through tonight without a fight or anything. She'd half expected him to go off with the Cinghiale.

Maybe he was behaving just for her birthday. It wouldn't be the first time.

Papa was gone. How was she going to keep Nico out of trouble *now*?

"Listen. Are you listening?"

She looked up, blinking fiercely. Everything was blurry. The last glass of champagne had filled her head with half-heard whispers, and the cold was all around her.

"Mithrus, Cami, don't *cry*. He's just transitioned. You'll see him again. But I'm *the* Vultusino now. I'm finishing out at Hannibal. There won't be any more problems there, I promise. When I come back, you'll finish at Juno's and go to college, right? And then—" He had finally found what he was rummaging for, and she wished he was still holding onto her. The world was tilting off-course even more, and she had the sneaking feeling it wasn't all the champagne's fault.

"Then," Nico said in a rush, cracking the small red velvet box open, "we can get married."

It was the Vultusina's ring. A blood-diamond glittered in clawed scrollwork cage, heavy white gold alive with charmlight to make it fit the chosen one, and Cami swayed again.

What? "What?" Why was she having trouble breathing? And why was there blackness closing in around the edges of her vision?

He had never looked like this before. As if she might snatch something he wanted away, as if she was the one who could tilt her head and say *let's go, kid* and be meekly followed.

"We can get married. If you . . . After, you know, college. Unless you don't . . . don't . . . "

Don't what? How could I not? A small seed of warmth bloomed under her ribs, and she almost swayed with relief. "Yes." Her cheeks were wet. *Nico. My God.* "Y-yes."

Maybe she should have thought about it. But it was Nico, the warmth under her ribs dilated, and the ring glittered as she touched it with a trembling fingertip. Its charmlight flushed a deep crimson as it popped a single spark.

If she hadn't been the chosen one, *his* chosen one, the ring would refuse. It was like the Heir's rings, or the signets. Sometimes things could be charmed for so long they seemed . . . alive.

The world righted itself, and the terrible cold fell away in invisible shards. The box snapped shut and she flung her arms around him, hugging so tight the charmstick in her hair tilted, and as he hugged her back, there was a pair of black eyes across the room.

Watching.

TWELVE

THE END OF OCTOVUS HAD ALWAYS BEEN A CELEBRATION, even before the Reeve. New Haven crouched under the lash of cold rain and spatters of sleet as Dead Harvest dawned, and curled itself down still further as the afternoon wore on under iron-colored clouds. Despite the wet and the keening east wind, last-minute costume-booths were still open on Southking, the thrift stores were crawling with customers—it was lucky to have something used as a part of your Dead Harvest attire—and the invitations flew fast and thick.

THE PLEASURE OF YOUR PRESENCE IS REQUESTED AT A COSTUME FÊTE,

so on, so forth.

No celebration at the Vultusino house, because of the observance of Papa's transition. But the invitations had to be sorted, and Nico didn't know how. It had always been Cami's job to go through them with Papa and make a plan for their separate appearances—the arcane dance of Family etiquette dictated some parties *must* be attended by the Head and some by the Heir, some by a junior member; others would be important but it could give the wrong impression if the Head attended, and above all there was the careful balance of power among the Seven to take account of. This year she didn't have Papa's comments to guide the whole process, but she'd been swimming in the Family's etiquette for so long there were no real problems.

It still took a while, even with Stevens making one or two helpful, if dry, remarks. Cami finally decided that since Papa had transitioned the only party that was absolutely *required* was the formal costume ball, hosted by the Stregare this year since one of *their* ruling family had transitioned too, just before May Eve.

The Vultusino would be responsible for the next May Eve party, because of Papa transitioning so close to Harvest. That was something Cami could worry about later. It would take months to make arrangements, but Stevens and Marya would help. So it ended up with only one Dead Harvest appearance to agonize over, the great Family costume ball.

Ellie was stuck home handing out candy to trick's-treaters while the Evil Strep attended the Charmer's Ball, and Ruby had plans with Hunter, Thorne, and some of the other Woods-downe clanboys. So there was no help there, and Cami's Moon costume from last year would have been fine . . . except her chest had gotten bigger, and she was taller. It looked ridiculous, and Marya muttered it was ill-luck to alter a Moon. Which meant the feywoman sent a few maids a-marketing for cloth and necessaries, and made the costume as she did every year.

Little mayfly, growing like a weed, Marya had said around the pins in her mouth. *Stand still, little sidhe. Be good.*

The sun slipped below the horizon on the last day of Octovus, and New Haven took a deep breath. The Dead Harvest had begun.

The gates of every great house—even the Seven's fortresses—stood open, the charmbell buttons and antique cold-iron knockers ready to be pressed into service. The Sigiled charmers' houses were alive with foxfire charmlight, shimmering veils through which ghostly faces pressed, half-heard whispers and screams spilling through cold night as the veil between living and dead thinned.

Every cemetery and graveyard was jammed with willo'wisps and families feasting in celebration, the gauzy shimmers of ancestral spirits hovering above the altars erected by their descendants, piled with hothouse flowers and sugar skulls melting in the damp even under the temporary canvas roofs. The first masked and gowned trick's-treaters rang bells or knocked, and the first cry of *Trick's-treating!* rang out; the first jewel-bright bits of wrapped candy showered into waiting bags. The first charmpoppers exploded against pavement, flung by shriek-laughing children.

The limousine slowed to a crawl, one of a line of shining glossy expensive cars flowing toward the Stregare's palatial main house. Cami shivered, her tissue-thin fey-woven veil tucked aside for the moment so she could breathe. The veil hung from a silver-tinsel crown; the dress's heavy length was brocaded with silver thread, the wand with its small golden crescent at the end, the reticule, and the fan secured at her belt. This year Marya had made Cami's costume in the style of the Renascence, high-waisted and bound with silver ribbons at the sweeping sleeves, as if she had known what the new Vultusino had planned to wear.

Nico lounged next to her, sipping at a whiskey and calf. The new Vultusino, ill-luck be damned, had chosen to dress as pallid Pierrot. White velvet tunic, white close-fitting breeches, white glove-boots, his face smeared with white and gray and his dark hair frosted, the red-thread bracelets at his wrists and the dagger-shapes of the black cloak alluding to the Little Lover's suicide, driven mad by the Moon-maiden who had promised… and left him.

Cami sighed. Nico was even being careful to sip instead of bolt his drink. If it spilled on him, the stain would never come out.

No fights, no running off, no explosions of temper. This was a new Nico, and one Cami wasn't quite sure about.

"You're worrying." He frowned, took another sip. The bloody gleam of the Vultusino's ring sent a dart of ruby light against the limousine's roof, and Chauncey whistled tuneless between his teeth, a familiar sound of concentration. "You look great."

The heavy weight on her left hand was the Vultusina's ring, its stone merely blushing instead of bloody. It clasped her third finger gently, lovingly, and the metal was warm. It should have been comforting, even if there was a party looming. Her tongue was a knot, so she didn't answer, just looked out the window.

At least *la Vultusina* couldn't be openly insulted. Etiquette would demand she be treated with distance if not warmth, and Cami was fairly sure she could handle smiling and nodding. It didn't take a lot to be agreeable, even in the Family.

Despite the rain and the fear, there was a throng on the wide pavements of the Helhurst neighborhood, where the Strègare had settled. It was lower on the Hill than the Vultusino residence, and older, but just as beautifully kept. The smaller trick's-treaters were in groups, with more adults hovering over them than Cami could ever remember seeing on a Harvest night.

Another disappearance had been all over the newscasts. A teenage girl, full of charm-Potential, vanished on her way to the corner market to buy a quart of fey-milk for her apartment building's concierge, a brughnie which couldn't have comfortably gone itself.

Brughnies, like Marya, were housebound fey. Marya went a-marketing, but always with a stone or three from the Vultusino household to anchor her so she didn't lose her way.

"Say something," Nico persisted. He drained the dregs, a slight flush rising up his freshly shaven cheeks and a dim red gleam lighting in his pupils for a moment before retreating.

What can I say? "J-j-just w-w-wishing w-w-we c-c-could s-stay. Home."

"What fun is that?" He grinned, and the crackle of the canines retreating and his jaw shifting was loud in the stillness. Outside, an adult dressed like an Armored Bear hunched his shoulders and "roared" for the delight of his childish audience, his broad paws spinning noisemakers, and charmsparks popping in a brief shower.

You're trouble tonight. And I don't know if I can stop you. So she said nothing, staring at the costumes outside the smoked charm-proof glass.

"Cami?" His fingers slid between hers. Warm and hard and familiar, the Family strength humming in his bones. Was he being careful of her mortal flesh, just as Papa always had been?

What would it be like to live with that strength, day in and day out? Sooner or later Nico was going to slip.

What would happen then?

"Th-thinking."

"Are you wondering if I'm going to run off with the boys

tonight? That's finished." It was the new tone, the one he'd used the night of Papa's transition. Almost questioning, as if he wasn't sure she would believe him.

If you get a few more whiskey and calf in you, will you still stay? But she nodded, touching her veil with her free hand. A twist of her fingers would loosen the silver clip, and she could spend the evening behind its blurring safety. Another group of children, all dressed as free fey, danced down the sidewalk, glittering with charm-sparkles carefully applied by their parents. A harried-looking mother in a wet mackintosh spread her arms, hurrying them along the sidewalk, and as her hood fell back her pale hair darkened under cold water.

Cami's heart leapt into her throat, throbbed there for a moment. She blinked furiously, and the traffic constriction eased. Chauncey touched the accelerator, a featherlight brush, and they slid forward.

"I mean it," Nico persisted. He squeezed her hand gently. The Vultusina's ring would scrape his palm, but maybe he didn't care. "Pierrot follows the Moon. All night, and always."

Her smile took her by surprise, and when he leaned over to kiss her cheek, his breath freighted with copper and the tang of whiskey, everything in her jumped again. The unsteady feeling went away, the world regaining its solidity. "All r-r-right, P-pierrot."

He looked pleased, and poured himself another drink.

Crush of lace and velvet of every hue, the newly finished dance floor whirling with color and motion—this was not a formal occasion, as her birthday had been. No, it was a revel, and the waiters and bartenders were the young ones among the Stregare, in their traditional blue and gold, instead of mere-human servants. The only mere-humans were security, like Trigger, and consigliere, some round and some stick-thin, all with the faraway look of those a Head could inhabit.

Cami kept her fingers lightly on Nico's arm, ready for him to give her that half-apologetic glance and step away, especially when the crew of lean Family youngbloods called his name and surrounded them in a warm haze of liquor and feverish heat, their canines out and their pupils holding sparks of high excitement.

"*Nico!*" Donnie Cinghiale clapped Nico on the shoulder, then swept Cami a wide, mocking bow, the black robes of his Haxemeister costume already disarranged and a drabble of spilled vodka and lamb splashed on his white shirt-front. "And the Moon Herself! Hey, bound for Taxtix tonight. Hot fight. You coming?"

"Only if *la mia signorina* wants to," Nico replied, hooking his arm over Cami's shoulders and giving a wide, brilliant smile. His other hand held a single glass—more whiskey and calf, but he'd been nursing it since they arrived. Which was *not* usual.

"Pierrot and the Moon, get it?"

Their laughter had teeth, and one of the Vipariane—Bernardo, the one who had cornered her once at a coming-of-age party and breathed *how sweet, how sweet* drunkenly into her hair—pressed close. "Ah, you're not hanging it up and leaving the nightlife to us, are you, Niccolo? We'll be lonely!"

Tresar Canisari, short and bandy-legged in his springhell-Jack costume, the oilskin over his dark curls knocked awry, let out a hiccupping laugh and slung his arm over his cousin Colt's broad shoulders. "Pierrot and the *Moooooon!*" he crowed.

Cami's breath came short and fast. She tried to step away, but Nico's arm tensed. "My *lady* Moon, Tres." Still with that bright, unsettling smile, both amusement and warning. The Vultusina's ring spat a single bloody spark, but the sound was lost under the waves of crowd-noise.

"*Lady* Moon!" Baltus Destra elbowed his cousin, lean dark Albin, and they managed wide drunken bows as well.

I hate this. She pinched Nico on the ribs, but gently, her fingers slipping against white velvet—her private signal for *I have to go.* "P-powder r-r-r-room," she managed, over the music. The beginning bars of a *tarantelle* had struck, and that was a man's dance. The wives and daughters usually retreated during the *tarantelle* and the *gipsicala*, and the young men were allowed to shout and misbehave while the elder men gathered in the smoking room to transact Family business. When the *moresca* played, the women would re-enter, and the boys would have had enough time to blow off their steam and act reasonably again.

That was what was *supposed* to happen. Some of the Family girls—the Wild ones—danced the *gipsicala*, but not many, and those who did were taken home early, if their mothers could drag them away.

Nico hugged her closer for a moment, before pressing his lips to her veiled forehead. The youngbloods hooted and cat-called, but he didn't seem to mind, and the veil hid Cami's blush.

At least, she hoped it did. Nico let her go, and Cami stepped away, a current of retreating Family women bearing her along.

Halfway to the powder room, a hard shove from behind in the crowd and someone stumbled into her. A flood of whiskey and calf splashed from a full glass. Cami staggered, almost falling—and whoever bumped her was whirled away on a tide of young Family men, their pupils gleaming with colored sparks and their heels, no matter what costume they wore, drumming the wooden dance floor in time to the driving beat.

"*Tarantelle!*" one shouted; the answering cry rose from the others' throats in a wave of copper-laced heat. A violin wailed, and the gitterns began to strum harder.

The veil stuck to her damp cheeks, and Cami struggled to breathe. The powder room *had* to be in this general direction; she felt along the wall for a doorknob, a latch, *anything*. Bumped and pressed, feathered masks and high tinkling laughter as the music spoke from the Family's distant past, igniting the creeping fire in their veins. The musicians, behind carved screens, were older Family men, and those who showed musical promise almost never developed the Kiss, even if they served the Family well. *You cannot serve the Kiss and the music*, the Family said, and the proverb meant much more. It meant being caught between a rock and a hard place, or trying to serve two masters. Sometimes it meant betrayal, and other times it meant Fate.

The Family had some funny ideas about Fate, and try as she might she could never get Papa or even Nico to explain them. Maybe you had to be born in to understand.

Sweat slid down her back, soaking into velvet. The dress was too *heavy*, and it dragged the floor. If she danced, it would have to be a slow waltz, or she'd trip over the material.

Oh please, come on, the powder room. Please. Her tongue was a knot, and so were her lungs, struggling against the noise and the glare and the veil's gauze, plastered to her face. Her questing fingers slid against a crystalline knob, she twisted savagely and shoved the door open. Stumbled into welcome cool, dark quiet, pushing the veil aside and gulping in dusty air full of neglect and stillness. The door swung shut behind her and she leaned against it, not caring where she was as long as she could *breathe*.

The darkness, after all the whirling color and motion, was a shock. Her ribs heaved; her wrists twinged sharply. It took a little while for her heart to stop pounding, and the dripping from her abused costume was loud in the stillness. Whiskey and calf, of *course*. It was never going to come out. Marya would scold and scold.

As soon as she could breathe again, she patted at her belt. The reticule was there, with all the supplies for the evening. She could dab at the dripping with the small charmcloth in her reticule, but it was all down her front. She probably looked like Bloody Scot Mary, for God's sake.

She clipped her veil aside and took stock. *Where am I?*

A parquet floor. Shrouded shapes of furniture, antique gas-jets jutting from the walls. Tall narrow windows choked with heavy rotting velvet drapes—what *was* this room? It looked like it hadn't been open for ages. The furniture was low, and there were high lamp-shapes with ancient, cracked tubing dangling from them.

Oh. It's a Borrowing room.

They didn't have them in all the Family houses anymore, just the older ones. There was the fireplace with its carved screen, and above the dangling tubes were the glass canisters, filthy with dust. The vessel, Family or human, would lie on the higher couch, the Borrower on the lower and wider one with the flowerlike cup to their mouth, and the red light from the canisters would grow dimmer and dimmer as the vessel was drained. This wasn't the private Borrowing between a Seven and one of their honored servants; this would be where the *Festas Scarletas* would be held and treaties would be cemented. It was also where an Elder would Borrow from a breathing Family member, with other Unbreathing in a circle around the two to make certain the Borrower didn't take too much.

The furniture was likely as old as New Haven itself, and the drapes were probably so rotten they would fall at a touch.

I shouldn't be here. She reached behind her for the doorknob, but it slipped against her sweating fingers. *I really should not be in here. Powder room. It can't be far away.*

But it would be full of slim bright-eyed Family girls and their lacquered mothers, all of them knowing who Cami was but few deigning to speak to her, and never without a sneer. At least they didn't actively *do* anything like some of the girls at school—it was beneath the pureblood girls to even notice the Vultusino foundling. It would be different if she'd been from a charming clan, married into the Family to cement an alliance or to strengthen the bloodline. Papa's dead wife had been a Sigiled charmer, a shining mortal star among them, from what Cami could tell.

What did they think of Papa giving her that name? She'd sometimes wondered. There was nobody to ask, and the wondering always led her to a deeper, more uncomfortable question.

What's my born name? Her wrists ached, sharply. She twisted at the knob again.

It refused to budge. Her sweating hand couldn't grip properly, and the music throbbing outside was oddly muted. Cami's dripping skirts brushed the deep dust griming the parquet. Nobody had walked in here for a long time.

Alcohol fumes rose from her ruined costume, she could almost *see* them; her Potential moved uneasily in the dimness around her, its heatripple haze almost visible as well.

What is that?

One of the curtains was slightly askew, and a cold white glow edged the folds of velvet. *An outside window? Not in a Borrowing room. And it's raining, there's no . . .*

A shudder slid through her entire body, crown to soles. The music had changed. It wasn't the *tarantelle* or the *moresca*, not a waltz or a foxtrot, not even a tango or a *capriccine*. It was a queer atonal moaning, several voices piled atop one another and echoing, a soft drip-drip-dripping with no pattern stitching the chant together.

And yet . . . it was familiar, in some way. The cold touch of her nightmares down her back began, ice cubes against sweating skin.

I can't . . . Cami stepped away from the door. The dust-thickened curtains moved slightly, as if touched by a hand or a vagrant breeze, and her footsteps—the Moon wore silver slippers with metal at heel and toes, so they chimed while she walked—were muffled and grit-crunched.

Skritch-scratch. Fingernails on glass, maybe? A small scrabbling sound.

The stone in her throat was dry. She smelled apples, wet salt, cold stone. Shadows moved at the window, brushing across the faint powdery silver light.

They're calling me, she realized. Chanting voices, the rustles and drips from her costume blurring, and there was another sound underneath it. Faint and far in the distance, a train's lonely whistle, perhaps.

No. Not a train. A howl, lifting cold and clear on a snowy night. Not a wolf's uncivilized cry, though. A dog's voice, a hunter's song, one she had heard before.

Skritch. Skritch-scratch.

A thumping. Cami took another step. How had she gotten halfway across the room? The crouched couches on either side watched her with no interest. Her footsteps had become silent, even the scratchy gauze of her veil not whispering as it rubbed against the Moon's dress, silver ribbons fluttering from her sleeves as if she was running. Her scalp crawled, her braided hair twitching as if every individual one wanted to stand up.

Apples. A breath of heavy, perfumed smoke.

The window was smeared with dust. Shadows and shapes moved behind it, whirling dancers and staggering drunks. A single bloody gleam—not the Vultusina's ring, but something else—pierced its foxfire glow, and the curtains shivered uneasily.

Wait. The cold was all through her, and a trembling like a crystal wineglass stroked by a wet fingertip. *It's not a window. Not in a Borrowing room.*

Glass. Flat glass full of light.

They were *mirrors*, behind the age-stiffened curtains. The crawling under her skin intensified, every inch of her alive with loathing but miserably compelled forward. The voices rose, a chorus with no music to it, echoing strangely as if the walls had pulled away. As if she stood in a vast cavernous space, the silvery foxfire gleam strengthening. Not moonlight, but a diseased glow.

The mirror. The calling was coming from the mirror. She couldn't decipher the word. *My name. The mirror's saying my name.*

Her *born* name. But she couldn't hear clearly. *Come closer . . .*

Her right hand lifted, trembling. The ring on her left was a millstone-weight, its stone cold and dead, and her fingertips hovered an inch from the glass. Half an inch, and when she touched it, she would *know*—

The locked door barged itself open. Giggling, a Family girl staggered in, a burst of golden haze behind her. It was Mocia della Sinistra, and one of her clan-cousins, the Sinistra boy who always wore calfskin driving gloves. They stumbled, his mouth at her ear, her hair half-undone, and his gloved hands had worked themselves into her bodice—she had dressed as

Esmerelda Gipsicana, and he was in a tuxedo and a shining mirrored half-mask, pushed aside as his face rubbed against her.

Their dance was a drunken whirl, and the music from outside was a blare that covered Cami's footsteps as she darted aside, taking shelter behind a long row of canister-trees and higher-backed couches. They would be dazzled from the sudden darkness too, and it looked like they were in a world all their own.

Her cheeks scalded. The inebriated pair fell on a low shrouded couch, and dust rose thick around them. Cami's breath jolted in her throat. Neither noticed her ghosting past; they were knotted together and murmuring with thick smacking sounds, and Mocia—she was Wild, there was no doubt about it—moaned as her cousin's fangs scraped her throat. Was he going to Borrow from her?

Her mother is not *going to be happy with that.* It was a sane thought, a comforting thought, and Cami clung to it as she hurried along, her skirts pulled up and the Vultusina's ring waking again with a ripple.

The door was closing, its slice of golden light and noise narrowing, but Cami ducked through just in time. The noise burst through her head, the clanging chimes of the *capriccine*—had she missed the other dances?

"*There* you are." Nico appeared out of the crowd. "Mithrus, Cami, what happened to you?"

She couldn't quite remember, her head full of buzzing noise

and her bones cold. Ice under her skin and muscles, chilling her from the core out, and it was difficult to think. "H-home." She could barely force the word out. "I. W-want. T-t-t-to g-g-g-g-go—"

"You're covered in it." He was a rock in the middle of the crowd, and she clung to his arm. He'd had more, it was obvious from the burning red pinpricks in his pupils and the way he too-carefully tipped his head back, avoiding the smell from her dress. "Did someone throw something? What the *hell*?"

"H-home," she kept repeating, but he wanted to stay with the Cinghiale boys and drink a bit more. In the end he handed her into the limousine and Chauncey drove her silently through Dead Harvest night, and when she woke Nonus Souls morning, Nico had already left for Hannibal.

Pierrot did not follow the Moon, after all.

THIRTEEN

THE MONTH OF NONUS WAS SERE AND COLD, DRY AND achingly bright. Icy flakes began falling a week after the Festival's orgy of candy and parties; Cami almost shuddered every time she had to walk outside. Ruby drove her home with mind-numbing incaution every day. Stevens, dry and sticklike, was looking particularly gray. Marya wore layers of fine thin spidery black, her long fine hair scraped back and her usually apple-blooming cheeks pale. Trigger and his security teams were unseen, but it didn't mean they weren't there—a prowler was chased away the first night it snowed, a Twisted beast found just at the edge of the property another night.

It was a sign that it was going to be a hard winter, Trig remarked, if things were so desperate to try even a Family estate's boundary.

The snow kept falling, and the plows and harnessed titons came out. Slump-shouldered, massive gray Twisted things, the titons were chained every winter, dragging plows along, their tiny yellow eyes alive with charmlight and their horny knuckles scraping the icy concrete. They ate bones and offal, as well as gravel and lumber with their broad flat black teeth, and were mostly docile if kept fed. They were trapped out in the Wastes between cities and provinces by teams of jack bounty hunters, and kept in pens on the edge of every city's blighted core. Rumor had it they were sometimes pitted against minotaurs in the cages, and the betting was fierce.

Nico would probably know. But he would never tell her.

"Mithrus *be careful!*" Ellie shrieked, grabbing at the dash. The radio reeled off names—it was the three-thirty newscast, and two more charmer girls had vanished last night, one right from her own bedroom. *No suspects*, the announcer said, as Ellie let out a short jolting scream.

Cami just held on grimly as tires spun, the car sliding. Ruby yelled a cheerful obscenity, goosed the accelerator, and steered into it. Tire chains and silvery octopus-leg catchcharms gripping again, ice crackling on the window as Cami, wedged uncomfortably in the glossy black Semprena's tiny concession to a backseat, found her lips moving silently.

Praying, she had decided, would not hurt.

"It's just *snow!*" Ruby crowed, and shot them through a yellow light with half a second to spare. The newscast crackled through the speakers.

—brings the total toll of disappearances to seventeen. The mayor's office had no comment, but Captain Ventrue of the New Haven Police Department—

Titons reared, their horns stabbing empty air, a plow behind them creaking as the zooming little car startled the giants, and Ellie and Cami screamed at the same time, in oddly perfect harmony. Their cries swallowed the end of the 'cast and the Red Twists came on, the bassline of "Born Charmed Enough" thumping the windows and rattling Cami's teeth.

Driving with Ruby was always an adventure, but it was better than the small, cushioned but stifling buses Juno used to take less fortunate girls straight to their doors. Private schools did not like losing their students, and if there wasn't a transporter or two on file you *had* to use a bus. Walking home in New Haven was risky—in other words, it was only for the public school kids.

Like Tor, Cami thought, and squeezed her eyes shut.

She'd seen him around the house, of course. Things weren't quite upside down with Papa gone, but they were definitely not the same. Some of the maids had been let go, Marya piqued about something or another they did wrong or didn't do right. Chauncey had caught the head groundskeeper "intoxicated, Miss Cami," and asked her if he should be fired.

Like she knew. But with Papa gone, Marya sulking, and Nico off at Hannibal, she was the only one to ask. *N-n-no*, she'd told him. *N-not unl-less it h-h-happens ag-g-gain.*

And he had nodded, looking profoundly relieved, and walked away whistling as if he'd heard it from Papa's mouth. She squirmed at the memory.

She'd even turned Ruby down when it was time to skip and head to Southking again. And Rube was not happy over *that.*

Stop being a foot-dragger, Cami. Mithrus, you're turning into an old lady overnight. Being engaged makes your brain soft.

Missing Nico was never pleasant. And before he left, he'd been odd. Treating her like . . . what, exactly?

Like she was something new. Something strange. And he hadn't even bothered to say goodbye. Just vanished like a Dead Harvest dream, and Marya had scolded Cami both for her own costume and for the shredded ruin of Nico's.

He'd gone out with the youngbloods after all.

Think about something else.

Something had happened to her at the Stregare party, but it had vanished just like the nightmares, and all she could remember was the Borrowing Room and the dust choking her as Mocia and her clan-cousin writhed on the couch. A bolt of queasy heat went through Cami's belly whenever she thought of it. Had Nico ever, with a Family girl . . .

Ruby shrieked, a wild joyful cry, and Ellie cursed with colorful inventiveness as the Red Twists harmonized about being born with flippers or fins. The car lifted as if it intended to fly.

Cami let herself think about Tor the garden boy instead.

He sometimes fetched things for Marya, carried things into the cellar, and the feywoman had started to ask for him. Not by his name, of course, she called him the Pike because he was long and dark.

Hearth-fey didn't like big changes inside their domains. Marya was . . . upset.

And me? What am I?

Nothing but the pin holding the house up. A tired, shivering pin. If she was a Family girl, would it be easier?

That was another incredibly uncomfortable thought, one she did her best to shove away. The Semprena slowed, banking like a plane and gliding to a stop. Ruby twisted the volume dial down to merely "overwhelming" instead of "minotaur roar."

"You can open your eyes now, Cami." Ruby sighed. "That wasn't even very *fast*."

"Death by cardiac arrest, induced by vehicular shenanigans." Ellie waited for a few seconds, unclicking her seatbelt. "There's the Strep."

Cami's eyelids fluttered open. The world poured in, full of the peculiar flat blue-white of snowlight. The Sinder house on Perrault Street was a fantasy of four stone spires and a sort of grim medieval feel, not helped by the tall curlicue wrought-iron gates. Ruby's Gran had a teeny, welcoming, very expensive cottage in Woodsdowne, but this was Perrault and the houses had serious, carnivorous faces. A tall line of firs frowned over the charm-smoothed stone wall enclosing the estate, and the glowing Sigil on the gates was a pair of high-heeled shoes.

The Strep was a famous charmer, after all.

Ellie's dad was a lawyer specializing in inter-province negotiations, and gone an awful lot. At some point the Strep was probably going to get herself knocked up, probably by one of the boyfriends she brought in when Daddums was working late, and the hormonal shifts were going to make her even *more* of a pain in the ass for Ellie.

In one of the towers, a shadow moved across the golden glow of electric light. The Strep had a carefully fertilized mane of frosted-blonde hair, and it always sent a shiver down Cami's back.

"Thanks for the ride," Ellie said finally. "Babchat later?"

"But of course. Let Cami out, it's her turn to pound on my dashboard."

Great. But she wriggled out while Ellie held the door, then hugged her. "C-c-courage," she whispered. "T-t-t-tis only the St-t-t-trep Monster."

The tired old joke wrung a tired old laugh out of Ellie. Her dad had been gone for two days, to New Avalon up north at the edge of the province, for high-powered negotiations. Something about inter-province trade agreements, fighting over who would pay to send rail-repair crews out into the Waste.

The smudges under Ellie's storm-gray eyes were getting awful dark. "Someday I'm gonna walk home and get kidnapped just to avoid her." She tried to sound light, but there was a terrible flat ring to the words.

"D-d-d—" *Stupid words.* "*Don't,*" she finally got out, her breath pluming in the cold air. The iron gate was opening, sensing Ellie's nearness.

"Shut the damn door, it's freezing!" Ruby yelled, but Cami waited, leaning on the car door until she saw Ellie trudge, slowly and safely, up the paved drive and heard the dull thud of the front door slam behind her. "Come *on*, Cami! She's not gonna get snatched in her own driveway."

You just never know. Some of the vanished weren't charmers, just young mere-humans, but the entire city was on pins and needles now. Cami privately wondered how many people would be concerned if whoever was doing the snatching hadn't started taking young charmers. None from Juno yet, but there were a couple girls gone from Hollow Hills. One had even disappeared between the Hills' bus and her family's front door, the snow scuffed as if a struggle had taken place and the branches of several nearby bushes broken.

The tabloids, for once, weren't screaming about celebrity follies or Twists. Cami avoided reading them, but there was only so much you could ignore.

She dropped down into the front seat, pulled the door to, and took Ruby's scolding all the way home with several nods, one or two *uh-huhs*, and five full minutes of cursing when Ruby opened up the Semprena on the straight shot of Grimmskel Boulevard. Remarkably, she didn't stutter once while she was terrified.

Ruby told her it was a goddamn miracle, blew her a kiss, and the Semprena vanished toward the downward slope of the Hill before the large iron gate had finished scraping itself open.

Camille shivered, the wind nipping at her bare knees. The gate groaned, creaked, ice falling from its scrollwork and the charm-potential under the surface of the metal running blue with cold. The defenses here were old and thick, laid in with the stones when the Seven had first come to New Haven and added in layers with each successive generation. Papa had remarked once that the Family had been in New Haven before it was New, and once a long time ago, when talking to the wide, perpetually smiling Head of the Cinghiale, he had paused and looked into the distance.

I remember when we were hunted, before the Reeve made us citizens. We should all remember thus.

And Marcus Cinghiale had nodded, his own iron-gray hair slicked back and his bullet-eating grin turning cold. *You are always cautious, old friend. We trust in that.*

Neither of them had noticed Cami playing in the corner of Papa's study, stacking wooden blocks.

She returned to the present when another gust of wind nipped at her knees, and the sound of cold air rushing over winter's surfaces modulated into an eerie wail.

Almost like a wolf-cry. Or voices in a chorus, rising through a word that would explain . . . what?

For a bare millisecond she toyed with the idea of turning away and walking down into town. Going into the core's diseased brightness, step by step, and seeing with her own eyes what the chaos-driven Potential in there would do to her. Would it make her a minotaur? Would she go running through the streets, bellowing, thick blankets of mutating Potential clinging to her body and her head swelling with bone and horn?

She was in-between, just like a jack. Not Family, not charmer-clan, not Woodsdowne clan, who knew if she was fully mere-human? Who would notice if she simply vanished? Would they say her name on the newscasts? Or would she be gone without a ripple?

Blank static filled her head, tugging at her fingers and toes. It formed words, spoken low and soft, so caressingly soft.

. . . nobody. You are nothing.

"You gonna stand out here all day?" he said, quietly, and she jumped, letting out a thin shriek. Her schoolbag almost fell, she clutched at it and found Tor the garden boy watching her, leaning against the gate.

FOURTEEN

THE IRON MOVED RESTLESSLY, SENSING HER AND ALSO testing him. He was allowed to be there, true . . . but the gate didn't like it, not the way it liked Family.

Not the way it liked her, either.

She dropped her gaze, suddenly acutely aware that he was in a battered, scuffed tan leather jacket and jeans that probably did nothing against the cold. Aware as well of her black wool-and-cashmere coat just long enough to cover her skirt, a gift from Papa at Dead Harvest last year, and her expensive silver-buckled maryjanes. She edged for the gate, and he watched her.

"I'm not gonna bite you." Now he sounded . . . what? Desperate? Angry, like Nico.

They're not even remotely alike.

Then why did she think of them together? And why was she blushing, uncomfortable heat prickling at her throat?

"I kn-kn-know." The words surprised her. She stepped over

the threshold and the gate stopped quivering. "S-sorry."

The snow was a blanket. Bare branches reached up, the driveway ribboning between their grasping hands. Hummocks and hillocks where there used to be gardens, a deceptive layer of white blurring everything. Waiting to catch an unwary foot, just like her goddamn tongue waited to trap the simplest words.

"You're not like them." His boots ground against the driveway, scraped free of ice and snow and sealed with charms. Had he maybe charmed part of it, too? She didn't see Potential on him, but then again, hers was invisible too.

At least for now, and maybe once it settled too. You couldn't ever tell with Potential.

What does he mean, not like them? Family? Of course I'm not. She shrugged, tucking her school scarf a little tighter and setting off for the house. Ruby *could* have taken her up to the door, but she'd been letting her off outside the gate instead. Cami didn't blame her. Of course Rube was pissed when Cami said *no, not today.* Because Cami could always be relied on to give in and go with. It was her *job.*

"Hey. Look, I'm always saying the wrong thing to you." He caught up with her. The gate screeched a little as it swung to, steel jaws closing gently. "I don't know what to do. Help me out a little here, huh?"

Oh, man. Here it comes. She swung to a stop and faced him, her heel digging into a patch of odd charming on the concrete, scraping roughly and striking a single colorless spark. A long strand of hair fell in her face, working its way free from the cap Marya had knitted her. "What." The word came out whole and hard, on a puff of frost-laced breath. "Do you. Want?"

"Bingo." His smile was instant, and it looked genuine. His nose was raw-red from the cold, and he stuffed his hands in his pockets, hunching his muscle-broad shoulders. "Hi. I'm Tor."

I know that, do I look subnormal? "I know."

"And you're Cami. You're beautiful, and you don't talk because you're nervous. So people end up talking to you a lot, because you listen. And because they want things out of you." He dug one toe into the pavement, stopped. Tilted his dark head. Snowflakes stuck to his hair, some melting. He was crowned with winter.

Well, don't you get a prize. Irritation stung her, but she kept her mouth shut. Instead, she just nodded. The wind grabbed at her knees, sinking into unprotected flesh—the cashmere was barely longer than her skirt, and the knee socks were pure wool but didn't help as much as they could. She spared another nod, and started taking mental bets about what game he was playing. Would he want money? A date? Something to do with Nico, maybe—more than a garden boy's scholarship?

If I went to public school, would Nico ever look at me? Or would I be invisible to him, like the maids?

More and more these days, Cami was wondering about that.

"I want to talk to you. And hear you talk, too." His shoulders hunched even further. "I want to hang out sometime, maybe. If you can stand to be seen with a poor kid. That's it."

That's never it. Her mouth opened. "That's n-never *it.*" *And maybe I was a poor kid too.* There was no way for him to know that, really, but it still bugged her. People always had all these *thoughts.* Assumptions. And her stupid tongue would never let her make them see, even if she felt like doing so.

A shrug and a wry expression, as if he understood. His nose was red from the cold and their words were clouds, hanging uneasily between them as if on singing wires. "Yeah, well, you can get me fired. You've got all the power here. I'm not even supposed to look at you. I know that."

Chip on your shoulder much? But she knew what he meant. She hitched the bag strap higher. A cup of hot chocolate and one of Marya's scones sounded *really* good right about now, and there was double HC Calc homework. Plus there was Ruby's French to get in before it was Babchat-time. "Why?" *Why me?*

"Because you're not *like* them." Patiently, but not as if she was an idiot. "I dunno. I just . . . it's stupid. Fine. Never mind." He took two steps back, then shook his dark head, dislodging little crystals of snow. Had he been waiting for her? Out here in the cold?

Maybe not. But she could ask.

"D-d-d-do you w-walk here?"

Tor actually blinked, as if she'd said something extraordinary. Another head-tilt, and those eyes of his *were* really black, she decided. Not just too dark to tell, not just a deep brown. *Black.*

Was it a Twist? But Marya was thorough and careful. Fey could *smell* Twists, and didn't like them. Some said it was because they were unpredictable, like the fey themselves. Marya was predictable, really, but she was a hearth-fey. Her world was the kitchen, her universe pretty much bounded by the house walls. Even Cami was only worth noticing because she belonged to the house.

"The bus drops me off on Hammer. Then I walk." He paused. "It's not bad."

"Aren't y-you af-f-fraid?" Maybe boys didn't have to worry so much.

"Why? This is a good neighborhood. It's not Simmerside. Or the core."

Simmerside. Where the Twists lived next to the normal too poor to live anywhere else. Where the sirens and gunfire spilled out of the core and into the waking world. "The c-c-core?"

"No, I haven't been *there*, you think I'm crazy? I'm a Simmerside kid, Joringel Street Orphanage. So out here, nothing much to be afraid of. Plus, those wackos kidnapping kids mostly go for girls. See? We're talking."

Kind of. But she nodded. She'd heard of Joringel; another

branch of the Mithraic Order used to run it before there was some scandal and the city had taken over administration some ten years ago. It was still a bad place to grow up.

Would *she* have ended up there?

"It's not so rough, right? You look like you could use a friend. Or at least someone to talk to."

And you're going to fill that gap, right? Riiiight. "I h-h-have f-friends."

"Yeah, ones that leave you on Southking alone. Or who don't even wait for you to get inside your gates." He made a dismissive gesture, his hand chopping down. A healing scrape across his knuckles was vivid red, the skin a little chapped.

"D-d-do y-you have f-f-f-friends?" At least he waited for her to get all the words out, and didn't act like waiting was a big deal.

"No." Quiet and very definite, like he'd thought about it. A *lot*. He unzipped his jacket, and she almost took a step back. When he lifted up his T-shirt—how was he out here in just that, without shivering too hard to speak?—Cami actually *did* step back.

Welts and burns crisscrossed his torso, most of them scars and a few still ugly-colored, as if his skin hadn't forgotten them yet. A wave of nausea pushed hot bile up to the back of her throat.

She knew those scars.

"No," he repeated. Not angrily. He pulled his shirt back down, zipped his jacket up. "Now you know about me. I'm angry, and I'm mean, and I'm halfway to Twisted, rich girl. I'm not gonna lie. Come on. Your nose is red."

He turned, and set off down the black streak of the driveway. Snow whirled down, and Cami finally made her voice work.

"Wh-wh-who d-d-d-did—"

That brought a scowl, and he was suddenly familiar. "Don't know. Had 'em when I got to Joringel. Come on."

He doesn't know? I don't know who did mine, either. So she followed. There was really nothing else to do. He silently walked her to the front steps, and as soon as she reached the massive ironbound doors he trudged off toward the side of the house.

To the servants' entrance. Leaving Cami standing there openmouthed, wondering what kind of friend he thought he was going to be.

FIFTEEN

The Queen, her long golden hair glowing, paces down a long corridor full of mirrors. Velvet swishes as her skirts swing, and everything around her is a soft glimmer. The smoke in the air is incense, perfuming the hallway; she halts before a particular mirror.

Writhing cherubs twist their wings together on the mirror's iron frame, flakes of rust drifting free and whirling down to the plush carpet. The Queen's white face floats in its water-clear depths, and it reflects nothing but her. This is her favorite one, you can tell by the way she leans in, smiling a little. The medallion at her chest glows, and the roundness of it is not quite perfect. There is something about it . . .

But wait. The Queen frowns slightly. She does not do so often, for it mars the perfection of her soft features. The skin, dead-white, is drier now. She leans much closer to the mirror, jerking back with a hiss as she finds what she does not expect.

For a moment the edge of the smoky heavy perfume lifts, and a sharper, drier scent underneath rises. It is an edge of rot, a fruit left in a wet dark corner for too long. The Queen's lip curls, and she whirls away from the mirror. Yet it holds her image as a cup holds wine, a long shimmering, and I can see what she saw. What she fears, what has struck her with terror and fury.

A wrinkle in white skin. A single line, at the corner of her right eye, radiating. And I know I am to blame.

There was no Nico. She sat up, clutching the white down comforter, her ribs heaving. There was no Papa either, and she must not have screamed because the house was quiet. Not even a breath of wind moaning at the edges, the absolute muffled silence of snow over everything. The nightmare retreated, and the blue gauze over the mirror fluttered slightly.

Cami didn't notice. She was too busy gasping, her throat a pinhole. No wonder she hadn't made a sound. She couldn't *breathe*. Her lungs were full of perfumed smoke. The chanting receded, a seashell-moan fading into the distance.

Constriction eased. She dragged in great gulps of clean air. No incense here. Her wrists twinged, and she caught herself hunching as if to ward off a blow. Her heels scraped against the soft sheets, and she was out of the bed before she thought of it.

Skritch-scratch.

A soft scraping at her door, loud in the hush. She padded

across her room, heart lodged firmly in her just-recently cleared throat, her fingers and toes made of clumsy ice, her nightgown fluttering. The silk was raspy with sweat under her arms, its straps cutting her shoulders and the hem behaving oddly, swirling as if it were heavier.

As if it was motheaten velvet, brushing her skin.

She twisted the crystal knob and jerked the door open.

Tor twitched back. His eyes were live coals, his hair a wild mess, and he was in a black tank top and hastily buttoned jeans.

She hadn't seen him for two days.

They stared at each other for a long moment, and she finally discovered what made her gaze catch on him all the time.

He looked familiar, somehow. He *reminded* her of something; she just couldn't figure out what with her head full of the rushing of a nightmare's passage.

The stasis broke. Tor pressed a finger to his lips, his boots dangling by their laces from that hand, bumping his chest. There was a hole in his white socks, right over his instep.

Cami's jaw fell. *He's not supposed to be here. How did he*—But then, she realized, he probably stayed overnight because of the snowfall. Some of the garden boys, like most of the maids, did. Especially if they lived in the Old City—the parts of pre-Reeve Haven that hadn't blighted into the core.

He held something out with the other hand. A thin black velvet case, worn down to the nap at its corners. She took it automatically, and his indrawn breath as their fingers touched was a twin to hers. His skin was cold, and he seemed to be trembling.

Am I dreaming?

She couldn't tell. Her hand curled around the case. It was too heavy. He nodded, gravely, and backed away before the smile broke over his face. It was oddly sweet, a winter sunrise all its own, white teeth gleaming. Then he went ghosting on quiet sock feet down the hall, melding with the darkness. There wasn't even a betraying creak from the floorboards.

Cami let out a long shuddering breath. She shut the door and brought the case up to her mouth. Velvet pressed hard against her lips.

I don't know him. I've never seen him before. Then why did he feel like a glove? Like a sock or a broken-in pair of charm-laced trainers, like the familiar faces of the books in the library or . . .

I don't know him. This is a dream, one I won't even remember tomorrow. She was sure of it.

Until she surfaced to her alarm tinkling "Wake Up Charm-girl," the streets plowed clean, school resumed . . .

. . . and a long thin bone hairpin, a fall of glittering crystals fastened to one end with smoky golden wire, sitting in its velvet case on the pillow next to hers.

SIXTEEN

There was, as usual, a steaming mug of hot chocolate and a porcelain plate with a delicate fey-lace doily spread over it, two fresh croissants nestled against the snowy paper. Sometimes Marya even did *pain au chocolat*, when she was feeling especially appreciated. But today the feywoman fluttered around the kitchen, her spiderweb shawl moving on invisible drafts of Potential, muttering to herself and obviously piqued over something.

Cami's nose and cheeks were stinging; she set her schoolbag down on the stool and slid into her accustomed place with a sigh. The surprise test in High Charm Calculus had not gone well, nor had the French quiz. Her braid, heavy and damp, lay against her back, and beads swung as she turned her head. The bone pin's point, carefully threaded through her braid that morning, scraped at her nape. "Y-yummy," she tried, tentatively, cupping her icy hands around the hot mug. It stung, but pleasantly.

"Yesyes." Marya stopped, put her hands on her ample hips, staring into the fireplace. "I cannot find it. The Gaunt will not be happy, but I cannot find it."

Stevens? I don't know if he ever looks happy. "What c–can't you f–find?" She blew across the top of the hot cocoa, her shoulders relaxing in tiny increments. Ruby had kept up a vociferous stream of obscenities all the way home, not letting Ellie or Cami get a word in edgewise. Her French test must have been just as dire, or something *else* was pissing her off. Ellie was wan and tired, and she kept giving Cami little sideways looks, as if she suspected her of something.

At least Cami had been able to sneak away at lunch and go to the office to arrange the surprise. *I hope she likes it.* The thought of Ellie's delight over a new blazer made Cami all but wriggle on her seat and smile.

Marya's glance was sharp, her mouth pulled tight. Her face was not so round now, the fey in her shining through sharp and glittering, a diamond under lace. The tips of her ears twitched. "Nothing. Not for little *sidhe*. Eat, eat. I make them special for you."

Fine. Another sigh, this one internal, and Cami stared at the small, delicate plate. Golden, buttery, and exquisite, the croissants were almost too pretty to eat. And she wasn't hungry, anyway.

Still, she dutifully nibbled one. Between sips of scalding-hot cocoa, she watched Marya flutter through the kitchen, touching the copper–bottom pots, fussing with the fire, the stove bubbling as usual and the heavenly aroma of fresh bread just beginning to fill the entire kitchen. It looked like beef stew for dinner, thick and heavy and seasoned with feycress. That was Trig's favorite, and since Nico was gone it was just Trig and Stephens and Cami at the too-big, highly polished rosewood dining table, unless there was Business.

Which there had been every night this week.

Which meant tonight she would probably be eating here in the kitchen, at the breakfast bar.

I like that better anyway. Any Business was kind of . . . troubling. There hadn't been any more disappearances the last few days—at least, not in the news. From what Cami could gather, the Seven had taken over from the police, even though they were only six in the city now. And Stevens had pleasantly asked if Miss Cami wouldn't prefer Chauncey to bring her home from school?

She'd just shaken her head, her braid bumping her back, and said very carefully, *N-no, R-ruby will d-dr-drive m-me.* And that was that, though Stevens looked . . . dissatisfied.

As dissatisfied as a man with a thin frozen face could look, that is. A consigliere without a Family Head to inhabit him, since Nico wasn't officially back from Hannibal.

When Nico did come back, would he have any time for her either? He'd be busy doing Family things. Things he would probably discuss with Stevens and Trig and the Family bravos and the other Seven . . . but most definitely *not* with Cami. She'd hear more on the news, if Ruby ever turned the radio on in her Semprena again, instead of playing Tommy Triton's debut tape over and over again.

Cami sighed, her skin prickling all over like it had been all damn day. Maybe it was her blazer. She was warm enough to take her coat off now, and was just in the middle of struggling out of itchy Juno wool when the swinging door from the servant's hallway opened and Tor stamped through, icy crystals caught in his messy hair and his arms full of firewood. "Hey, Miz Marya. Figured it was time."

"Pike!" Marya stopped fidgeting and fussing, beaming through the careful examination and placing of each chunk of firewood in the big beaten-copper holder on the hearth. She dusted her hands together afterward while her shawl-fringes waved lazily and her black skirt fluttered on an invisible draft of Potential. "Cellar. Will you go into the cellar? Old Marya's knees are not good."

"Absolutely. Just give me the list." He stole a look at Cami as Marya bustled to the shining tomato-red refrigerator, its gloss alive with preservation-charms and yellowing pictures held with magnets and stickcharms.

She sat up straighter, pulling the blazer's shoulders back up defensively and shaking her head a little so the pin's colorless beads shivered. His answering smile was shy and warm, and

Cami found herself grinning, ducking her head and staring into her cup.

Marya plucked a sheet of paper covered with spider-scratches from under a stickcharm. "Wait. Wait while Marya thinks and writes, yes?"

"Take your time." Tor straightened, brushing wood debris from his leather jacket. His nose and cheeks were bright red, and the melting ice in his hair made him into a faunlet. Except he didn't have fangs, or claws. "Hello, princess."

Oddly enough, she didn't mind the name now. "H-Hello." She peeked up from the cup's depths. "W-want s-some hot c-c-cocoa?"

A shrug, the snow-darkened leather creaking. He looked miserably cold. "Maybe in a bit. How was school?"

She shrugged, then raised her eyebrows. He caught the question—not as quickly as Nico would have, but still. He was paying attention.

At least *someone* was.

He laid a work-roughened hand carefully on the countertop, moss clinging between his fingers. "Some kid got knifed in the bathroom, and one of the girls in my Chem class is pregnant. The History teacher had to shout over a bunch of jack-yobs to tell us about the Battle of the Marne and the first wave of the Reeve. Just another day." But his expression robbed the words of any anger. "I was glad to get out."

I'll bet. Was that what happened in public schools? She'd heard stories, but never anything like this. She searched for something to say. "Y-you l-look n-n-n-nice." *Oh, Mithrus. Can't even talk, and when I do, I say something useless.* His jeans were soaked to the knee from snowmelt, and he was covered in wood guck. But it was the only thing she could think of that didn't seem likely to get her in trouble.

His smile turned lopsided, but his black eyes were warm. "So do you."

Everything inside Cami loosened a fraction, then a fraction more. The feeling was so new and unexpected she actually grinned, forgetting to duck her head to hide her expression.

Marya's forehead was creased as she turned away from the sink, the paper in her hand covered with yet more scribbles. "List! Pike, tall and dark, down into the cellar with you. Big *brughnie*-shouldered boy, to lift for poor old Marya."

"Yes ma'am." But he was still looking at Cami. He seemed about to say something else, but just then Trig slid in from the other hall, his step light and ghost-quiet, his baggy sportcoat red and green today and deep smudges under his tired eyes.

Every night a different something, Twist or strange or *other*, pressed against the borders of the Vultusino house. A hard winter, indeed. As soon as dark fell the security teams were working harder than they ever had.

As if everything in New Haven could tell the Vultusino

were without a Head. Some of the younger cousins were showing up at the house at odd hours, too, the boys eyeing Cami and
the girls trying to be friendly. Stevens dealt with them, but she
just wished Nico would come home.

When he did, what would happen? The Vultusina's ring was
safely locked up; occasions and parties were fine, but she wasn't
going to wear it to *school*.

The loosening inside her clenched up again. Tor disappeared
on the other side of the kitchen, and Marya immediately began
fussing at Trig about whatever she couldn't find. Cami sipped
at her cocoa, hoping the bright red on her cheeks wasn't too
visible. Trig barely glanced at her, just nodded at Marya's nervousness and set about soothing the feywoman, and ten minutes
later, neither of them noticed when Cami escaped, carrying her
bag and her coat, the croissant and sugary milk curdling in her
stomach. All the way up the stairs to the warm white bedroom,
she thought of that funny lopsided smile, and the tinkling of the
beads from the pin was ice chiming against glass.

So do you, he'd said.

Did he really think so?

SEVENTEEN

TWO DAYS LATER, CAMI WAS STILL THINKING ABOUT that funny smile of his. A present, from someone who didn't have a whole lot. Someone who couldn't really afford a bunch of presents. Someone she didn't owe something to.

It was a new thing. Unfortunately, she wasn't left to brood in peace.

"You don't look so good," Ruby whispered, reaching over to touch Cami's forehead.

Cami ducked away, her braid swinging. "I f-feel fine." The stutter wasn't so bad today. The bone pin, slid through her braid, was oddly heavy, and everything seemed too colorful to be real.

She hadn't seen Tor since. There had been another alarm in the middle of the night, Trig and his security team arriving to find that charms laced through the ancient stone walls had forced something back, *again*, from the Vultusino grounds. She wouldn't have known if she hadn't been already awake from yet another bad nightmare, sweat-soaked and gasping, hearing soft commotion elsewhere in the darkened house.

But Marya wouldn't tell her what had happened, and Trig didn't show up. And Stevens only asked her again if she wouldn't prefer Chauncey to drive her to school?

No, she'd snapped, without the stutter for once, and he had nodded and retreated.

Weak winter sunlight slid through high windows; Sister Grace-Redeeming's classroom was brimful of the quiet murmur of girls bent over paper, pencils scratching. Ruby shrugged, the gold dangles on her earrings winking. She hunched back over her Provincial History book. It was odd—the only thing looking washed-out today was her friend's bright copper mane. Every other edge pressed against Cami's skin even through empty air. Even the dust was painful.

Plus, Cami was itching all over. Maybe it was the wool of the blazer, or just her wanting to be *gone*. She didn't even want to go back home, it was too far. Just a closet, or maybe a forgotten corner. Any quiet dark place would have done, just so she could sit and breathe a bit.

She tried to read, but the letters were dancing on the page. The itch was somehow *under* her skin. A steady irritation, building, a hot prickle of temper.

If I'm angry, why does it scare me? She took a deep breath, staring at the paper in front of her.

The door opened, and a ripple passed through the classroom. Ellie, her eyebrows drawn together and a terrific bruise glaring on the left side of her face, shook her sleek blonde hair down and stamped for the head of the room. She handed a slip of pink paper to Sister Grace, who woke up long enough to nod and murmur something that sounded kind.

Ellie shrugged and hitched her schoolbag up on her shoulder. Turned, her skirt flaring, and stamped to her seat. Her knees were bruised too, and the way she held her bag said that it hurt.

Ruby was bolt-upright. "*What the hell?*" she mouthed, but Ellie wasn't looking. She dropped down on Cami's other side, fishing a pair of shades out of her blazer pocket and jamming them on.

It didn't hide the fact that someone had socked her a good one. The Strep didn't hit her in the face often. Maybe it was one of the boyfriends. Who knew?

I know. A terrible, nasty, guilty heat bloomed behind Cami's breastbone. The blazer.

Maybe it wasn't that. Don't leap to conclusions.

She slid her book over, so Ellie could get the page number. She also silently slid her notes over. Sister Grace went back to dozing, the girls went back to scratching with their pencils— and whispering about Ellie's arrival. The ghoulgirls were hungry for gossip, the bobs would be asking about it, and the fluffs were ready for talk-meat, as always. Gossip was juicy, and even Ruby's glower couldn't keep all of it away.

The irritation under Cami's skin mounted another few notches.

Ellie just sat for a few moments, her shoulders shaking imperceptibly. Cami's heart was in her throat. Her friend was in her ancient school blazer, shiny-collared and wearing down, fraying beginning at the elbows.

She could suddenly *see* it, in vivid color—the Strep tearing the new blazer away. *You little slut, where did you get the credits for this?* Ellie's hands like little wounded white birds as they fluttered ineffectually, the Strep screaming as Potential flashed and the new blazer shredded to ribbons.

Anger, hot and vicious, sank sharp claws into the back of Cami's throat. The itching all over her threatened to pop out through her skin. She fidgeted, and Ellie's head slowly, very slowly turned.

The mirrored lenses of Ellie's shades showed her reflection. Cami didn't look like herself—her eyes too big, her face dead-white, the stray bits of hair pulled free from her braid lifting on a breeze from nowhere. The bone pin stuck out, its little colorless dangles gleaming, and its sharp tip jabbed at her nape again. There was a little raw spot where it kept rubbing.

God damn *it.* She reached up, yanked the pin free, and laid it carefully in the pencil groove at the top of the ancient wooden desk. Ellie shifted, her blank lenses following the pin.

Cami flipped to a fresh sheet of paper. *You OK?*

Ellie fished a pencil and her history book out. Her notebook was battered too, but she opened it and made the date notation. She leaned over, and Cami's anger evaporated like steam from one of Marya's kettles.

NO, Ellie scrawled on Cami's paper. *Later. Who gave you that?*

Cami shrugged. Now that the terrible fury had subsided she was queasy, her head aching and the discomfort all over her like crawling razor-legged insects. *A guy*, she wrote.

Don't take anything else. Ellie flipped her textbook open. Cami swallowed her retort—she could feel the stutter knotting just behind her lips, a brick wall between her and anything she might want to say. Ellie paused, then leaned over and wrote carefully: *There might be charm on it.*

Ellie was just slopping over with Potential, wasn't she. She'd be able to see charm Cami wouldn't.

But Tor wouldn't charm her. He just didn't have the Potential. Besides, he didn't have to. She was halfway-charmed already; she liked him. Whatever he was after when he talked to her, at least she knew she didn't goddamn well *owe* him anything.

So now I'm stupid. Can't do anything right. She hunched her shoulders, and the prickling all over her went away as she took a deep breath. Her fingers, tense around the creaking pencil, relaxed a little, then a little more.

Ruby peered around her, a tendril of curling russet hair falling in her eyes. She blew it away irritably, and there were two bright fever-spots high on Rube's cheeks.

She was *pissed*.

Sister Grace finally resurrected herself at quarter-till, announced a quiz for the next day, and smiled pacifically at the wave of groans. Her round, plump face, flour-pale, framed in black and white, was a serene moon. The Mithrus beads tied to her sash clicked as she passed to the board and wrote the night's homework in her flowing copperplate script. Cami's shoulders twitched and she inhaled deeply—chalk dust, a touch of sweat, the funky smell of a room used to corral kids for long periods of time, a breath of clove and invisible fuming from Ruby on her right. From Ellie, nothing but the faint aroma of harsh soap and the also-invisible smell of misery.

The crystals on the bone pin glinted. She was going to have to ask Tor about—

The pin twitched. Ellie tensed.

It hopped out of the pencil groove. Cami let out a soft sound and grabbed for it, but Sister Grace was saying something, and the slight noise was lost. Also lost in Sister Grace's droning reminder that *chapel is after lunch, ladies, don't be late*, was the sound of the pin splintering as it hit the blue-flecked linoleum.

What the— Cami sank back down in her seat. Broken in three pieces, the bone pin rolled away. She grabbed the edge of the desk to keep herself from diving for it, since Sister Grace had turned around and was scanning the classroom intently, looking fully awake for the first time in months.

Ellie's breathing had turned rapid, her fists clenched. A tear glittered on her bruised cheek, and Cami could see where the back of her earring had scraped on her neck, probably when whoever–it–was belted her.

It was *the Strep.* Sudden knowledge rode a cresting tide of nausea. Sweat had gathered in Cami's armpits, dewed her lower back and her forehead. Everything was too *bright*, and Sister Grace's gaze passed over them all like the shadow of a giant drifting bird.

"Ladies," Sister Grace finally said, "you are excused." The tinkling charmbell rang to signal the end of third session and the beginning of lunch, and Ruby sighed dramatically.

"'Bout damn time," she announced as a surfburst of chatter swallowed the room. "Who do I gotta kill, Ellie?"

Cami wriggled out of her side of the desk. The shards of the bone pin were numb-cold, frost-burning her trembling fingers, and the crystal beads had disappeared, rolling away under desks and feet. Her stomach cramped, then eased all at once, and she couldn't bring herself to throw the remains of the pin away. So she simply jammed the pieces in her bag while Ellie began explaining what had set the Evil Strepmother off this time. Ellie's cheeks were wet, Ruby was furious, and Cami was secretly, shamefully glad that nobody was paying any attention to her.

EIGHTEEN

Ruby was a ball of simmering rage from lunch onward, swearing to give the Strep a taste of her own medicine; Ellie admitted it was the new school blazer that had set the Strep off.

The blazer Cami had brought in the money for, so it would arrive charm-boxed at her door the next morning. Which meant Cami was responsible. Though they both kindly refrained from pointing this out, the knowledge churned at her the whole time, hot and sour.

And then there was the pin. Tor's gift, broken. He'd just *given* it to her, and he wasn't asking anything in return, right? Nothing except being her friend.

You need a friend that listens.

She hadn't stuttered so much when the pin was in her hair, had she? She'd been feeling fine for the entire two days. *Better* than fine, even. Secretly pleased.

And he wasn't a charmer—his Potential would be low. He was only a garden boy, after all.

The last bell rang and she dawdled, Ruby and Ellie at their side-by-side lockers. They didn't stop to preen today—with Ellie's face the way it was, of course they wouldn't. So Cami just waited until both of them had their heads deep in their lockers and let the crowd of girls whisk her away, around the corner from the main stairwell.

Today of all days, she couldn't stand the thought of getting into the Semprena and listening to Ruby fume.

You weren't supposed to go off Juno's grounds by foot, but there were ways. She took the back stairs to the gym, slid out past a chattering gaggle of cheersport girls—bright-eyed, smooth-haired, and chirping like Twisted cockatiels. The fire door was supposed to be locked and alarmed, but Ruby had shown her how to slip a bit of charmed tinfoil—*one of those things a girl should never be without if she intends to be up to no good*, Rube always said—over the connector and slip out while it was resetting itself.

The sudden cold was a blow. The sky was a featureless iron blanket, and the metallic smell of a hard freeze filled her nose. She shivered, but it was too late now—the door thudded closed, and she was faced with a narrow strip of pavement between two frowning brick walls. At the far end, a dustbin crouched, and past it there would be a way down the hill, screened from the lacrosse and football fields by thick spiny heartsthorn, naked without its glossy summer green and bright red berries. The bushes were defense-charmed too, so she had to be careful not to brush against them.

She edged along, carefully, past the dustbin breathing out a reek of garbage even through the killing cold. The heartsthorn rustled a bit as she passed, not-quite-sensing her. Juno's thick stone wall lifted on her right, veined with long fingers of red ivy. Cami tightened her scarf, her knees already chilled and her coat flapping as she hurried.

But careful, cautious, just like a little mouse.

There was the gate—tiny, wooden, overgrown with heartsthorn. To the side, there was a gap between the post and the wall. It wasn't used *too* often—just enough to keep it clear. If it started getting worn through, the Sisters would find out and patch it, and everyone would have to find a new way.

Cami wriggled through, holding her breath.

Outside was a narrow alley, frost-slick cobblestones that probably dated from the post-Reeve rebuilding of New Haven. The windowless back of a warehouse loomed, unmarked except for the occasional schoolgirl graffiti traced down low where Juno girls could reach. *Sheela sucks* something-scratched-out, and *Kill Juno*, in black, with arrows pointing to it to show agreement. Something about a Sister Mary Clarice, though there wasn't a Sister of that name at the school now. Other scrawls and symbols, none of them alive with charm but managing to glow with feeling just the same.

Her feet crunched and slid, and by the time she reached the end of the alley and peeked out into a weedy, snowbound vacant lot, she was shivering from fear *and* cold.

This is pretty anticlimactic. What did I expect, monsters to eat me the moment I stepped off school grounds?

Well, yes. Wasn't that what was supposed to happen?

Did Tor feel this cold and alone when he walked? Was he used to it? She could ask him, she supposed. If her stupid tongue would let her.

The wind picked up, and she heard dogs barking.

No, not barking. Baying. *Hate that sound.* It reminded her of snow, of headlights, of a rat's plated tail and bright red eyes. She pushed the memory aside, but it didn't want to go.

That was one thing about school and Ruby and Ellie. They kept her head so busy the nightmares couldn't creep up through waking consciousness and poke at her.

Another galvanic shudder worked its way down her spine. She pulled her mittens on and set off around the edge of the field. Her maryjanes slipped and slid, and at least her knee socks were wool, but this was looking to be a very long and uncomfortable walk home. New Haven wheeled around her, cold blighted core radiating bright charmed streets, and she put her head down. Her braid lay heavy against her back, as if the pin was still thrust through it.

He walks all the time. It can't be that hard. She settled her schoolbag higher on her shoulder. *Besides, I've come this far. I might as well keep going.*

PART II: Waking Up

THE IRON IN THE SKY HAD BLACKENED. NIGHT CAME early in winter, and it was so close to dusk the streetlights were beginning to flicker into grudging life.

Legs on fire, feet raw, her back aching, she rounded the corner and sighed. The Hill had been a bitch—it seemed so *simple* in a car. Someone else would just press the accelerator, the engine responded with a throb, and up went all the metal and charmfiber and glass, and the people inside it too. Her right heel slipped a little bit inside her shoe—it was numb; she didn't know why it was sliding around so loosely. Her shoe didn't seem to be broken.

The dogs kept barking. Maybe she was the only one that could hear them, full-throated howling or pathetic whimpering. There were a lot of them, and sometimes they were nearer, sometimes further away. If she rounded the wrong corner she might *see* them, and that had made her run before she figured out running just tired her out more.

Almost there. The gate was three blocks away, scrolled iron dripping with icicles. It had never looked so wonderful. Her schoolbag weighed a ton, and homework tonight was going to be a—

"What are you *doing*?" He appeared out of nowhere, and Cami shrieked, backpedaling despite her exhaustion. He grabbed her arm, and she found herself faced with a tall, trembling Torin Beale, who was dead pale and breathing as hard as she was. "Mithrus *Christ*, do you know what *time* it is? The whole house is—" He broke off, and for a second Cami thought he might shake her.

"I d-decided to w-walk home." Her heart thudded, and her head felt clearer than it had all day. "The p-pin. T-t-t-tor, I'm suh-suh-sorry. The p-pin b-b-broke."

"The *pin*." He addressed the air over her head. "She's worried about the *pin*. They called the Vultusino. Whole house is like an anthill. Miz Marya's roaming around looking for you, checking the study every five minutes and wringing her hands. The security guys are . . . " He made a quick movement with his head, tilting it.

She heard it too. Dogs barking, hysterical yaps and yowling. She didn't know if any of the neighbors had security hounds. It wasn't out of the question, they were popular even if they could be charmed.

But she had never noticed them before.

"D–d–dogs," she whispered. "A–all afternoon."

He stared at her like she'd just grown another head. "All afternoon?"

She nodded. Wiped at her nose with a mitten, not caring if it was gross. She was cold, and tired, and apparently they had noticed she hadn't come back.

Well, you kind of thought they would. Was that the point?

Tor let go of her arm, as if it was Twisted, or red–hot metal. "You . . . "

Telling him about Ruby and Ellie was out of the question. But at least she could tell him how she'd scraped together enough guts to do this. "I'm s–s–sorry. I w–wanted to s–s–see what it w–w–was l–like to w–walk home." Even her teeth were numb. "L–like you." She pointed at his chest, hoping he would understand. *We're more alike than you think.* "S–scars," she managed. "Th–th–they *hurt*. I–i–i–ins–side."

"You . . . " He kept looking at her like she'd Twisted, or something. He finally shook his head, his leather jacket creaking. Snow caked his jeans all the way up to his knees, and there was a scratch on his cheek.

Maybe from thorns.

Cami swayed. "I h–have t–to g–g–g–go."

That snapped him back into himself. "I'll say you do. Come on."

NINETEEN

THE SECURITY TEAMS MARKED THEM AS SOON AS THEY were through the gate, but it was Trig who appeared at the bottom of the front steps, lanky and older than ever, deep lines graven on his lean face. His sportscoat was the baggy yellow, orange, and brown one with shiny patches at the elbows he wore sometimes to shoot skeet, and his knife-sharp cheekbones were blushed with cold.

He didn't say a word until they were inside. "You found her." Flatly, brushing snow from his shoulders. His hiking boots were clotted with mud and snow, and he took in Cami with one passionless, sweeping glance. "Thank Mithrus. Miss Camille, honey, what the hell *happened*?"

I don't know. She shrugged, miserably. The foyer was warm, and her fingers and toes were tingling with pain. Her socks were probably ruined. *I couldn't explain it even if I tried.*

"Mr. Nico's on his way home. You . . . " Trig visibly

groped for Tor's name. The butt of a Stryker showed briefly under his coat as he ran a hand back through his thinning hair. "Beale, right? You found her?"

Oh, no. If they'd called Nico from Hannibal, they must've thought *something* bad was happening to her.

Maybe even a kidnapping.

She should have thought of that. Miserably, Cami sighed. He was going to be unmanageable when he got here.

"Down the street, sir." Tor's sullen politeness was at once normal and terribly embarrassing. "My shift was over, I was walking home. Since the road's cleared."

A relieved smile, and the tall man clapped the garden boy on the shoulder, gingerly. "Well, head to the kitchen. Marya will be overjoyed. Get something to eat, huh?" With that, Trig seemed to forget Tor's existence, and he offered Cami his arm. She took it, grateful for the support.

The high narrow foyer was all at once terribly alien and familiar as well. The parquet floor was alive with crackling charm, and the whole house was seething. Little whispers ran between the walls, and the sense of hidden motion and hurrying swamped her.

Tor didn't take himself off to the kitchen *just* yet, though. He paused, his fingers on her elbow, digging in through the black cashmere and the navy Juno wool underneath. Not brutally, just to get her attention. "You gonna be okay?"

Braced between them, she tried not to sag with relief. "Y-yes." *Now that I'm here.* "T-t-tor. Th-thank y-y-you."

"Anytime." He let go, took a step back, two, staring at her face. "I mean it. *Anytime.*"

Thankfully, her flush could just be a reaction to the sudden warmth. Her fingers were cramping, her toes felt wet. Trig had gone very still next to her, but she didn't care. "T-t-tomorrow. After sk-k-k-school. Okay?"

"You got it." He made a curious little movement with his right hand, stopped himself, and turned on his heel. This time he didn't vanish, he just took the hall that would lead him back to the kitchen.

"Well." Trig sounded thoughtful. He stared after Tor for a long moment or two, and his face was set. "You walked? From St. Juno's?"

Cami nodded. *Now* she was shivering, great waves of shudders gripping her. Her skirt and shoes were dripping with melted snow, and her hair was a heavy frozen weight. "I w-w-w-wanted t-t-to—" Her tongue just would *not* work. Even if it did, how could she explain to Trig? It wasn't the sort of thing he'd understand. "S-sorry," she finished, lamely. "I'm s-s-s-s—"

The old man took an experimental step, bracing her as she hobbled. "No need. Just glad you're safe. Let's get you upstairs."

Her socks were ruined. The blisters had broken and bled,

and the blood had greased the inside of her shoes. That was why they were so slippery. Marya, her white-streaked dandelion hair standing up and writhing, black shawl-fringes moving on an angry breeze, made little spitting sounds as she bandaged Cami's feet. "*Walking.* All the way from school. What were you *thinking*? Silly, naughty little thing." The cameo at her throat shivered uneasily, its carved surface changing.

"S-sorry." Cami sucked in a breath as the antiseptic stung. For all her scolding, Marya's hands were exquisitely gentle.

"So worried!" Marya's long fingers flicked, and the gauze crackled with charm. "Late little girl, and your redheaded friend came. She told the long one you had disappeared. The Gaunt was beside himself. Whole house upside down. Looking and looking for our naughty little *sidhe.*" Wrapped with deft quick movements, Cami's feet began to resemble mummies. "The long one" was Trig, and "the Gaunt" was Stevens. Most fey were bad with names. Cami could look forward to being "naughty little thing" for a while now.

"Going wandering, hmm? Wayfaring blood in our naughty girl. Terrible worry, little mayfly." Marya sighed.

"W-w-wayfaring b-blood?" *Does she know where I came from?* Cami had never asked.

There had never been a need.

"Oh yes, it's all over you. She smells like a wanderer, our little thing." Marya glanced up. "Eat, eat!"

The tray on the small table at Cami's elbow held a small mountain of buttered toast, hot chocolate steaming in a charmed bone-china cup, and strawberries like bloodclots in a thin crystal dish. The white bedroom held its breath, purple-gray dusk gathering at the window, touched with orange citylight as the snow began again.

"Wandering. With *dogs*, too." Marya sniffed. She'd insisted on Cami taking a bath, even though the hot water stung so bad she could have cried, if there had been any tears left. Now, warm and dry, clean and bandaged, crunching on toast and sipping hot chocolate, the afternoon seemed like a bad dream. Her Babbage glinted on the stripped-pine desk, waiting for her to switch it on and enter chat. Ruby was just going to tear her *ears* off.

Cami settled back into the chair. The bleeding had stopped now. She had a rash on her shoulder, where the schoolbag's strap had been rubbing and rubbing, even through her coat and blazer and blouse. *God.* The watered-silk footstool with a plain white towel draped over it was just right for her battered feet, and every muscle in her body was twitching a little. The twitches ran through her like the shivers did, and there was a coldness down in her marrow where the bath and the house's warmth didn't reach. "D-d-d-dogs," she echoed, softly, hoping Marya would say more.

"Hounds. They were hunting you, naughty thing." Marya nodded. "Hear them all the time. Worse in winter, always. I told *el signor,* he heard them too."

An unpleasant jolt. "P-p-papa?" *He never said anything about dogs.*

"Oh, yes. Yesyes." Marya capped the antiseptic and finished wrapping Cami's left foot. Flicked her fingers again and feycharms crackled blue-white, to stave off infection and speed healing. "Nasty dogs. Hate them. Won't have them here. *Cats.* Cats are proper, yes? Not dogs."

"The P-p-pike," Cami breathed. *Tell me about Tor. Have you noticed anything on him?* If Marya was disposed to be chatty, she could probably—

"Told him too. No dogs. He reeks of them. He's a hunter, that one, lean and angry." Marya shrugged. She gathered up her materials, whisking the towel gently from under Cami's feet. "Sit, eat. Little wayfaring naughtiness."

"W-wayf-f-faring?" *Tell me something else, anything!*

"Said too much." Marya clapped a hand over her mouth. She stared at Cami, the oddness on her suddenly pronounced. Sometimes she looked more human, but right now she was all fey, the tips of her ears poking up through wild white-streaked hair, her cheeks bloodless-pale. She shook her head, long jet earrings swinging, and rocked to her feet.

Good luck getting her to give anything more *now.* But Cami was going to try, opening her mouth and taking in a deep breath.

There was a single splintering bash on the door before it flew open. "*Cami!*"

It was, of course, Nico. Fangs out, eyes blazing, he hadn't even changed out of the Hannibal uniform. His white button-down was torn though, his tie askew, and his hair stood up anyhow. Little crystals of snow had caught in it—he had probably run from the car to the front door.

"I'm ok-k-k—" *I'm okay. Calm down.*

"Leave," he snapped at Marya, who bowed her head and hurried past in a wash of floating spidersilk. "Mithrus *Christ*, Cami. What the hell?"

Deep breath. "I w-w-w-walked—"

"*Walked* home. Yeah. Do you have any *idea* what could have *happened* to you? This is *New Haven*, Cami! And you're Vultusino!"

I wasn't born Family. She looked down at her pajama pants—Marya had insisted on the pink silk pj's. A flannel robe too, the belt securely knotted. As if she would freeze to death sitting in *here*.

Nico took another two steps into the room. His anger filled everything up, made it hard to breathe. "I'm *talking* to you! Mithrus *Christ*, Cami—"

"*No!*" Her own yell took her by surprise. "You're n-not talking!" Shocked silence rang between them. She wet her lips, quickly, with a nervous flicker of her tongue. "You're s-s-s-screaming," she finished. The last syllable broke, and a tear trickled down her cheek.

So she did have a few left after all.

"*Fuck* it." Nico rocked back on his heels. "Do you know what it's like, driving from up-province and worrying over where you are, what's wrong, if someone's snatched you? And you're *walking* home! You're *bleeding*, too!" Of course he could smell it. "Tell me what happened." Dangerously quiet, now. "You'd better start, Cami. Or I'm gonna . . . "

Apparently no threat was too dire. He ran out of words, for once, and stared at her. Another tear slipped out, ran hot and shameful down her face. Was it just because the room was warm? Or was it relief that he was finally here? Irritation? The empty hole in her chest, aching to know where she came from, where she belonged?

She couldn't tell. She searched for something to say. To *make* him understand. He'd understood plenty before, why not now? What was *wrong* with him?

Or was it wrong with her?

"I d-d-don't know wh-who I a-a-m." The words tripped over each other. "I w-was j-j-just f-f-found—" *Just found in the snow. Like trash, picked up and carried here.*

"I know who you are." Quietly, but everything in the room rattled. Or maybe it just seemed like it did, because when Nico got quiet like this, it was just before he went over the edge and nothing would calm him down. Once, when she'd been trapped in the hallway to the bathrooms in Lou's by a Family bravo who reeked of whiskey-calf, Nico had gotten this quiet. "I know exactly who you are, and if Papa hadn't found you, *I would have.*"

You don't know that. "Y-you c-c-c-can't—"

"*Oh yes I can.* I'm the Vultusino, Cami, and I am telling you, *I would have fucking found you.*" His tone dropped still further, and the deep growl behind the words was enough to drain all the air from the room and leave her gasping. "Whoever did that to you, I'll find them too, now that I'm old enough. And I'll make them *pay.*"

"I—"

Instead of the stutter stopping her, it was *him.* She couldn't get a word in now, for love or hexing.

He was, quite simply, too determined. "I'm finished at Hannibal. I'm staying home. I'm taking care of things now. Don't you *dare* pull another stunt like this, Cami. I swear to God I'll . . . " He ran out of threats again, his fists clenching and unloosing, like he wished there was something caught in them.

Do what? "You'll what? H-hurt m-m-me?" *Because when you get like this, that's what I'm afraid of, Nico.* The idea was as crystal-line and terrifying as the first howl she'd heard, a few blocks away from St. Juno's, lifting on an icy wind.

That brought him up short. He actually sagged, deflating.

The growl behind his words stopped. "I would *never* hurt you." Whispered, as if she'd been the one shouting and raging.

"You're g-g-going t-to." As soon as she said it, she knew it was true—and she wished she hadn't. "If you d-d-don't learn to c-c-calm d-d-own."

It was a day for guys staring at her like she'd lost her mind. Nico's gaze burned, locked with hers for long endless seconds.

Then he turned and stamped out, slamming the door so hard she was surprised the crystal knob didn't shatter. Cami let out a long, shaking breath and sagged into the chair. She shut her eyes. The darkness was better than the glare of the white bedroom.

But it made the sound inside her head worse. The roaring. The howl of dogs, the clicking of their nails on cold pavement, the deep huffing of their breath as their reddened tongues lolled. Dogs—and Marya said Tor reeked of them.

All the noise in the world boiled down to a single question, stark and black as the night pressing against the windows.

What is happening to me?

TWENTY

DAWN ROSE GRAY AND PINK AND GOLD, AND FOUND her stutter-stepping toward the window seat. She could hobble with the bandages on, and it made her think of the Eastron section of World History, the little inset about lotusfeet girls. Charmed cloths around a baby's tiny feet, and the deformity, a chosen Twist.

To make them more beautiful. Was that what it took?

You do, too.

The snow was blank, featureless, deceptively smooth. Unbroken, it poured over the gardens—or, no. Not unbroken.

Someone had trudged through the snow. She could tell because of the line of footsteps, their edges chipped free of a layer of ice forming on the drifts. She could *also* tell because he was still there. A sword of darkness against all the white, his leather jacket inadequate against the cold, his hair a wild blue-tinted blackness. His breath plumed, and he looked up at her window.

Even at this distance, his gaze was a dark fire.

Cami's breath fogged the glass. She lifted her right hand, pressed it against cold translucence.

Tor lifted his. Five fingers, spread, just like hers. A star of flesh. The frozen glass burned, and she found herself shaking. A thrill all through her, Potential rippling like heat-haze. Or maybe it was an ordinary electricity, like the natural, predictable stuff lightbulbs burned.

What is he doing?

There was no way to ask him, and he turned and trudged back the way he'd come, stepping carefully from footprint to footprint. The fog of his breath turned to ice, falling with tiny flashing tinkles. How cold *was* it out there?

The sound inside her head was a deep chanting, voices lifted in a sea-swell of ecstasy. She smelled fresh-cut apples, and salt, and a peculiar heavy incense. It scraped the inside of her skull clean, filling her with cotton. Whatever name they were singing, she couldn't . . . quite . . . hear.

Cami turned. The sun's red rim lifted over the horizon, and she could almost *feel* it, as if she was Family. Directionless blue winter-morning light pushed past her, filling the white room to the brim. The gauze over the mirror fluttered, and she found herself stepping gingerly across plain carpet.

She tore the scarf down. The mirror, clear and flawless, was a blank screen, not even reflecting her.

Not a mirror. An eye.

A gleam in the depths of the thin glass. Trembling, Cami lifted her right hand again.

There was a *snap*, felt in the chest more than heard through the ears, and the white room glared at her from the mirror's surface. She blinked, and found herself standing, fists curled, her hair messed by the restless tossing she'd done instead of sleeping, her face hectic with color and her eyes blazing blue.

It was there, standing and not-quite-thinking, her brain humming with the sharp edges of a puzzle forming around her, that Cami had a very odd thought.

I need an apple.

The kitchen was curiously deserted. Marya was not humming near the hearth, nor was she at the stove. She could be anywhere in the house, dusting or flitting from room to room, engaged on whatever charms a house-fey used at dawn. The important thing was she wasn't *here*, and the copper-bottom pans hanging shiny from their rack were still and quiet.

The fridge was tomato red, its door fluttering with yellowed photographs—a shyly smiling nine-year-old Cami in white eyelet lace, Nico glowering behind her in his small but exquisitely tailored suit, his hair slicked down. Papa with Cami on his lap in a white silk sundress, squinting slightly in the garden sunshine, and Nico tall and straight-faced at his left shoulder.

A baby Nico, with a rare smile, lifting up a dirt-clotted bulb of garlic from the herb garden and shaking it. Papa, younger and solemn, straight as a poker and holding the hand of a smiling young mortal woman with Nico's proud tilt to her head. Papa and three of the other Seven, their mouths all the same straight line.

The pictures of Cami herself were newer, and they fluttered uneasily, interlopers against the red enamel.

She found what she needed in the crisper. She pulled out the cutting board, selected Marya's favorite wood-handled butcher knife. Placed it, gleaming-sharp, next to the scarred block of oiled wood and weighed the apple in her hand. Satiny and red, it was too heavy. She set it down and looked at it, her brain still caught in that peculiar humming, head cocked, ink-black hair a river down her back.

Tip it over.

So she did, one trembling finger touching the apple until it toppled. It was not perfectly round, so it rolled with a bump and lay there, as if it knew a secret.

It does. Are you sure you want to know one, too?

Her fingers curled around the knifehilt. She blinked.

Cloven horizontally, the apple fell open. She saw the seeds, each nestled in its own hollow, making a five-pointed star. Deep foulness bubbled up in the recesses of her memory. A screaming, a hissing, gouts of perfumed smoke that filled the cup of the skull with cotton numbness, and the crisp scent of a just-sliced apple all mixed together.

That's what she smells like. Smoke and fruit. Because she's the Queen. Shudders rippled down Cami's back.

Not just any queen. The White Queen. The shaking was worse. It held her in its jaws, snapping her back and forth. The knife clattered against the counter, and her left hand smacked the apple halves and sent them flying.

It was too late. The knife's poison-polished blade flashed, a dart of white cruelness straight into the center of her skull, and Cami let out a soft birdlike sound. She couldn't scream because she couldn't *breathe*, it was too bright, there was smoke in her throat and the chanting was full of nonsense syllables instead of meaning and she couldn't . . .

Her legs gave out. Her head clipped the edge of the tiled counter on the way down, and the brief starburst of pain turned into wet warmth. The knife spun, teetering on the edge, then fell with another chiming sound. It missed her nose by a bare half-inch, but she never knew.

Her muscles locked, and the sound wouldn't stop. It was a child's voice too broken to scream any further, and its chirping made words as she curled into a ball on the russet floor.

"Mommy no Mommy no Mommy no Mommy noooooooooo . . ."

TWENTY-ONE

"SHE PASSED OUT." NICO, BUT ... DIFFERENT. LIKE there was something caught in his throat.

"Are we sure that's what it was, sir?" Stevens, now. Dry and reedy, his throat needed oiling. Would he be Nico's consigliere too, a glove for Nico's consciousness, the well that a new Vultusino would drop secrets into?

What secrets would he have now that he couldn't tell *her*? Plenty. Even Papa had sometimes sent her to Marya, when things were happening a little girl shouldn't hear. She'd been able to guess around the corners, but to be the Vultusino was to have secrets. Lots of them.

Bad secrets.

Are mine bad too? They must be.

Cami sighed. She was warm, and it was soft around her, and the noise had stopped. *All* of it, even the roaring and the barking dogs. Her head was only full of ringing silence.

They were quiet, and she kept her eyes closed. Her breathing came in deep even swells. She was so glad she wasn't choking that she just kept doing it, drawing the air in, letting it out.

"If you have something to say, Stevens, spit it out." Nico *still* sounded different. She couldn't figure out just how. The question kept her occupied much as breathing did.

"Black as night. Blue as sky. Red as blood." Stevens paused. "*White.* As snow."

"We'd know, if she was—"

"Would we? Would *you*?"

"Be careful." The difference was sharp and hurtful now, but without the usual edge of flippancy. "Be very careful what you say, ghoul."

That's it. She was so pleased she moved, turning over and pulling the covers up. *He sounds like Papa. Won't he be surprised to know that.*

But she wouldn't tell him. Not yet. He was still too angry.

They were silent until she had settled.

"She is far too young, and there are none of the signs. Still, she may have been . . . marked." Stevens, ponderously slow and so dry. If Papa was angry, or speaking quickly, Stevens would space his words further apart, stringing them between pauses to force Papa to slow down. She could have told him that wouldn't work with Nico.

"Just what the hell are you saying?" Now he was more

like himself. Angry—and she wasn't sure when that anger had become a comfort. If he was sharp and furious, at least she knew what to expect.

"I am saying caution is called for, if we are not to lose what we have."

She could almost *see* Stevens clamming up, pursing his thin lips. The air was heavy, oddly dead, but it still tasted wonderful. A ghost of bay rum, a familiar comfort, and the softness all around her.

"*Biel'y.*" Nico all but spat. "They can have anything else in the goddamn city, but not *her.*"

No answer from Stevens. Had he nodded in agreement? Cami buried her face in a pillow. *Why don't you just go away so I can sleep? I need it. I don't feel good.*

Not good at all. Clear-headed, certainly. Like a broom had swept through her jumbled thoughts, pushing them out and away, smoothing her like Marya would smooth a sheet of phyllo dough.

I dropped the knife. She'll be furious.

No, Cami did not feel good. She felt like she'd just run a race, one too fast and too long for her. Her legs were still going and the rest of her hadn't caught up.

Nico finally spoke up, decisive. "My calendar should be clear today. Did you call St. Juno's?"

"I did. Sir, the Stregare wish for your—"

"They can *wait*." Impatient, now. "Get out. She's waking up."

I'm already awake, thanks. It was no good. Cami stretched. It wasn't her bed. It felt all wrong. Too soft, and the covers were too heavy.

A door closed, softly. "He's gone. You can open your eyes now."

It was the Red Room, still holding the silence of Papa's transition. Nico was in the chair by the bed. Cami pushed herself up on her elbows. *Someone must have carried me here. Marya probably found me in the kitchen.*

The silence was immense, and there was a new thing in it. A breathlessness, like the static just before a Waste-born lightning storm. His anger had never felt so . . . unsteady before. As if it might be directed at *her*, instead of just dangerous on its own.

But that was ridiculous. If he was here, she was safe.

"I'm not gonna ask what you were doing." Nico leaned forward, elbows on his knees. His eyes were dark, no colored sparks in the pupils, and narrowed. "I'm not even gonna ask if you're okay, because you're obviously not. I should take you to the hospital, except I know you don't like needles and poking. Trig says you didn't give yourself a concussion, so I suppose that's all right." He paused. "I am, however, gonna ask you about *him*."

About who? She stretched, pulled the covers up. Her pajamas were all rucked around. "Who?" The word came out whole, surprising her.

Nico's gaze was dead-level, but there were no pinpricks of red in his pupils. "The boy."

What boy? "W-what?"

"The garden boy. Beale, right? The Joringel scholarship boy."

Oh. Tor. How do you know he came from there? But of course, he would. She gathered herself. How could she even begin explaining?

Nico kept going, though. "Because I really don't mind you hanging out with the help, babygirl, but you should know what he's probably thinking."

She pushed her hair back, strings of darkness clinging to her fingers. *Why here? It's on the other side of the house from the kitchen. And what do you think Tor's thinking? It's not like you've asked. I know you better than that.* "What w-w-would he b-be—"

"You're a sweet girl, Cami, and you could be a lot of help to a kid from near the core. You're *la Vultusina*, all right? People are going to see that. They're going to want things."

They always have. You don't know, you're always away. Doing important things. Family *things.* "N-nico." She sounded annoyed even to herself. *And I'm not* la Vultusina *yet.* "He's m-m-my f-f-friend."

"You may be *his* friend. But I don't think he's yours." Nico leaned forward. There were shadows under his mossy eyes, and his fangs were out, just delicately touching his lower lip. "It doesn't matter. Just be careful. Wouldn't want any accidents." His smile widened, and it was the grimace he used when he wanted to scare someone. An animal showing all its teeth, white and sharp and perfect.

The unsteadiness was all through her instead of just underneath her feet. She couldn't even figure out what to call it, when it was vibrating in her own bones. Her back straightened. The covers fell away. The room was utterly still, and it had even begun to smell a little neglected. You could tell nobody had breathed in here for a while. "L-l-leave h-him alone."

"If he behaves himself, I'll be his new best friend. I'll take him out with the boys and give him a taste of real nightside." The grin didn't go away. "If he steps out of line, though, Cami, there's gonna be trouble. I guarantee it."

"Why a-a-are you b-b-being l-like this?" *He doesn't even matter, he's just a friend! He's just . . .*

What, exactly, *was* Tor? Every time she talked to him, she ended up confused. And there were the dogs.

What about the dogs, Cami? Marya said . . .

To hell with it. She pushed the covers aside further, sliding her legs out of bed. The bandages were still crisply charmed; their whiteness dyed by the Red Room's gloom.

"Like *what*?" Nico didn't move. If she wanted to stand up, she would have to push past him. "You tell me exactly what I'm being like."

Like . . . this. I don't even know how to say it. "L–like m–mean."
*Like you think you can order me around too, or something. Or like you
don't even see me, you just see . . . what?*

He didn't flinch, but his stillness became its own creature,
hunching between them like a titon hunched over a pile of cow
bones. "I don't want to be mean to *you*."

Then why are you being nasty? Everything was knotting up
again, the inside of her head getting all jumbled. So she just
shrugged, and pushed her feet out further. Her toes brushed his
leg; she scooted for the edge.

He didn't move.

"Cami." His fingers touched her knee. They were hot
through the silk of her pajama pants, and the hurtful strength in
his grip was restrained.

Still, it was there. He was *Family*.

And she wasn't. She was something else, from somewhere
else. Cami halted, staring at the nightstand. The bone comb
wasn't there, but the candles in the two heavy iron holders were
flaming steadily. The room was trying to be the same, but it
couldn't.

Papa was gone.

Nico exhaled softly. "I'm not gonna let anyone hurt you."
The grin was gone. The words were serious, very quiet, and suddenly everything inside the Red Room suffocated her. "*Ever.*"

Except you, right? You won't be able to stop yourself one of these days. And you'll be sorry about it. But you'll do it, and I'll be the one hurting.

Unless I do something about it.

She pushed forward and he finally moved, sliding the chair back on the plush carpet. Her feet weren't too bad, she only hobbled a little. Nico made a frustrated little sound she knew from long experience—he was annoyed, but he wasn't going to explode.

Well, thank God for that, at least. She made it to the door. Her bandage-shuffling footsteps fell into the dead silence.

"Say something. Mithrus, Cami, get mad at me, throw something, do anything, just *say* something!"

I can't. Haven't you noticed? "I'll b-b-be c-c-c . . . " She stopped, her own frustration rising bright and metallic to her back teeth. Took a deep breath, tried again. "*Careful.* I'll b-be c-careful."

It probably wasn't what he wanted, and she probably shouldn't have left him in there staring at the Red Room's paneling and the red bed. But she had to get out of there, because the buzzing in her bones had mounted another few notches, and she still didn't have a name for it.

And for once, Nico could deal with his own fury. It was, Cami thought as she headed grimly for the stairs, about damn time.

TWENTY-TWO

SHE PRETENDED SHE WAS SICK AND STAYED HOME FROM school, and Nico didn't push. Neither did anyone else. Marya's careful charming took care of her feet. Stevens kept bringing up messages from Ruby, from Ellie, written in his crabbed hand on the traditional thick linen paper; Cami just glanced at them and nodded. She didn't even turn on her Babbage.

Nico was angry. Ruby and Ellie were probably angry too, but who cared? Let them go on without their third wheel for a while. It wasn't like they would miss her deadweight.

Plus, Nico was busy with Family business, too busy to care what Cami did or didn't do. Marya kept sending lunch and dinner to the study on trays; they returned uneaten. There was a steady stream of visitors from the other Families, and from the lower ranks of the Vultusino.

They were hunting the child-takers, since the police had no clue.

Cami avoided them. Let Nico take care of that. If he was going to start working like Papa always had, it was probably high time. She heard enough whispers around the edges to know the vanishings were still going on, but there was nothing on the news. Whoever was snatching kids had to know *that* meant the Family had been asked to step in.

Or maybe they didn't. Either way, it was only a matter of time. Once the Family began hunting, you couldn't hide. Even Papa said so.

We are the scouring of the earth, he had said once to Stevens, as an eight-year-old Cami perched in his lap and played with his tie. *As we always have been.*

What was there to do all day, when you didn't go to school? A pile of nothing and brooding. Which left her sitting up in her room staring out the window at the snow. High stacked billows of iron-gray cloud moved in every evening, the temperature rose slightly, and from a flat-beaten sheet of metallic dark infinity the flakes would come whirling down. After midnight the sky cleared, and the drifts were frozen stiff.

Tor didn't show up, even when Cami dragged herself down to the kitchen. Where Marya, when she wasn't happily scolding everyone, was humming to herself as she fussed over the stove, supremely oblivious to Cami's sullen silence. Of course, the benefit of sullenness was taken away when you couldn't talk much anyway. If it had been *Ruby* shutting up, everyone would have noticed.

So, Tor wasn't going to come to her. Fair enough. One day after lunch, she decided she might as well do a little scouring of the earth herself, and look for *him*.

What did you wear when you went chasing a scarred garden boy from Simmerside? She decided jeans were acceptable. A chunky green wool jumper Marya had knitted her for Mithrusmas last year. The black boots with the fake fur at the top, doubled socks over her tender still-healing feet, and her cashmere coat.

She cut through the empty, quiet ballroom and found a back hall, letting herself out through a servant's door. The problem of where to find him solved itself—the groundskeeper's barn and its sheds were just down the hill from here, tucked out of sight behind a high hedge of windbreak firs but still close to the puzzle-garden, which needed constant babying in spring. She could remember being lost with Nico in its depths, her heart beating high and wild in her throat, and Nico's grin.

I'm Family. I'm never lost, he always said, his hand warm in hers and his presence banishing all fear. *Come on.*

Not this time. This time, Cami crunched along alone, her boots breaking the icy crust, her nose and cheeks immediately numb. Her fists, stuffed deep in her coat pockets, were slippery. Her breath came short, the air was knife-cold, and the clouds for the afternoon snowfall were riding in fast, low in the sky like a steel-colored headache. Winter sunlight thrown back from the drifts scraped through the inside of her head, left it aching.

Even if it wasn't expressly forbidden, she'd never dared to play much in the barn. She'd played *banditti* with Nico there, sometimes. He was the fearless bandit, she was the girl from the town, smuggling him food and drink or aiding his daring escapes. The barn was good for that, but the groundskeeper would shake his gnarled fist if he found them among the machines and implements, fascinated by the riding mower or the oozing, dozing gray grinmarches whose job it was to eat pests, insect or rodent—and sometimes, bigger things.

Stevens wasn't the only dark hole to drop a secret, and once something went into a grinmarch, it didn't come out except in tiny gray pellets spread on the gardens in spring. And they ate anything organic.

The side door was unlocked, and she heard male voices, laughter. A clanging, the crack of a leather strap.

Cami grabbed the knob, twisted it firmly, and stepped into the hay-smelling dimness. It was cold, but not as frozen as outside. Her breath plumed, and she blinked, trying to adjust.

Dead silence. For a moment she thought the place was deserted, but her vision cleared slowly and she saw the lean brown groundskeeper, his mouth ajar, staring at her from where he bent over a red-shining mower, its hood lifted and the engine a collection of fascinating alien metal bits. Two garden boys were feeding the sluggish gray-skinned four-legged grinmarches, pilfer husks drifting from the shovels, crawling with charm-caught insects and the occasional small mouse. They stared at her agape as well. The oil-sheened grinmarches snorted and champed, snuffling in the husks and making little crunching noises when they came across anything with a skeleton or carapace.

Tor straightened slowly. He was crouched by a pile of shiny things, and as he stood, she saw they were blades. He had a whetstone in one hand, and his messy black hair was shaken down over a glower. Another garden boy, this one blond and husky, was hanging up bits of leather—she didn't know what they were, but they looked important, with jingling metal bits.

Embarrassment flooded her cheeks with heat. "Hi," she managed, awkwardly. "I'm l-l-looking f-for T-tor."

The groundskeeper cleared his throat. "'E's done." Gruff and gravel—was this the same man who had been a figure of terror while she tagged behind Nico, never daring to look at his face? Now he was a stick with scanty white hair and a pair of overalls hanging loosely on his frame, a bulky colorless jumper underneath and his hands spotted with black grease. "G'on."

Does he stutter too? She regarded him curiously, and Tor dropped a shiny blade and the whetstone. Metal clanged, and she almost flinched.

Tor zipped his jacket up—it was the same dun-colored leather jacket with its scuffs and missing hardware, and she suddenly longed to see him in a new one. Would he take it the right way?

You got Ellie in trouble, you want to get him in trouble too? You're good at that, Cami. A spot of hot acid shoved behind her breastbone, an accusing finger.

Tor's scowl didn't change. "Clock me out, Derek?"

"You bet." But the blond was staring at her, as if she was a summerfey appearing past the Dead Harvest—a violation, something that shouldn't *be*.

Like a minotaur. Or a Twist.

Tor approached with long loping strides, and there was a dark bruise on the side of his neck, peeking past a ratty red knitted scarf. She stood, not quite sure what should happen next, and he tilted his chin a little at the door. She groped for the knob, and in a few heartbeats the cold hit her afresh. So did the glare of sunshine, and she began to shiver.

He barely waited to sweep the door closed before snapping at her. "You shouldn't be here."

Well, isn't that welcoming. "I th-thought—"

He apparently didn't care what she thought. "It's dangerous."

"I w-w-won't l-let N-nico do anything." *To you. Just so you know.*

A dismissive movement. His boots, at least, looked sturdy. Not tattered like the rest of him. "You think I'm worried about him, princess? Not likely."

This time, she minded the name. She raised an eyebrow, an imitation of Ruby's do-you-know-who-you-are-addressing expression, and for once her tongue didn't eat a word whole. "P-princess?"

"Up in your tower, watching the rest of us. Never mind. Come on."

I thought you said it was dangerous. "Why? If I sh-sh-shouldn't b-b-be here."

"We can talk. A little, at least." He raised a hand, flattened it against his chest—high up, just where a pendant would rest. A curious look of relief passed over his sharp, wary face. "But after that, we shouldn't. It's not safe."

"I th-thought you w-w-were the r-right k-kind of trouble." *I can't believe I just said that.*

I can't believe he stood there and let me get it all out.

"I thought I *was*, for you." He glanced around. "Not anymore."

The shed by the south pond was ramshackle, and unlike the barn, it was familiar territory. Near the wall at the very edge of the property, it was as far away from the house as Cami could comfortably go on a summer's evening—which meant it was too far while winter lay on New Haven.

Afterward, she wasn't quite sure if Tor led her there, or if she led him. They just . . . set out, and naturally arrived there in the middle of the brambles, a slice of land left fallow inside the Vultusino's massive wall. Every house of the Seven had a charmed property boundary, gray stone from the quarries upstate threaded with ancient barriers against trespass and stray charm. The security crew walked the boundaries every dusk and dawn, with wooden daggers and other weapons, searching for any attempted breach.

It was frigid inside the shed, and the weight of snow on the roof was about to cave it in. Thorny vines clasped the walls—they had played Reeve and Wasteland here as children, Nico as hunter and Cami as herbalist, fighting off mutants and wild Twists. She knew the floor was sagging but not quite ready to give yet; the hole in the ceiling where the swallows nested spilled a trickle of diamond snow.

The coils of rope on the wall, slowly rotting, were old friends. The stain in the back, on the packed-earth floor, still gave her a chill deeper than the cold outside. *Just the size of a body*, Nico had said once, casually, and she was never sure if he knew something she didn't.

"We can't do this again." Tor folded his arms. "It's dangerous."

What's so dangerous about you? "What if I don't c-c-care?"

"Maybe *I* care."

"M-maybe you d-d-don't." But she had other questions. She pointed at his throat—no, slightly below, where the pendant would gleam, "An apple. C-c-cut in h-half."

He actually went white, even the rawness at his nose and the corners of his mouth paling. "You don't know anything *about* it."

"I d-d-don't. But I n-n-need—"

He took two steps toward her, and his hands curled into fists, dangling naked at his sides despite the cold. "What do you think you need? Take my advice—stay where it's safe. Don't go outside. Don't go places with strange men. Stay away and hope . . . " His throat worked. He'd run out of words, so maybe she could get one or two in.

So Cami swallowed hard, and went for it. "Wh-what's *B-b-biel'y?*" She couldn't pronounce it like Stevens had.

She didn't need to. If she thought he was pale before he was ashen now. His throat worked as he gulped. His shoulders hunched too, defensively. "Do they know?"

Know what? I don't even know, how can I tell what they *do? I'm not one of them. You said it yourself.* She swallowed, the bitterness all through her hard and frozen as the ground outside. "I h-heard them t-t-talking." *I don't have to say what they were talking about, now do I? Or even who "they" are.* "I d-d-don't know anything. B-b-but I *n-n-need* to. I . . . I h-have d-d-dreams. *Bad* ones." Her fingers shook as she unbuttoned her coat. "W-wait." Even though he wasn't going anywhere. The cashmere fell open, and she lifted the thick woolen jumper and her T-shirt underneath.

Her belly showed, so pale the veins were blue through the skin—and not only that, but the scars from burn and welt and slice were plainly visible.

The breath left him in a rush, a white cloud. The wind rose, fingering at the shed's edges. A low moan, eerie and unmodulated.

"Y-y-you're n-not the only o-o-one with sc-c-cars." *God, why can't I just* talk?

He stared until she lowered her shirt and sweater. It was too cold, but she didn't feel it. Her fingers shook even more as she buttoned her coat back up, her gloves making her clumsier.

"They f-f-found m-me in the s-s-snow." Now it was easier, because she had his attention. He was listening like Nico did, leaning forward, the rest of the world shut out. "I'm not F-f-family. N-not a p-princess. I w-want to know wh-what's *h-h-h-happening* t-t-to me." *Because something is. Something terrible.*

He stared for a long while. She fidgeted, shivering, wishing she could shake him and *make* him start telling her things.

Finally, Tor let out a ragged sigh. "Okay." He nodded, his shoulders slumping. "Okay. But not *here*, for Chrissake."

Uneasy relief and fresh nervousness mixed inside her stomach. "Wh-where?"

"Not tonight, either. Let me think, all right? Just let me think." He actually turned in a full circle, looking at the shed's walls covered with coils of decaying rope and the black hanging driblets of moss that would green in spring.

Just like a dog settling down for the night. Cami shivered even harder.

When he turned back to her, he was still pale. His hands were fists again, and he thrust them in his jacket pockets. "Fine." As if they'd been yelling, and the fight was over. "*Biel'y.* Okay."

"D-d-do you—"

"I said *okay.*" Quick as a flash of lightning, and the irritation gone just as fast. "I'll tell you what I know, but not *here.* The moon turns tonight. Waxing moon's much safer for . . . both of us. Can you get out after dark? Two days from now?"

She nodded. *Nico's going to be angry.*

But only if he finds out. And besides, she had to know. If she wasn't Family, this wasn't his business, was it?

Tor nodded, once, sharply. You could tell he was used to planning things, once he made up his mind. "Here's what we'll do, then."

TWENTY-THREE

QUIET, DARK, AND MUFFLED BY THE SNOW, THE HOUSE on Haven Hill crouched.

She carried her shoes down the stairs, holding her breath whenever one thought of squeaking under her weight. Slowly, softly, a mouse in a dark hole, she kept glancing in every direction, nervously halting whenever a breath of sound brushed her ears.

Nico was out, with some of the Cinghiale boys. Clubbing, or who knew? Family business, and Trig was gone too. They'd left that afternoon, and the house was just like when Papa was gone—absent its breathing, beating heart. The Vultusino was missing, and even the walls knew it.

If Papa had been alive, she never would have dared to do this.

The front door grimaced at her, so she turned aside and crept across the foyer. Trig gone with Nico, Stevens already in bed; Marya was in the kitchen humming, and would be for a long while. The servants were bedded down; precious few of them wanted to trudge home through a New Haven winter. It was best just to stay on the Hill. And security wouldn't do another circuit until dawn—or unless the protections on the walls woke.

The side door was locked, but it recognized Cami and opened with no fuss. The charms were uneasy, but she was allowed.

At least, this once. If she got caught, things might change.

Did Ruby feel like this when she snuck out? Did Ellie feel the risk breathing on her back, tingling in her fingers, her heart beating so hard she thought she might faint? Or was it just Cami the coward who cringed at every sound?

The cold ran down her body like oil. The leggings were good, the skirt was okay, and her coat was warm—but she was looking at being half-frozen already. She pulled the door shut, heard it click, and heard the charmbolt slide back into place.

Well, I'm outside.

Down the steps, around the corner, the snow wasn't too bad. Expeller charms kept it mostly whisked away, and the wind drifted it against the north side of the house. She crept to the corner and peered out at the driveway.

"Don't just stand there." Tor's breath touched her ear. She jumped, almost letting out a shriek, and saw the white gleam of his teeth as he grinned. "Sorry."

She balled up her fist and socked him a good one on the

shoulder, as if he was Nico. He stopped short, still grinning. Her clenched fist tingled.

That was probably not a good idea.

"Really, I'm sorry." He even sounded contrite. "Got carried away."

With what, dammit? Her heart finally settled, pounding high and hard in her wrists and throat. At least with her pulse going like this she wasn't cold. "F-fine. Where are w-we g-g-going?"

He was an ink-drawing, from the smudge of his hair to the paleness of his hands. "Someplace I'm sure we won't be overheard."

"O-o-over—"

"There's ears everywhere, princess. Let's go."

It wasn't easy to get off the grounds without using the gate, but Tor climbed a tree near the periphery, put his hand down and braced her as she scrambled up. The protections scented Cami and vibrated a little, but subsided, and she finally let out the breath she'd been holding.

He dropped down on the other side, caught and steadied her as she tried not to fall into a snowdrift. His hands were warm against her waist, even through her coat, and a different heat went through her, along with a curious comfort.

Why did he feel so familiar?

He let go of her, slowly, and they trudged along the wall

until they reached a small enclosure, saved from the worst of the snowfall by a huge cedar tree. Under its low-hanging branches, in the fragrant chilly dark, stood a motorcycle.

It was sleek and shining, slung low to the ground, and its front wheel was covered with a shield shaped like a silver horse's head. Its wheels were alive with silver grabcharms, hissing slightly as they touched the cold air.

"You like?" Tor's grin was proprietary and uneasy all at once. "He was a junked-out hulk. I dragged him halfway across town, remade him from the inside out."

"Wow." Cami touched the horse's head, her gloved finger scratching behind an ear. As if it was real. Charmlight ran in the silvery metal, and she snatched her hand back. Tor, right behind her, was so close his breath was a cloud over her shoulder.

"He likes you."

"H–how c–can you t–t–tell?"

A shrug she felt in her own shoulders. "I rebuilt him, I can tell. You know how to ride?"

She had to shake her head. Motorcycles weren't safe. Nico would have a *fit* if he knew—but she pushed the thought away. He was out, doing God knew what. It was Cami's Personal Choice to be here, and if he didn't like it, well, he could just . . .

Bravery only went so far. It would be much, much better if he just didn't find out about this. It was *private*, she decided.

Tor's fingers, awkward, touched her elbow. "It's easy. I did the charming myself, all through him, he's pretty safe. You'll have to lean with me, and you'll have to be close. Still want to? You can get back into the house if you—"

"N-no." She stepped back, blundering into him, and the contact sent a shock through her, even through layers of clothing. "I'm n-not going b-b-back." *I've come too far. I have to know.*

And for once, she was a necessary part of an expedition. *She* wanted to know, *she* had sought him out, and *she* had snuck out of the house on her own. This whole thing wouldn't be happening without her, and that was a frightening—but kind of pleasant—change.

"Okay." He pushed past her, swung a leg over the cycle's padded seat, and leaned it, popping the kickstand free. Another quick motion, and the purr of an engine rasped under the snowy quiet. "Climb up, princess."

I wish you wouldn't call me that. It was probably useless to ask any questions, so she didn't. She clambered carefully up, sliding her arms around his waist. At least she knew that much.

"Closer," he said over his shoulder. "You've got to hold on tight."

His jacket smelled of leather, but without the bay rum and Nico's fiery pepper-temper it wasn't a quite-safe aroma. The cold lay over them both, an almost physical weight. The purr of the engine ratcheted, and the cycle jerked forward. The snow was churned about, broken and dangerous; he half-walked the purring thing toward the road. The grabcharms flung themselves out in sticky lightning-snake tentacles, digging into the frozen surface and tossing up tiny bits of it.

The wind rose, tugging at her braided hair, wringing tears out of her eyes. She wondered how he could see to steer, and laid her head on his shoulder. He tensed, but then relaxed as the motorcycle reached the bottom of a shallow hill, whinnied, and hopped up onto the road as neat as you please.

Cami caught the trick of it—you did have to lean close. Pretty indecently close.

Ruby would love this. The thought made her grin, and she hugged Tor fiercely as the icy, dangerous road slid away underneath them. He gunned it, leaning forward as the grabcharms spat, and the chrome horse leapt to obey.

TWENTY-FOUR

HER CHEEKS STILL STUNG FROM THE COLD OUTSIDE, and she tried to look like she walked into a smoke-dimmed, charm-and-neon lit, bass-thumping inferno every day of the week. The club was on the edge of Simmerside, and Tor was known here—at least, the jack bouncer nodded him and Cami past. Thick with muscle, mirrored shades over eyes that glowed through the polarized lenses, the shaven-headed jack presided over a line of other jacks and Twists, inadequately dressed against the cold, none of them daring to step much out of line under his glare.

Inside, it was a crush of throbbing music, and the smoke drifting around was from burning tobacco and other substances. A few *actual fausts* were on the dancefloor, jerking as if possessed.

Well, technically, she supposed they *were* possessed. She had never been this close to real live fausts before, and was surprised to see they looked just like regular people, except for the constant smoke wreathing them. And the way their hair stood up, writing madly. Even the lone female faust's waist-length mop tried to rise on an invisible draft.

There were their eyes, too, glowing dull punky unnatural colors as the dæmon crouching inside its human host looked *out*.

There were Twists here too, most of them congregating along one wall of the club where iron bars ran from floor to ceiling, part of the Age of Iron chic the whole place had. Odd shapes lurked in the shadows as limbs corkscrewed by Potential moved restlessly; shoving and snapping, their eyes glitter-crackling with stray sharp unhealthy charms, the Twists were given careful space even by the fausts. The iron would scorch them, but every once in a while a Twist brushed against it deliberately, and the sick-sweet roasting smell that arose added a sharper note to the funk as the Twist exhaled luxuriously.

What would it be like, Cami wondered, to love pain that much?

The bar was a mess of tubing; the bartender wore goggles pushed up on his sweat-greased forehead; polished sprockets and gearwheels glittered from the circulating waitress's skirts. The tables were covered with dingy linen, and the jacks on the dancefloor sported feathers, fur, lizard skin, a whole cavalcade of Potential-spurred anomalies that would keep them hidden or creeping in the shadows during daylight.

None of them elbowed Tor, though, and she followed in his wake to the bar. He leaned over and shouted something; the tender gave him a brief dark glance, looked over his shoulder at Cami. The bartender was a charmer, the edge of his Potential flaring with a faint green wreathing glow as it reacted with the charged atmosphere. His dark hair and wide dark eyes made him into an inquisitive river otter, and he yelled something over the noise at Tor, who shrugged. "*She's with me,*" the garden boy yelled back, and picked up something shiny from the counter. Two glasses of something fuming with steam were handed over. Tor nodded, didn't bother paying as he turned away and forced a fresh route through the crowd.

There was another Twist bouncer at the staircase, but this one just stood aside, holding the end of a frayed red velvet rope. The music—if you could call it that—was a migraine attack, but Cami thought she heard Shelley Wynter singing again. Or maybe it was Bronwinn and the Titons, floaty female vocals over a pounding beat and wailing charmesizers.

Nico really liked Shelley Wynter, had every tape she'd put out, even the limited-release demos from when she was a torch singer in New Bransford, a couple province-states south.

When Cami was thirteen, she'd wished for her hair to whiten just like Wynter's. She'd nerved herself up to ask Marya about bleach and dye, but had never quite scraped together the last drop of courage necessary to actually *do* it. Ruby had said there would be no problem, but Cami didn't want to trust her hair to Ruby's enthusiasm at that point. Not after the Great

Clippers Incident earlier that summer. Of course Rube had just looked gorgeous and ethereal, but still.

Behind the rope was an archway, and stairs going up. She climbed after Tor, blinking. Her eyes kept filling up—from the cold, and the smoke, and all the noise.

I'm out, at night, with a strange boy. Near the core, too. Her heart pounded so fast she thought she might have some sort of attack.

Was this what freedom felt like?

There was a close dim hall upstairs; Tor took a sharp right and set off down it. He shouldered open a door to his left, jerked his head at her, and she stepped inside.

It was, of all things, a sitting room. There was a fireplace, but it was cold and empty. Two overstuffed chairs that looked pre-Reeve crouched dispirited in front of it, and a small table sat between them. Peeling yellow-brocade wallpaper hung in strips from the walls, and the whole thing made Cami's throat close up. If the Red Room was a comforting weight, this sad little room was a strangling crush of poverty and disrepair.

If Papa hadn't found her, who might have? Or if Chauncey hadn't bothered with the brakes, what would have happened? Or what if Nico decided, sooner or later, that she wasn't Family enough, if she made him *too* angry? He was the Vultusino now, and if he decided she didn't belong in the house on Haven Hill . . .

It didn't bear thinking about. But sooner or later, Cami supposed, she *would* have to think about it.

"Sit down," Tor said, sweeping the door shut. "I'm pretty sure we won't be overheard here."

I doubt anyone could hear through all that downstairs. The music and crowdroar from below was a giant beast's dozing pulse, as if they were above a rumbling titon pit. "I d-d-d-don't—" she began, but he just pushed past her, set the drinks down on the table, and stamped back to the door. There was a click, and she realized he had locked it.

Her throat, in addition to closing up to the size of a piece of spaghetti, was now slick and dry as summer-dusted glass.

"Got to be careful. You start talking about *Biel'y*, people get nervous." He brushed past her, dropped down in the chair to the left. Reached for one steam-fuming drink, and poured it down in a long swallow. "Gah. *Nasty.*"

Cami's boots were still wet with melting snow. His tracks and hers showed up dark on the threadbare, flower-patterned carpet.

"Before I forget." He dug in his jacket pocket. "Something for you. Since the pin broke. You seemed awful worried about it."

She lowered herself down in the other chair. "I f-felt b-bad. S-s-since you—"

"I'm not broken up about it. But I figured I'd get you something else, pretty girl. Here."

It was a velvet bag, deep black, the nap worn in a few places. She opened it gingerly, and the shimmersilk spilled out.

Opalescent, charm-woven by Waste-witches, the rumor ran—it was pretty rare. The threads were fine, but strong as iron, and the lacework of it could be doubled, turned over itself to make a belt, opened for a shawl. She'd never actually *held* shimmersilk before.

It made even fey-woven lace look coarse and ugly. Her small wondering sigh was lost under the thumping from below. "W-wow," she breathed. "H-how d-d-did you—" She was just about to ask *how did you afford it*, stopped herself. "Th-thank y-you."

For a bare moment, he grinned without anger, shyly ducking his head. "I saw it in a pawnshop, thought it belonged to you. Took a couple paychecks, but it's worth it." He eyed the second drink. "You want that? It's called a minotaur. Rat-tooth gin, strawberry juice, and cornswell charm. Just the thing for nerves."

"N-no. Th-thank you, Tor." His name managed to wring its way free of her lips, whole and undamaged.

"You're welcome. I . . . *Mithrus.* I like you." Did he look uncomfortable? Maybe just a little. He grabbed the second drink, bolted it too. Steam drenched his face for a moment; he wiped it away with his free hand and set the second glass down. The gleam in his hand was the door-key, he set it on the table, pushed it with a fingertip until it was on her side. "Okay, so. *Biel'y.*"

The shimmersilk slid through her hands. It had tassels, made of smoky floss. Nobody at school had one.

Ruby would just *die*.

"I only know a l-little," she hedged. *Wait. Did he just say he liked me?*

"Look, I was an orphan. I didn't know. Sometimes it happens, one of them gets lost and grows up outside the cult."

It's a cult? There were a lot of them around, leftovers from the Age of Iron, coalescing around charmers gone bad, or Twists with charisma. You couldn't swing a hexed cat in some provinces without hitting a cult or two. Papa said that even some branches of the Family, like the Stregare, used to be worshipped sometimes, back before the Reeve.

Papa's gone. A chill touched her back. The shimmersilk was cool, like supple living metal against her sweating fingers. It was waking up, coming alive in her hands as her Potential filled it with heat. Music thumped away below, the beat changing a fraction, becoming more insistent. "Okay." *I didn't think there were cults here in New Haven, though.*

"I'm not one of *them*," he persisted.

She nodded. Her braid bumped against the back of her coat. She was beginning to warm up a little. Maybe she *should* have had the other drink. A buzz would probably help right about now. "I b-believe you."

Maybe it was the dimness, but he suddenly looked years older. "Well, don't. *Biel'y* lie. That's the first lesson about them—don't ever trust one who says they're not, especially a man. Once the Queen gets hold of them, they'll do anything, say anything, to get her what she wants."

Her hands cramped. The shimmersilk bit, its thin threads able to slice flesh if enough pressure was applied. She had to force her fingers to relax. "The Queen." It was a bare, numb-lipped whisper.

An answering whisper, from the well of darkness her night-mares hid inside. *You are nobody. You are nothing.*

"The White Queen." Tor was pale. Sweat stuck his messy black hair to his forehead. "The boys serve her, they grow into her huntsmen. The women serve her too, if they come in from outside. But the girls . . . she *takes* them." He wet his lips, a quick darting motion of his tongue. "It's old magic, older than the Reeve or the Age of Iron. Didn't anyone ever tell you this ghost story?"

"N–no." *Not until now.* "They t-talk around the edges. B–but not out l-loud."

"Sometimes she takes in orphans. There are some kids born into the cult, born underground where they live, like Twists. If they're not Twisted, if they're not jacks, if they're plain human or charmer, they're kept." He shuddered. "The born-below boy babies are *special* huntsmen. Her *Okhotniki*." The word was funny, swallowed into the back of his throat, almost French but not quite. "The girls . . . when they're six . . . it's not pretty."

How old are you, bambina? Where is your momma, your poppa?

Tor's black eyes glazed. He stared at the empty fireplace like he could see the story he was telling played out in its shadowed depths. "Sometimes, only sometimes, the White Queen consents to her most favored *Okhotnik*. Sometimes after that there's a baby, and sometimes, only sometimes, a special baby girl born. A princess. When she's six, the Queen takes her. Then the Queen's renewed, not just for a little while like with the other girls, but for a hundred years or more."

"R–r–renewed?" Her hand stole toward the key.

"Oh, yeah." He blinked furiously, like there was something in his eyes. "It's not easy, being the Queen. She gets ... hungry." He shuddered again. "That's why there's *huntsmen*. They, and the *Okhotniki*, bring her things. To ... eat."

Oh, God. The cold was all through her now. The music below mounted another frenetic notch, a vibration running through the floor and the chair, rising up her spine.

This one's heart is fiery.

You were dead. She ate the heart.

The apple, cut in half, its seeds forming a star. A flat medallion, sparking, a red stone in the middle—the only one with a jewel, because she was the Queen.

The others had medallions too, but they were plain. Plain silver, not-quite-round.

"You h-had one," she whispered. "A n-n-n-necklace." *A huntsman. Bringing her things to eat.*

"Since I was in the orphanage. I was an *orphan*," he said. He was shaking now, his hands clamped on the chair's arms. "I was—"

But whatever he would have said next was drowned in a crashing from below. The music rose on feedback-laced squeal, and the screaming started.

Cami grabbed for the key. Her fingers scraped the table, draped in shimmersilk, and Tor's eyes rolled up into his head. Under the sudden chaos from below, the sound of the chair's arms cracking as he heaved at them, struggling against something invisible, was only guessed-at, not heard.

She let out a high-pitched cry, lost under a wave of cracking that shuddered through the frame of the nightclub, and bolted for the door, the shimmersilk waving like seaweed as she ran.

Down the stairs in a rush, her wet boots smacking, Cami hit the bottom and went over the frayed red velvet rope with a leap that would have made the gym teacher, Sister Frances Grace-Abiding, *very* proud. Landed, skipping aside as a faust crashed to the floor right in front of her, for a moment she couldn't understand why everyone was screaming . . .

. . . then one of the steel-toothed dogs leapt, foam splashing from its muzzle and its fawn-colored hindquarters heaving. It crunched into the fallen faust, chewing as the dæmon inside the flesh let out a shattering wail. Bone splintered, and the faust curled up, throwing the dog aside with a snapped charm that sparked red in the gloomy interior. The charmlights had mostly failed; the bleeding neon glow was barely enough to see by, and the crowd pressed for the doors as the dogs bristled, leaping at will.

A lean half-familiar figure in a tan trench coat stood in the middle of the dance floor's writhing mass, dogs flowing around him in a stream—brindle, black, splashed with white, big and small, all of them with the same mad gleam in their white-ringed eyes, crunching and howling as their steel-laced teeth champed. Cami skidded to a stop, nailed to the floor as the hounds set up a belling, braying cry that punched through the feedback squeal and swallowed it whole.

The door. But it was choked with fleeing Twists and jacks, a melee breaking out as they panicked and elbowed for room. The fight was going to spread; she'd seen enough of Nico going crazy to know *that*.

If things go sparky, babygirl, look for the back door.

It was something he always said when he took her into Lou's on a particularly nasty-tempered day, or to the dives and bars he could prowl with relative immunity as one of the Seven's boys. She heard it now as if he was right next to her, his lips skinned back in the most dangerously amused of his smiles, the good-natured one that said he didn't much care who he hurt next.

There. It was to the right of the bar, a fading exit sign that guttered and went out just as the feedback died and the only sound was the dogs' crunching and yapping, howling and snarling. She bolted for it, her boots squishing, and the shimmer-silk in her hands turned treacherous again, its fringes somehow lengthening, waving wildly and jabbing at her eyes, scraping at her wrists, tearing at the cashmere coat.

She hit the door *hard*, and it opened—thank Mithrus *Christ*—spilling her out into a cold close darkness. The latch clicked as she shoved it shut, and she gulped in a reeking mouthful of frozen outside. It was sweeter than the fug of breath and smoke and terror inside.

The howling behind her ratcheted up a notch, and she didn't have to be told they had seen her.

It was the man. The wooden man Nico had thrown out of Lou's.

She ate the heeeeeeeeart!

But Cami's heart was pumping in her chest, knocking like it wanted to break out through her ribs and escape the crunching of dogs piling into the jammed-shut door behind her. Her breathing came in quick hard white puffs, and she found herself in a trash-choked, narrow alley, the door behind her shuddering as more dogs hit it, and the sound of sirens lifting in the distance as someone noticed there was a riot starting on the edge of Simmerside, too close to the core for comfort.

This kind of spreading chaos so close to the blight could even trigger a minotaur.

Shimmersilk bit at her hands, its fringe turned to claws as it struggled, a live thing in her grasp. It was trying to eat her *face*, for God's sake. She struggled free with a despairing little cry, every inch of skin crawling with revulsion, and flung it to the cobbled floor of the alley.

It rebounded, alive with charm and spitting peacock-colored sparks, nipping at her knees. The edge of Cami's Potential flashed, a colorless ripple; she skipped aside, banging into a metal dustbin. Fine snow sifted across the alley, icicles festooning the walls wherever heat leaked out of the buildings arching overhead, and her breath came harsh and tearing in her throat.

"*NO!*" she screamed, and tore away from the shimmersilk. It bit through her leggings, opening bloody stripes and scratches all the way up to her knees, but she managed to kick it loose just as the metal door groaned, buckling.

The dogs might not be able to open it, but the wooden huntsman could—and if enough of the beasts crashed into it, even a fire door wouldn't hold. Sooner or later one of them would hurl itself against the bar that freed the latch.

Cami let out a sob, her cheeks slick with hot wetness, and gave one last kick. The shimmersilk went flying, hissing in frustration. Sirens howled—the cops had arrived, thinking there was a riot starting. Maybe there was.

She put her head down, and ran.

The holding tank wasn't that bad. Well, sure, it reeked of cig-arette smoke and stale vomit, and it was full of a crowd of jacks, some of them bloody and bruised from the scramble inside the nightclub. Still, it was brightly lit—and there were no dogs.

Her wrists throbbed with pain, and so did her shoulder—one of the cops had bent her arm back, savagely, snapping charmed cuffs on her. Cami hadn't resisted. She was sobbing too hard, anyway, and besides, she *wanted* them to take her away from the thin stick of the huntsman and the leaping, yapping, barking, steel-toothed—

She shuddered, pushed her back more firmly into the con-crete wall. The benches were for the people who would fight for them, so she had just picked a corner and retreated into herself. A few catcalls and pokes, but as soon as they figured out she wasn't going to respond they left her alone.

It was kind of like school. Except they didn't throw burning cigarettes at her there.

The holding cells were jammed. The Twists were on the other side, behind bars crawling with vicious bright golden charmwork; the charms on the jack cages were dull red. She had no idea why they'd put her in with the jacks; maybe they thought she was one, even though she had no mutation? Or maybe there hadn't been any mere-humans left? Or charmers? She hadn't seen any but the bartender, maybe he . . .

Just don't think about it.

She wanted to squeeze her eyes shut, couldn't afford to. The harsh buzzing light was her friend, it kept the shadows away. And if she closed her eyes one of the jacks in here might think she was sleeping, and try to do something to her.

Clash of keys, screams and a rising mutter.

"You! Girl, in the back!"

She raised her head, strings of damp black hair falling in her face, free of her braid and tangled into knots.

It was a heavyset jack cop, his skin scaled in rough patches and the low ragged edge of his Potential sparking against the bars. He jingled the keys again, his yellow fur-hair smoothed down under the uniform cap; his brass badge held a mellow gleam. "Yes, you. Come on."

She hauled herself to her feet. The jacks quieted, bright-eyed with interest. The hallway pulsed with noise, burrowing into her head. It was preferable to the other sounds, the ones she wasn't sure were actually physical.

Like the chanting, and the dripping. Plink-plink, water against stone.

The jacks edged away, and she made it to the barred iron door.

"Back *up!*" the cop snapped. "No, not you, kid. *You're*

coming out."

"She got bail. Lucky charmer girl." This from a gawky male teen, bone spurs on his cheekbones slicing out through peeling skin, the wounds suppurating freely and by all appearances perpetual. He was one of the loudest inmates, and the others in the holding tank mostly did what he said. Behind him, two other jacks—his friends, maybe, since they wore the same multicolored jacket he did—grinned and mouthed nasty words.

"Cryboy, if I want shit out of you, I'll squeeze your fuckin' head," the cop snarled. "Back *up*, or we take you to a room."

Cryboy laughed, made little kissy noises . . . and turned his back, took a couple of mincing steps away. His friends laughed too, hyena noises and crude jokes about things they'd like to do to the charmer-girl.

The door clanged and clattered, slid sideways just enough for Cami to slip out. She did, stood blinking in the hall while a fresh wave of hysterical screaming went through the cages on either side.

"Come with me, ma'am." The jack cop actually touched the brim of his hat, and the imprisoned jacks burst into derisive laughter, catcalling madly. Her cheeks were hot. Some of the things they said were pretty anatomically impossible, but it didn't stop her from wondering if they would, somehow, perform these weird acts if given a chance.

There was another heavy metal door with a barred window

at the end of the hall; the observation slit darkened briefly and there was a clatter from the other side. It opened, Cami was prodded through—not ungently—and she found herself in a quieter hall floored with peeling gray linoleum. The guard—another cop, this one pure human—took his hand off the butt of a gun, and she was absurdly comforted. The motion reminded her of Trig.

There was also a burly, graying man, pure human, in a cheap suit. He looked almost relieved to see her, and Cami stared at him curiously. She'd never really seen a detective before, and he didn't look at all like a creature deserving of the scorn sometimes heaped on the cops among the younger Family, especially at parties where the whiskey and calf flowed freely.

"Miss Vultusino?" The detective held up the student ID. It had been yanked from her coat pocket after they cuffed her, before they lifted her and threw her bodily into the van.

Abruptly, she ached all over. The cuts on her arms and legs were singing with pain, and her head was heavy. She managed a nod, and almost swayed.

"I'm Detective Haelan. Let's get you out of here."

"No shit?" The pure human cop eyed her like she was an exotic pet. "It's one of *them*? Why wasn't—"

"Shut up, Sullov." The detective ran a hand back through his hair, a fume of cigarettes and cheap cologne clinging to him. His stubble was salted with gray too, and the pouches under his eyes could have held soup. "This way, Miss."

So she was *Miss* now. Well, that was good. Except they'd found out who she was. Cami approached him carefully, held out her bruised hand, and the laminate of the ID crumpled slightly in her sweating fingers. He also had her coat, which he handed over.

"Would you like some coffee? A Danish?" He had kind eyes, she decided.

"Why not just give her a foot massage, too?" the blond guard muttered. When Cami glanced back, though, he was peering through the observation slit in the door. "Animals," he said, a little louder. "Look at them. A bunch of animals."

"Don't mind Sullov. He's subnormal, that's why we have him working down here." The detective's half-grin was not pleasant at all, and the words had the quality of a challenge. He ushered Cami past another heavy locked door, swiping his hand over a charmplate near the handle and nodding as it clicked. "They've sent someone to fetch you. Not often we see Family in this part of town."

She winced inwardly. Would it be Nico? No, he was the Head, he couldn't come down here personally. Nor could Stevens—even though the Seven owned the law, there were appearances to be upheld. One of the younger Vultusino? Trig? Maybe, but that would mean Nico knew about this, too.

Haelan kept talking. About how they hadn't known who

she was, and how he hoped the holding cell hadn't been *too* bad, and was she sure she didn't want a cup of coffee? She finally agreed, just to make him be quiet, and the relief passing over his face when he heard her stutter was thought-provoking.

However mad Nico got, it was better than the dogs. And the way things inside her head were opening up. Curtains lifting, the things behind them leering and capering, full of scorched skin, the blossoming of red pain, the filth and the chains.

This one's heart is fiery.

She ended up perched on a battered leather couch in a paper-choked detective's office, listening to the phone ring and clutching a paper cup of boiled, ash-smelling coffee. Haelan had disappeared, and after a while Trigger edged into the room, his hair stuck up anyhow and his jacket dusted with melted snow. He gave her a brief look, nodded, and cocked his head.

That was, at least, one signal she knew how to decipher. She was on her feet somehow, tossing the slopping-over cup of coffee in the overfull wastebasket with a splash.

Time to go.

TWENTY-FIVE

The house on Haven Hill was dark.

Chauncey brought the limousine to a soft, painless stop before the front steps. Older now, but still a careful, competent driver, was he thinking about another snowy night and a shivering girl in the car?

Trigger hadn't said a word the entire way, and Cami, huddled on the seat across from him, wasn't sure if that was a good sign. Or . . . not.

Her head hurt. Everything else hurt, and she just wanted to lie down somewhere. Just to think about all of this, or ignore it, without the jumble in her head getting worse and worse.

Trig sighed, heavily. "He was . . . upset." Slow, evenly spaced words. "Was all set to come down himself."

"He c-c-c-can't." *How can I sound so normal?* "I'm s-s-sorry, T-t-trig."

A shrug, his jacket rubbing uneasily against the leather

upholstery. His first act on getting into the car had been to slip a gun into the holster under his arm and let out a sharp relieved breath. "Figured sooner or later you'd want to run a bit, Cami-girl."

I ran all right. I ran for my life. If she told him, what would he do?

Nothing, probably. I'm not Family. There it was, as plain as day. Trig was loyal to Papa, and to Nico by default. Even though he was there each time the punishments had been meted out.

Did Nico hate him for it? Was it any of Cami's business?

I'm not Family. It can't be my business.

The smoked, bulletproof glass between them and Chauncey lowered a little. "Is the Miss all right?" A sleep-roughened voice, familiar as her own. She could still remember sitting on Chauncey's lap as the car jerked forward, thinking she was controlling the limo as his broad hands covered the wheel and his foot eased off the brake. *A born driver*, he would say, and Papa would beam, hearing Cami laugh and crow with delight.

"A little shaken, but she seems okay." Trigger rubbed at his face. He must have been yanked out of bed to come fetch her. Had someone figured out she was gone, or had it been someone the Family owned on the police force—maybe the detective, maybe not—calling to let them know one of their possessions had wandered?

She had a name for what she was, now. And it was not

Vultusino. It had never been, but now she was old enough to know.

"Mr. Nico will be relieved." Very careful, as well. Like she might break if they said the wrong thing.

Or as if they were warning her.

She reached for the handle, ignoring Trigger's sudden surprised movement, and the lock obligingly chucked up before she pushed the heavy armored door wide. Fresh snow was falling, the flakes spinning lazily, and her stomach did a queer double-hop inside her.

She slammed the door, maybe a little harder than she had to. Scuffed her still-damp boots across the pavement, the whiskaway charms on the stairs waking in brief flurries to push the snow aside before it could ice the stone and make it dangerous.

Is that why I don't like stairs? That memory wouldn't come. Instead, the smell of fresh-cut apples and thick cloying incense spilled through the cold, and a dark curtain filled her head.

The wind cut off as she stepped inside the house. The foyer was hushed and dark. Maybe she could get up to her room before he—

"Cami." Nico sat on the stairs, a shadow in the dimness. His hands dangled loosely, his forearms braced on his knees. Only the gleams of his eyes and the paleness of his throat showed. No—there was the gleam of the signet, too. Just as bloody as when Papa had worn it. The Heir's ring was in the ancient

strongbox in the library, behind the painting of Vidario Vultusino, the Eldest of the Seven of New Haven.

Waiting for an Heir. And *la Vultusina*'s ring was right next
to it, probably waiting for a Family girl to wear it. Once Cami
was . . .

. . . what?

What am I thinking? Immobile, frozen, she waited for the
explosion. Her coat was sliced, her leggings torn to ribbons, her
boots sodden with melted snow and alley ick, her skirt ripped
too. Strings of black hair fell in her face, reeking of the smoke in
the nightclub, and she probably smelled like the holding cell too.

"Say something," he persisted, soft and coaxing. She
couldn't see him well enough to find the anger in him; the
sense of the world sliding away underneath her returned,
her knees loosening and her breath coming short and hard.
"Mithrus Christ, Camille, I'm not mad at you."

Was he actually *lying* to her? The whirling inside her intensified. "Y-yes y-you are."

"Nah." Now he moved, but very slowly. He straightened,
touching the banister, and her heart thundered as he stepped
down, paused, stepped again. "I never thought of what it's like,
for you. Watching Papa go. You were in there every day with
him, weren't you?"

You think this is about that? Her teeth found her lower lip,
sank in. The pain was a bright star, a silver nail to stop the

whirling. It didn't make it go away, but at least it gave her something to hold onto.

Nico kept talking. The very softest of his voices, the one he kept just for her. "I was gone. And when I *was* here, you were holding me together too. Being brave." He reached the bottom of the stairs. Stepped cautiously toward her. "Hell of a job, babygirl."

If you knew what I was, would you be saying this to me? "N-nico . . ."

"I'm listening." Another step. Edging up to her. What did he think she was going to do, run? That would be like dropping a burning lucifer into gasoline.

"I w-w-went w-w-with T-t-tor." Her heart was going to explode.

He went very still. Red sparks firing in his gaze, deep in the back of his pupils where the Kiss would eventually burn through after years of service to the Family. He would belong to them even after his breathing stopped.

Where would *she* belong?

"I f-found out. I'm *B-b-b-biel'y.*" She couldn't get the word right. But it was close enough. "I esc-c-c-caped. I-in the s-s-snow. N-Nico—"

"Was it Stevens? Did the ghoul open his mouth?" His hands were curling into fists, she could see that. The dimness was hiding less as her eyes adapted. There was a moment's worth of comfort—if he was angry, she knew how to deal with him.

Or do I? "T-t-t-tor—" How could she even *begin* to explain?

"I'll kill him." Very quietly.

Oh, no. "N-n-nico—"

"Shhh." The bloodring glimmered as his hand came up, as if he wanted to put a finger to his lips. Stopped. "*I will kill him.*"

Why won't you listen? "I'm *B-b-b-biel*—"

"You're *not*. They can't have you." Still very quiet, the words drained and pale but still smoking. Like a faust, something inside them too furious to be corralled. "You're *not* one of theirs."

"N-n-n-nico—" *I remember. I remember being chained after I tried to escape. I remember the handcuffs and the beatings, then there's something horrible, and I can't remember, but then I was in the snow and there was Papa.* The enormity of it stuck in her throat, her traitorous tongue strangling the words as she tried to force them out past a snarling maze of blackness, the ground tilting and a Tesla-thunderstorm direct from the Waste, one nobody else could hear, drowning her out.

"It's *arranged*, babygirl." Still so quiet, she had to strain to hear him over the rushing in her head. "I've promised. I'm going to kill *him*."

Then he was gone with the inhuman speed of a Family member, leaving only a trail of unsteady charm-sparks in his wake. She was left alone in the darkened foyer, the cuts and bruises all over her throbbing viciously, her head full of noise, and her cheeks—again—hot and wet, the tears dropping onto her ruined coat as she swayed.

TWENTY-SIX

THE LOCK ON THE WHITE ROOM'S DOOR WAS ANCIENT and flimsy, but she threw it anyway. Hot water in the bath stung the cuts on her arms and legs—the shimmersilk's claws had been *sharp*.

Found it in a pawnshop . . . it belonged to you.

She sat shivering in the steaming cast-iron tub for a long time, hugging herself as the bathwater rippled with her trembling. Her hair flooded over her shoulders, dampness sticking it in tiny curls and streaks to her abused skin, and when she slid under the surface it floated around her just like a mermaid's.

She stayed under a long time, everything above the water blurring as the heaviness in her lungs mounted. Burning crept into her nose. She surfaced in a rush, splashing, and the sound of her gasping echoed against white tile, charm-scrubbed white grout, the ecru towels and the blind eye of the misted mirror, the sink like an opening flower, and the gleaming toilet.

None of this is mine.

Even the hot water wasn't hers. It drained away with a gurgle.

Still dripping, naked because the nightgowns and pajamas weren't hers either, she crawled into the bed like a thief. Some other girl belonged here, a girl with clear unmarked skin and a carefree ringing voice, one of the Family girls with their bright eyes and disdainful smiles. A girl who could make Nico less angry, a girl who could have kept Papa on the breathing side of transition, a girl the house could close around like the well-oiled machine it was.

She curled up and stared into the darkness. There was a faint edge of gray under the curtains—sunrise approaching, a late winter's dawn. The gauze over the mirror, a stolen thing like everything else in this bloodless room, fluttered teasingly.

What will you see if you take the gauze off and look? Dare you to do it, Cami.

Except that wasn't really her name, was it? She didn't even have a *name*.

My Nameless. A slow, easy hissing whisper, a familiar stranger's voice, in the very center of her brain.

Another steady whisper rose from the cuts and bruises, becoming audible in fits and starts. The gauze rippled, rippled, and behind it the mirror was a water-clear gleam. The muttering from the mirror mixed with low atonal chanting, blended with the throb and ache of contusions, scrapes, and thin slices, and now, at last, she knew what it was saying.

You are nobody.

Over and over again.

You are nothing.

And it was true.

The light under the curtain strengthened. The door rattled. Someone said something on the other side of it, but she closed away the sound of the voice.

They weren't talking to her, anyway. Maybe to the ghost of the girl who should have had this room.

The girl she had tried, and failed miserably, to be.

After a while the sound stopped. It came back, twice, then the light under the curtains faded and welcome darkness returned.

It was dark for a long time. Her stomach growled, and she tried not to move until she couldn't stand the jabbing pains, muscles protesting.

Soft taps at the door. "Cami?"

She squeezed her dry, burning eyes shut. Hearing *him* hurt almost as badly as the stiffened-up bruises and drying scabs.

Nico said other things, but she turned her brain into a soft droning hum. The door gave a sharp banging groan, shaking on its hinges, but she counted the words inside her head, rolling them like small metal balls on a dark-painted surface.

You are nobody. You are nothing.

It was almost a relief. No more struggling with her stupid tongue. No more being the third wheel. No more jumping at shadows. No more flinching.

Yelling, finally. But she clutched her hands over her ears. They, at least, belonged to her, and the yelling ended with a thud. The doorknob screeched, the ancient lock groaning against the doorframe. She curled even more tightly into herself, around the empty rock of her stomach, the smell of her own body wrapping in a close comforting fog.

My hands. I can't be nobody if I have hands.

She tried to shove the thought away, but it wouldn't go. Her bladder ached too, a steady relentless pressure. Her lungs, stupid idiot things, kept going even though she tried to stop them. Her hair lay damp-sticky against the back of her neck—she was sweating.

You are nobody, the whisper insisted. *You are nothing.*

Then who the hell was it talking to? Her fingers tensed, fingernails digging into her scalp. *Her* scalp, and the stinging was welcome. Some of her nails were broken, she could feel the sharp edges. Her mouth tasted bitter and nasty, there were crusties at the corners of her eyes.

My eyes. My hands. My mouth. She shifted restlessly, every part of her jangling a discordant song of ache and pain, and her bladder informed her once again that it was *not* happy. Her stomach rumbled loudly, insistently.

Her stomach didn't stutter. Her breath moved in and out, despite everything she could do. There was a thumping, regular and insistent, and she kept her eyes shut. Traceries of false light burned against the inside of her eyelids.

You are nobody. You are nothing.

The *tha-thump, tha-thump* irritated her. It interfered with the whisper, shoved it aside, and demanded to be heard along with the need to pee. What was it? Someone banging on the door again?

Don't be an idiot. It's your heart.

Tha-thump. Tha-thump. The rhythm didn't vary. She felt it in her wrists, her throat, the backs of her knees. All through her, scarlet threads twitched as the beating in her chest went on. It was whispering too, and as soon as she realized it she moved again, restlessly, trying to figure out what it was saying.

Her bladder was going to explode, and the murmur from the mirror was getting more insistent. Was it hoarse now, a little desperate? It was scratchy, like a smoke-filled throat. She shook her head, slowly, every muscle in her neck shrieking, trying to figure out what the thumping in her chest was saying. It was a song, maybe? One of Nico's favorites, with thumping bass shaking her into jelly?

No.

Her arms spasmed. So did her legs. Muscles locking, moving restlessly, annoyed at her. The whisper from the mirror pushed against the gauze; the torn material billowed, fingernail-scraping the wooden frame.

Cami scrambled out of the bed, tripping and going down, banging her knee on the floor. She lunged up, bare feet smacking the carpet, and just barely made it to the bathroom.

It was there, sitting on the toilet and a glorious relief filling her, that the noise in her head died down, and she figured out the thumping in her chest.

Tha-thud. Tha-thud. Tha-thud.

I am. I am. I am.

The pace quickened. The aching and cramping in her bladder subsided.

I am. I am. I am.

She flushed, her hands moving automatically, and the chugging cascade of water drowned out the mirror's fuzzy static-whisper. As soon as she stepped into the white room, though, she could hear it. The gauze fluttered to the floor, stroked by an invisible hand, and the mirror's surface was full of gray vapor, pouring out from the glass in defiance of its own unreality. Heavy, perfumed smoke. It crawled along the floor, reaching for her with begging, sharp-nailed fingers.

White fingers, on a broad soft hand.

Nobody. Nothing. You are nobody. Nothing! YOU ARE NOBODY NOTHING NOBODY NOTHING NOBODYNOTHINGNOBODYNOTHING—

"*Noooooo!*" The wail burst out of her. She flung herself across the room.

Punch from the hip, Nico said in her memory. Teaching her how to fight one lazy summer day, while they played *banditti* in the woods. *That's my girl. Hit 'em so they know they've been hit.*

Her fist met bulging, smoke-bleeding glass. Her scream spiraled up, drowning out the other cry of female rage—the one coming from the mirror as it broke, crashing, a red jolt all the way up her arm.

The White Queen stumbled back, almost tripping on her long dress, her face graven, runneled with lines, a contorted picture of hatred. She screamed, and the mirror in front of her showed a withered, slobbering hag, the jewel at her throat dark heartsblood, flickering as her life faded.

Cami came to on her knees, her bleeding right hand clutched to her chest, the pale carpet silvered with glass. Running feet in the hall, a splintering jolt against the door. She hugged herself, sobbing, as the acrid smoke in the room thinned.

And through it all, her heart thundered.

I am. I am. I am.

TWENTY-SEVEN

IT WASN'T NICO. IT WAS STEVENS, WITH TRIG RIGHT behind him. The gaunt consigliere stabbed two fingers at the broken mirror, snapping a charm that flashed venomous-red in the darkness as the broken shards on the floor quivered; Trig's hand closed around Cami's arm and he lifted her bodily out of the glass, fingers slipping against blood and sweat. Her hand bled freely, and there was a stinging in her knees.

Stevens hissed a curse in another language, a long sonorous filthy-sounding term that ended with him jabbing his fingers at the mirror and hissing once more. Glass shards trembled as if they wanted to fly up from the floor; a shudder worked its way down the consigliere's dusty, black-clad back. "Avert, *Bianca mala*," he muttered, finally. "*Avert.*"

"Mithrus *Christ!*" Trig had a handful of material—it was her old terrycloth bathrobe, and he bundled her into it with quick efficient movements before half-carrying her toward the bathroom. He reached around the edge of the bathroom door and flicked a switch; sudden golden light stung her eyes. "Are you okay? Are you *hurt*?"

"I do not like this," Stevens said, slowly but very loudly.

"S-s-s-s-s—" The stutter matched her frantic pulse. *Sorry. I'm sorry. I don't know what's wrong with me. I just know I—*

"*CAMI!*" Nico broke what was left of the door, skidding on the carpet, bare-chested and in his ragged pajama pants, his hair standing up and the red pinpricks in his pupils guttering like candleflames in a draft. He stopped dead, thinning smoke shredding and cringing away from him.

"*Biel'y.*" Stevens turned on his heel. Even at this hour he wore mirror-polished wingtips, and his suit wasn't creased or wrinkled. The only thing missing was his tie, his collar unbuttoned instead of cutting into the papery skin of his throat, and it made him look, for the first time, oddly fragile. "The maggots are *here*. In New Haven, yes, and they dare to break the sanctity of this house."

Nico's nostrils flared. He wasn't listening.

He inhaled, deeply, and Trig went very still.

"Oh, *fu*—" Trig shoved Cami through the bathroom door. He didn't even get to finish the word before Nico was on him, a thundering growl throbbing in the new Vultusino's chest and his fangs out.

Cami fell, barking both bleeding knees on white tile. Nico

tossed Trig aside like the older man was made of paper, Trig's head hit the doorframe with a sickening *crack*. A blink and the Vultusino was there, his fingers sinking into her arms like iron claws, and Cami kept screaming breathlessly, scrabbling to get away as his teeth champed just short of her throat.

It was Stevens, one thin knee in Nico's back, who wrestled the Vultusino away from her. He had paused to grab the gauze from the floor and twisted it into a noose, pulling back on Nico's throat as if dragging the reins of a maddened titon, his face set and still as it always was. He heaved Enrico Vultusino's son back, and the scream of a blood-maddened bloodline Family member turned the air so cold Cami's breath turned to a white cloud.

Trigger Vane lay very still, across a shattered door, his eyes closed. And the copper-smelling crimson tide, maddening Nico with its perfume, was *everywhere*.

TWENTY-EIGHT

BOTH KNEES BANDAGED, HER RIGHT HAND BANDAGED too—Marya hadn't even scolded her, just observed a stony, worried silence—Cami clutched at her schoolbag and wiped at her cheeks. Behind her, the limousine purred.

Nico was locked up in the Holding Room, probably with Stevens standing guard at the door. It was a good thing the walls of the house on Haven Hill were thick, otherwise they could have heard the new Vultusino's screams in the next province.

The cries had ceased, as if cut by a knife, the instant she closed the front door behind her.

Chauncey slept in a small apartment over the cavernous garages; Cami's tentative knocks hadn't even woken his wife Evelyn.

I need to go to Ruby's, she'd told him. *It's an emergency.*

Chauncey hadn't asked any questions, just rubbed the sleep out of his eyes and yawned, grabbing the limousine's keys off the pegs. He was used to being awakened to drive someone somewhere.

Now her stomach growled, and she lifted the brass knocker again. The garden lay under snow, the ruthlessly trimmed holly along the east boundary glowing green under a scrim of ice. The fountain, its snout lifted and its concrete jaws wide, was festooned with artistic icicles.

The gate was wooden and the fence was low, but you got the idea it was because she *liked* it that way, and furthermore, that Mrs. Edalie de Varre, Ruby's formidable grandmother, needed no wall or gate to bar and no security guards to eviscerate any Twist or jack who stepped onto her property.

There were powers in New Haven even Family respected, and one of them rested here in Woodsdowne.

The locks clicked, the door opened, and a pair of bleached-gray eyes under a fall of bone-white hair, braided and banded across the top of her head, peered out. Gran was in her high-collared dragon-patterned silk housedress and embroidered slippers, and she examined Cami for a few moments before stepping back.

"Camille." A faint smile, her parchment skin barely wrinkling. "Come in."

She really does have very sharp teeth, Cami thought, and stepped over the threshold. The limousine dropped into gear out on the street, and Chauncey pulled away.

Inside, it smelled of hot griddle and blackcurrant jam, frying eggs and bacon. "I'm making breakfast," Gran said briskly, taking Cami's coat and stowing it in the cedar-scented closet, just like usual. She never seemed surprised or ruffled, which was probably a blessing since she had to deal with Ruby all the time. "You like them scrambled, I recall. Ruby will be down as soon as I make coffee."

"Th-th-thank y-y-y—"

"Oh, don't," the Wolfmother of Woodsdowne said, her faint steely smile widening a trifle. "Nobody has good news this morning, my dear. I can smell as much on the wind. Come and eat."

It took some time. Gran didn't make coffee until near the end of Cami's stuttering recitation—unlike Ruby, *she* couldn't lie to Gran, and she didn't want to. There was just something about those pale eyes and the way the old woman moved, with such precise economy, that warned against any such impropriety. Spending the night at Ruby's meant walking on eggshells, though Mrs. DeVarre had never even raised her voice in Cami's presence.

You got the feeling you didn't *want* her to. At the same time, there was a curious comfort. Gran hadn't batted an eyelash when Ruby brought Cami home one day after school. *Yes, the Vultusino girl,* she'd said. *You are welcome in my house, young one. Sit down, have a scone.*

Cami left out some things, certainly—the flush that went through her every time she said Tor's name, just how blood-crazy Nico had gone, the wooden huntsman's blue, blue eyes, the dreams . . . and Trig's awful stillness, lying in the shattered doorway.

But she told about Tor and the pin and the shimmersilk, the mirror, and the smoke. Gran listened, her eyebrows coming together fractionally as she refilled Cami's glass—*milk for a growing girl*, she always remarked—and snapped a charm to flip the pancakes on the griddle.

"And so," she finally said, switching the coffeemaker on, "you came here."

I couldn't think of where else to go. I just need to sit for a little while. Just get myself together.

And even if Nico wanted to, he couldn't step inside Gran's door without her blessing. Not even Papa would have. Here was the safest place Cami could think of, even if she wondered just what might follow her out to Woodsdowne.

If some bad charming, bad magic, could reach through a mirror in the house on Haven Hill, it might be able to come here too. Cami's midsection clenched at the thought. "I n–need h–help." Her tongue had eased. At least Gran was invariably *patient*. She let you get everything out.

"Help. Well. Hm. You did well, coming to me. Shows you have some intelligence." Gran poked at the fresh strips of bacon sizzling in their pan. Dawn, creeping through the wide window full of terracotta pots holding green herbs, was iron-gray. More snow before long. "But . . . *them.* The Pale Ones. Theirs is an . . . old magic."

Here, in the cozy sun-yellow kitchen, warm and chewing on pancakes with blackcurrant jam, it almost seemed like she could handle all this. Maybe. "O-older than th-the R-r-reeve." She nodded. Her scalp itched, her hair felt greasy. But her stomach had quit growling. It wasn't like Marya's oatcakes, but then, nothing was.

Marya probably wouldn't ever talk to her again.

If Trig hadn't been there, if *Stevens* hadn't been there . . . Nico'd never Borrowed from Cami before. Ever. But still.

The coffeemaker gurgled, and a thread of heavenly scent stitched every other fragrance together. "It may be possible to buy you passage to another town. A place to hide." Gran tapped one finger alongside her nose. "But they have very sensitive noses, *les Blancs.*"

Like dogs, you mean? "L-leave N-New Haven?" *Go through the Waste, maybe? To another province, another city?*

It was another nightmare. Only this time, she couldn't wake up.

"Perhaps. I don't know, Camille. And it is no guarantee." She snapped at the pancakes again, and they obediently charmed themselves off the griddle and onto a waiting, charm-warmed yellow plate. "*Les Blancs n'oublient rien, ma cherie.*"

Her accent wasn't the same as Sister Mary Brefoil's, but Cami had no trouble with the words.

Les Blancs, they forget nothing. "Is ..." She reached blindly for her milk glass. "Is th-th-there ... I m-m-mean, h-how m-many of th-them *are* th-there?"

"They are carrion." A slight wrinkle of Gran's aristocratic nose. "There are as many as the suicides and the desperate will support. If a woman survives long enough in their halls, she may become a Queen herself. Like ants, or another insect. It is ... not easy. Or pleasant. Good morning, *ma petite fille.*"

Ruby halted in the kitchen doorway, yawning, her hair a tangle of bright copper curls. She blinked and stared at Cami, pulling up the strap of her blue pajama tank-top.

She's going to be so mad. Cami searched for another apology, her tongue tangling over itself. "R-r-r-ruby—"

Ruby let out a whoop and leapt across the intervening space, flinging her arms around Cami. "You *bitch*!" she finally yelled, laughing, attempting to shake Cami and kiss her cheek at the same time. Gran made a spitting noise and rescued the dangerously toppling milk glass. "I should have suspected when I smelled bacon! God*damn* I've missed you!"

It was classic Ruby. Gran sniffed. "Language at the table must be cleaner, Ruby. Let the poor girl eat. She has enough problems."

"Did you hear about Ellen?" Ruby could barely contain

herself, plonking down in her usual cane-bottom chair at the breakfast bar. "Her dad. Train crash, out in the middle of the Waste. The Strep has custody. It's horrific."

The bottom dropped fully out of Cami's stomach. *Mithrus. Oh, Ellie.* She stared at her plate, sticky with blackcurrant jam and half-eaten pancakes. "Oh."

"*Ruby!*" Gran didn't quite raise her voice, but her tone could have sliced through the walls. Every dish in the kitchen rattled. "Do *not* add bad news to her troubles!"

Ruby's jaw dropped. Her eyes narrowed, and Cami braced herself for the explosion. Gran turned back to the coffeemaker and the griddle, the straight bar of her spine somehow expressing disdain and disappointment.

"Mithrus Christ," Ruby breathed. "Cami, honey, what kind of trouble are you *in*?"

The heat and prickling behind her eyes almost overflowed. She took a deep breath.

Maybe, just this once, Ruby would let her talk.

"I f-f-found out wh-who I am."

Gran vanished halfway through Ruby's breakfast, reappearing in a long black coat and a jaunty blue hat perched on her pale, rebraided hair, and left them with the dishes. "Sparkling," she said sternly, and Ruby waved a hand. "And no, your friend will not do them all while you chatter."

"*Mais oui, chère grandmère, mais oui.*" Ruby's accent was cheerfully atrocious, and Gran sniffed again before sailing through the kitchen without even glancing at Cami, moving through the utility room and into the garage. An engine roused with a sweet soft purr, the garage door rumbled unhappily, and she was gone.

"Thank God for bridge club. If she had to stay home Saturdays I'd kill myself." Ruby applied herself to the rest of her breakfast. "What did Gran say? I mean, *really* say?"

"Th-there m-might be a w-way." *I'll have to leave New Haven.* She shivered. She knew there were other provinces outside the city's borders, but it was like knowing there was a moon. She'd never expected to *visit.* "It's d-dangerous."

"Well, if anyone can get you through the Waste or overseas and into another province, the Valhalla Bridge Club can. But what about Nico? Why doesn't *he* get off his ass? Family's got to be good for *something*, right? Plus, you're Vultusino. This charmwhite bitch, queen, whatever—seriously, Cami, you think you might be *related*?"

Maybe I just belong to her. She shivered, staring at her coffee cup. "I d-d-don't know. T-t-tor s-s-said—"

"Oh, yeah. The garden boy. I'm with Nico on this one. Shame, too. He had nice shoulders." Ruby crunched at bacon with her strong white teeth, so like her grandmother's. You could see other similarities, their high cheekbones and long eyelashes.

What would it be like, to look at someone and see her own face reflected? Or even just a piece of it? It nagged at her. Something familiar; if she could just sit and *think* she could tease it out.

Why bother? You know what you have to do.

But oh, she didn't want to.

"Seriously, though," Ruby had her stride now. "Why doesn't Nico just *deal* with this?"

He can't. Besides, he . . . She ran up against the memory of his teeth snapping close to her throat, his arms stiff as he held her down and away, struggling with himself and the bloodrage. The screams as Stevens locked his blood-maddened Vultusino in a safe room, until the hunting insanity wore off. But there was a simpler reason.

She found out she could say it, after all. "I'm n–n–not F–f–f–family." *I wasn't ever supposed to be here.*

Ruby actually stopped chewing and stared. After a full ten seconds of silence, Cami began to wonder if she had, in fact, struck her speechless. It would be the first time ever.

She'd dreamed of such an occasion for *years*, but it didn't seem quite worth it now.

Ruby took a giant mouthful of hot coffee, winced, and swallowed. "He said that?" Very quietly, and her dark eyes narrowed.

"N–n–no. B–b–but—"

"But *nothing*. You're *his* family, dammit, and if he's not gonna step up it's his loss. You're *my* family too, Cami, and if these child-beating weirdos want you, they're going to have to come through me." She nodded, coppery curls falling in her face. *That's that*, the motion said, *now don't be silly, Cami. I know best, I always do.*

Except this time Ruby didn't. What if the dogs came while she was here? Or something worse? Gran's house was seriously charmed, but so was the house on Haven Hill. The White Queen had reached through the mirror with . . . something. If she could do *that*, break into the Vultusino's fortress, what else could she do?

What could she do to Ruby? Or to anyone Cami turned to?

I shouldn't have come here. But where else was there to *go*, for God's sake?

Only one place. You know where.

"Now." Ruby crunched on a fresh piece of bacon. "Drink your milk. We'll do the dishes and set up the guest room for you. I'll see if I can call Ellie. I might be able to sneak her out, or talk the Strep into—"

"No." It burst out so hard and clear Cami didn't have a chance to stutter. "D-d-dangerous. It's t-t-too d-d-dangerous, R-rube."

"So's her stuck in that house with the Strep, dammit. I've been planning a jailbreak for a while, this is as good a time as any.

And she'll have *ideas*. She's all practical and shit. Drink your milk."

Cami just sat and stared at it. White milk in clear glass, and a sudden sweat broke out all over her. She probably smelled unwashed and desperate, too.

Was Nico still screaming, locked up and crazed by her mere-human blood?

Or was she mere-human? So far, nobody had told her exactly what the *Biel'y* were, except a cult. *Maggots*, Stevens had said.

Well, wasn't that a lovely thought.

The man in the tan trench coat definitely wasn't just-human, though. At least, not completely. Wood and sap and sawdust, and his blue, blue eyes.

Huntsmen, Tor had said. *Okhotniki*. Gripping the arms of his chair, shaking. Giving her poisonous presents, scars all over him.

Scars like hers.

The boys are Okhotniki.

Ruby kept up a running commentary. Cami just put her head down and did as she was told, washing dishes while Ruby dried and put them away. She was thinking so hard she even let Ruby bully her upstairs into the blue guest room, and the mirror at the vanity with its frame of enameled water lilies gave her a chill all the way down to her bones.

TWENTY-NINE

Ruby switched her Babbage off with a practiced flick. "Ell's sneaking out a window, the Strep is on a charmweed bender and won't notice until tomorrow. Now's the best chance I have to spring her, and then we'll fix this right up. *All* of it." She shrugged into her black woolen school-coat, pulling her hair free of the collar with a quick habitual yank. "Don't open the door to *anyone*."

Cami nodded.

"I mean it. Don't answer the doorbell or the phone. Just hang tight."

Cami nodded again, following her down the stairs. Her scalp itched. She wished she'd had time to take a bath, at least. But the idea of water dripping from the tap made her cold all over.

"It's iced over bad out there, so it might take some time to get her out and back here. Take a nap, paint your nails. You can wear anything in my closet."

You must really be worried. Cami assayed a bright smile, picked a piece of invisible lint off her friend's shoulder.

Ruby bit her lip. "Stop trying to look so brave." She picked up her schoolbag, swung it once or twice to gauge its weight. *Supplies*, she'd said grimly, shoving various odds and ends into it. *I don't care if I have to break a window or two, I'm getting Ellie. I've had enough.*

"S-sorry."

"We'll figure something out." But she was pale, and she only had one gold hoop earring in. The asymmetry bugged Cami—it was Ruby's version of a nervous breakdown. "You know where the liquor cabinet is. I'll be back soon."

"I kn-kn-know. G-go on. I'll b-b-b-be f-f-fine." *Go, so I can think. I need to figure out what to do. Coming here was fine temporarily, but . . .* The inside of her head tangled, and she traitorously wished Ruby was gone already.

Gone, and safe. The more Cami thought about it, the more she realized bringing all her trouble here wasn't a good idea.

"You'd *better* be. Look, don't drink *everything*, all right? Save some for Ell. She's gonna need it." And with that, Ruby was gone through the utility room. The garage door opened and the Semprena slid out, its chains and grabcharms rasping against churned-up, broken ice and packed snow. Cami made it to the living room window to watch, and was just in time to catch a flash of the sleek black car disappearing around the corner at a reasonable speed.

Never thought I'd see that. But there she goes, to rescue the fair maiden.

Was this what it was like to be a ghost? To watch everything arrange itself neatly without you, like a puzzle without the misshapen lump of an extra piece forced into it?

She took a deep breath. The ghost of breakfast lingered all through the cottage. Everything in here was trim and tidy, except for the explosion of Ruby's room. The living room was deep blue starred with gilt-silver and touches of full-moon yellow, overstuffed chairs and a tapestry of a charmer's sun-and-moon along one wall. The hearth was wide and scrubbed clean, a burnished copper kettle set precisely on the stone shelf before it and firewood neatly stacked in a holder shaped like clasped hands.

Sometimes, imagining where she came from, she'd pretended she was the heir of a great Sigiled charming clan, stolen by a competitor. She would daydream about her faceless birth-parents living in a cottage very much like this, searching for her tirelessly, only the evil competitor had sent her to another city across the Waste, and it would only be through some stroke of luck that they saw her and recognized her. Then there would be crying and hugging, and she would have a family of her own, and . . .

That was a kid's dream. Like playing *banditti* in the barn.

Cami wiped at her cheeks. Stood staring at the empty

fireplace. Gran, like most really strong charmers, didn't want a lot of open flame while she was working. There was too much Potential that could just latch onto a fire and do odd things.

She could go up into the spare bedroom and lay on the tightly made blue and white bed, maybe. Or take up Ruby's suggestion about the liquor cabinet. Go up to Rube's room and turn on the stereo, hope that the noise would drive away the sound of Nico screaming inside her head. Or . . .

A chill raced down her spine, drawing every inch of skin tight. She hugged herself, and the cottage shivered too. The tapestry rippled, and from the kitchen she heard dishes clinking and rattling.

What is that? But she knew. Instead of a daydream of a Sigiled charming clan, the nightmare of reality was slinking closer and closer. You couldn't run from that. It would sniff you out.

Like a dog.

Three raps on the front door. Cami's mouth went dry.

Another two. It was four steps to the window, and she made them on rubbery legs. Tweezed part of the curtain aside—the Semprena's tracks were already lost in a mess of churned-up white. The front garden was just the same, still and secretive under a white blanket.

And there was a shadow on the front porch. The angle was wrong, she couldn't see.

No more knocks, but she could feel the waiting. A deep

pool of it, ripples of silence spreading out. *Don't open the door,* Ruby said.

But where could you hide when this came knocking?

And if I don't answer, will they tear the house down? The trembling was all through her. She realized she hadn't taken her coat off, though the cottage was warm and snug, and she still had her boots. The same boots that had carried her through snow and filth and the holding cell.

I wanted to know where I belonged. Now it's calling me . . . home? Is that the word for what you can't escape?

Her hand reached for the knob. The foyer rippled around her, and the charms in the cottage walls made a low warning sound.

The locks slid back, each with a faint definite sound, bones clicking together. A sliver of white winter sunlight glared through a crack, widened, and Cami blinked in the sudden assault of light.

They regarded each other for a long few moments.

"I'm sorry," Tor whispered. The bruises on his neck were livid, and the cut across his cheekbone had leaked blood, dried to a crust. He was shivering too, steam rising from his skin—he wore tattered jeans and the remains of a white T-shirt, sliced and burned. "I'm sorry. *She* knew I could find you."

Cami's hands were numb. His hair was stripped back, plastered down with crud she didn't even want to *think* about, and she finally saw what had snagged her gaze on him all along.

His jawline was heavier, but it was familiar. So was the arc of his cheekbone, and the shape of his mouth, especially the space above his top lip. There was the shape of his eyes; their color had distracted her, but they were catlike and wide.

And just like hers.

I look like him. We're the same. That was the feeling of hand in glove, of broken-in trainers. They looked . . . similar.

Related.

His Adam's apple bobbed. "Don't step outside." The whisper came through cracked lips. "Please. She can only push me so far. You're safe in there."

I'm not safe anywhere. She found herself touching her face, wonderingly tracing the shape of her upper lip. Just like his.

Why hadn't she seen it before?

"Run." Tor coughed, and something moved in his black eyes. Sharp alien intelligence peered out of his drugged gaze, and he shuddered. "Please. I don't . . . don't want . . . *Run.*"

I ran once, didn't I. Ten years ago, Mithrusmas Eve. Not far enough, though.

Never far enough. What was it the Family said?

Blood always tells.

If he went back without her, what would happen to him? And what would the Queen send next time?

I have to stop this. Cami braced herself. She slid out of her coat, and stepped outside into the cold. It was too small for him, but she wrapped her coat around his shoulders as his shivering infected her.

Tor's hand closed around her wrist, unhealthy feverish heat scorching her skin. He let out a tired, hopeless sigh. Their footsteps crunched on the charmed path, and as soon as they stepped past Gran's gate, his head dropped forward like a tired horse's. Woodsdowne was deserted, and in the distance, the baying of dogs began.

The first fat flakes of the day's snow began to whirl down.

PART III: *The Sacrifice*

THERE WAS NO SNOW UNDERNEATH.

The dogs hadn't come after all. Instead, Tor had led her through the maze of Woodsdowne, west toward the core. Not for very long, though—he'd stopped at the intersection of Columbard and Lamancha Avenue. The piles of snow and ice to each side, broken by titon-plows, imitated small mountain ranges. The buildings were tall and dark here, festooned with icicles and whispering with the chill breeze. Any one of the boarded-up windows could have exploded outward, giving birth to a jumble of dog-shapes salivating and snapping their steelstruck teeth.

But it was in the very middle of the crossroads that a round slice of frozen street had silently opened its dark eye—a manhole cover, ice crackling away from its circumference, pushed up by an invisible force. Tor moved her toward it, not ungently, and she'd seen the iron rungs going down.

New Haven's surface swallowed them, pleating closed

overhead and smoothing itself like a freshly-laid sheet.

Tor took her wrist at the bottom of the ladder again, and her coat fell away from his shoulders, landing on a sodden pile of something stinking. It was almost warmer down here, but her breath still came in a cloud and thin traceries of steam. Cami stopped, and he tugged at her arm.

"N-n-n-no." She tried to peel his fingers away, but they wouldn't come. "I'm n-not g-g-going to r-r-run." *She would follow me. There's no point.* "H-Here." Her voice echoed oddly, and she managed to work his hand down so his fingers laced through hers.

We're Family, too. Every scar on her twinged heatlessly, and she wondered if he had nightmares too. Who held him when he woke screaming?

Did anyone?

A curious faraway look came over his face. There was no shadow of the garden boy there. This was an automaton, stumbling like a broken-stringed puppet through a labyrinth of concrete passageways. Pipes ran overhead and alongside them, some groaning and hissing; the floor kept steadily sloping down. She had to duck to avoid some of the pipes, Tor ducking as well with weird mechanical grace. Icicles dripped down from the infrequent gleams of light above, turning to a crusted seeping on the walls.

He took a hard right, and his fingers tensed. "Hard," he muttered. "Interference Underneath. *Bring* her."

"I-i-it's a-all r-r-right." Cami squeezed his hand. *You can't* stop this. *It's not your fault. It's mine. I ran away, and everything is falling apart around me. Because of me. I went where I didn't belong.* Cami's chin raised slightly. "T-tor. It's ok-k-kay."

"Don't wanna." He shook like a rabbit, but his legs kept going. "Don't make me."

Oh. He's not talking to me. So she simply followed him, going down and down, away from the light.

It never got completely dark, though. Once the glimmers from above faded and the concrete changed color, traceries of pale glowing fungus appeared on the walls. Growing in curves and sharp dots, they looked like decoration—but Cami did *not* want to brush against them. They smelled. Not of anything bad, just a faint breath of spice and fruit.

And smoke.

Another sharp corner. His skin was cooler now, and Cami had stopped shivering. A faint breeze, warmer than the knifing wind above, touched tendrils of her hair, fingered the walls with their glowing patterns. The fungus was like brocade, fuzzy flower-shapes soft and plush against the roughness. Down and down, and the breeze was redolent of fruit now, a summer orchard with a tinge of perfumed burning. It was warm and moist, and Cami's skin crawled steadily. Little ant feet crawling all over her—tiny little feet of apprehension, nausea, familiarity.

I know this place.

Stairs, going down. The concrete was ancient here, and

New Haven crouched overhead. How deep were they? She had no idea. Her feet ached; her fingers, locked in Tor's, were slippery with sweat. Her boots slipped a little, and they passed through an archway. S**vAY, it said overhead, except part of it had crumbled.

Dingy tiles that had once been white, cracked and falling. It was a much larger tunnel, the breeze whooshing through it with a low hungry sound. The floor was ancient and filthy, the domed ceiling draped with long shawls and gauzy runners of that pale glowing stuff. Was it a fungus if it hung in sheets like that, intricate glowing lacework?

It reminded her of the shimmersilk scarf and its poking, slashing tassels, but she was past wincing at the thought. Instead, she stared, wide-eyed, and her heart was an insistent drum in her ears.

I am. I am. I am.

Had she stumbled this way before, six years old and terrified, forcing her small legs to pump, smelling smoke and fury? The black hole in her memory would not tell her. It just pulsed, soft slithering sounds coming from its well-mouth.

No, the noise wasn't from inside her head. Tor halted, a fresh thread of blood soaking into his T-shirt from a ragged slice on his back, and she heard rippling. The gleam on the floor wasn't the fungus; it was a reflection of the light from the ceiling on slowly moving water.

A canal. And as the breeze chuckled to itself, creeping fringes of perfumed smoke stringing from the left-hand archway where the water disappeared, she heard another sound. A rhythmic splashing.

Oars, dropped into water.

The boat was coming.

Tor stepped to the very edge of the canal. Chips of ancient yellow paint under the crusted dirt leered up at them. She stared at the ceiling, her mouth slightly agape, and as the splashing intensified a sodden gleam appeared.

It was a small flat-bottom boat, its draping of rotting white velvet trailing the scum-laden surface. Dimples showed in the water where invisible oars dipped, disturbing the weird scrim of paleness, probably some algae related to the fungus all around.

The boat was empty—or anyone inside it was invisible, too. It nosed gently up to the side of the canal and halted. Cami's throat had closed up. Her eyes prickled.

The worst part wasn't the alienness of Underneath. It was the *familiarity*. No wonder the house on Haven Hill wanted another girl, a different girl.

This was where Cami—or whoever she was—belonged.

Tor stepped off solid land and onto the boat. Her arm stretched out, their fingers linked, and he glanced over his shoulder at her. The bruises and welts on him showed up garish and hideous in this directionless foxfire light, and the rippling reflection turned him into a monster for a moment. A jack, or a Twist, the bruises peeling skin and the blood on him black.

He's just . . . he's like me. Cami stepped forward. *He is me. We're the same.* The boat gave a little underneath, swaying, and Tor steadied her. A splash and another lurching, and his arms were around her as if it were the most natural thing in the world. The boat almost-spun, righted itself, and drifted for the left-hand tunnel, where the wreathing smoke was incense, and the smell of it filled her head with blind numb buzzing.

The archway swallowed them. *Here* it was dark, except for the algae's weaker glow.

"Princess." His breath was hot against her ear. "I tried. Sorry."

She shook her head, carefully, hoping he'd understand.

She was the reason he'd been beaten like this. *She* was the reason the Strep had snapped and started in on Ellie. *She* was the reason Nico was screaming with blood-madness, locked away. *She* was the reason Papa Vultusino had Borrowed and come downstairs . . . and transitioned to Unbreathing.

If anyone should be sorry, Tor, it's me. But her tongue was knotting up, she could *feel* it.

Book. Candle. Nico. The charm wouldn't work now. She was going to fix the problems she'd made for everyone. Take the extra piece out of the puzzle, and throw it into the trash where it belonged. Where it had always belonged, no matter how far it had been flung.

THIRTY

WHEN THE BOAT BUMPED AGAINST THE BOTTOM OF A high sweeping flight of stone stairs, she was almost—but not quite—ready for the terror.

The stairs.

They had sharp polished edges, each step mirror-shining. She knew how they bit when you fell down them, stabbing and slicing. She also knew what the fresh red streaks bubbling on the glossy stone were.

She gets . . . hungry.

The doors were tall, made of the same polished black stone. Their carvings shifted with faint scratching noises, apples and dogs and faces with long flowing hair and foxfire-glowing eyes. The bad place in Cami's head bulged again, and she heard tinkling laughter.

This time she stepped off the boat first. Felt the sharp edges under her bootsoles, and the idea that she might faint and fall on them kept her upright. Tor's arms dropped to his sides; he hopped with eerie grace to the steps too, balancing.

Her hand flashed out, she steadied him.

He didn't even look at her.

The doors creaked, a soft musical sound. Tor stepped up once, waited for her. She took a step, and her breakfast rose in a hot acid gush.

She retched, milk-curds and blackcurrant jam splattering on the bright clean steps, and her heart was going to explode. She could feel it tightening before it shredded into useless scraps, her entire chest full of clawed wriggling dread.

The doors flowed outward, and the hounds poured free. They were almost silent, only the occasional yip as they bolted down the stairs and surrounded Cami's swaying and Tor's poker-stiff frame. They didn't press close, and she struggled to stay upright.

Just at the threshold, the man in the tan trench coat stood. Only now he was in leather, different tones of brown matching his wooden skin. The Huntsman's face was wooden too, blue eyes afire with a different light than the pale diseased glow. That light dimmed as he gazed down, and behind him, like a pale moon rising, was a shadow of white.

"My runaway children," the White Queen murmured. Dulcet honey, her voice scraped like the smoke and made the bad place in Cami's head shudder and squeeze down on itself. "Home at last. How I've missed you."

A dog snarled and jumped. Cami let out a miserable vomit-scented little cry and took the next three stairs in a rush. Tor began to climb, and the reek of spoiled honey and rotting fruit was quickly swept under a pall of spiced, numbing smoke. The inside of Cami's head began to feel very strange—too big, an empty ballroom with nobody to take her hand or start the scratchy ancient Victrola.

The dogs drove her through the door, and as she passed the wooden man he twitched. Not much, but the Queen laughed.

"One happy little family," she purred, and one broad, soft white hand touched his shoulder for a moment. "Greet your father, little Nameless. After all, he gave his heart for you."

The warm draft was from tall greasy-white candles with oddly pallid flames, serried ranks of them on either side of the high-ceilinged hall. Blue gouts of incense rose from powdery dishes, veiling the ceiling. The *Biel'y*—tall spare men and women with blank eyes holding only *her* reflection, there were no children—wore gray robes, and each throat held a silver gleam. The medallions were eager, avid little eyes too, and Cami, her mouth full of sourness, stumbled miserably up the center of the aisle in the White Queen's wake.

She was so tall, the Queen. Her parchment hair was piled high and elaborate, ringlets bobbing and bone pins with dangling colorless crystals thrust artfully through. The other women were shaven-headed, the men short-haired, and their feet were bare while the Queen swayed on lacquered sandals with funny wooden blocks on the soles that went *tic tic tic* against the stone floor. She wore white velvet and silk, but the hems dragged on the dusty floor, little motheaten bits showing.

At the far end, there was a low wide padded bench on a dais, under a great fountaining fall of crystallized glowing fungus. It pulsed and glittered, this colony of light, and its glow bleached the Queen still further.

Cami stopped dead at the bottom step of the dais. Her arms and legs shook, the tremors spilling through her in waves, her bandaged knees and hand throbbing. Every hair on her body was trying to stand up.

Imagining that pale slimness with a baby was . . . Cami's stomach cramped again. Heaving nausea passed through her and away, an earthquake in numb flesh.

The Queen turned, sank down on the bench, and Cami realized it was her throne. A sigh went through the assembled *Biel'y*. More were coming, their robes shushing and their bare feet padding.

She knew that sound. The black bulge inside her brain swelled a little more. The faint tang of acridity under the incense's spice coated the back of her throat, and that was familiar too.

"My newest *Okhotnik* may approach," the Queen murmured,

and a rustle went through the assembled. The candleflames bowed.

Tor staggered mechanically up the three dais steps. Cami's hands itched to help, but she was nailed in place. His black hair, still slicked back under a mask of crud, gleamed wetly, and the rags of his T-shirt flapped.

She still could not look at the Queen's face. Her eyes simply refused. Instead, she stared at the hands, lying folded in the velvet and silk of her lap. The soft fingers, the dimpled knuckles—but there was something wrong.

There were marks on those hands. They had always been plump and soft and *young* before. Now there were pronounced veins, and shadows of age spots. And a tremor that had never been there before.

"Good boy." The Queen's chuckle was soft, but so cold. "You brought My Nameless back to Me. I had my doubts, young one. But you will make Me a fine husband. I will not need another."

A cracking sound. Cami flinched, whirling. The dogs had crept up the aisle, red tongues lolling and their coats washed pale by the weird directionless light. The wooden man stood in the aisle, slump-shouldered and stiff; another rending cracking noise echoed and he listed to the side. His blue eyes were closed, and a rivulet of splintering crawled through him, crunching and creaking, tiny pieces falling from his face and grinding themselves into dust. The leather of his clothes sagged obscenely, sawdust pouring from sleeves and legs, and collapsed inward.

The memory of Papa's slow crumbling folded through her brain, slid away.

"Such a strong heart he had, and given so thoroughly." The Queen sighed, and the *Biel'y* sighed too, a susurrus passing through candleflames like wind through wheat. "Now, My Nameless. Come here."

She's talking to me. Dread choked Cami. Little black spots danced in front of her. The dogs crept closer, on their bellies. One whined, a high nervous sound.

Silence stretched, thin and quivering. The candles hissed, and even the crystalline mass over the throne was making a sound—a felt-in-the-teeth ringing, like a wineglass stroked with a wet finger just before its singing shivers it into pieces.

Until one word broke it. "N-no." Cami dug her heels into the stone floor. The Queen's will wrapped around her, pulling her toward the steps, but the sourness in Cami's throat and the sudden pain from her bandaged left fist, its knuckles throbbing with the feel of glass splintering underneath them, both refused the urge to obey.

I'm here. You can have me instead of Tor. But I'm going to make you work for it.

The silence returned, but changed now. This was the quiet of utter shock.

Cloth moved. The sandals tip-tapped. A draft of clove and

numb smoke, the taste of fruit edging into decay, brushed Cami's hair. The Queen loomed over her, and the shudders went away.

The terror was so huge it could not shake her. Or she had become so small the whole world was aquiver, and she could not tell. The only thing left was to tip her head back and back, her gaze traveling up silk and velvet grown dingy, pinprick holes in its splendor, the subtle silver trimming tarnishing.

The Queen's ravaged face bent down, a grinning moon. Wrinkles spread from the corners of her eyes, no matter how immobile she kept her expression. Fine lines bracketed her mouth, but they were not Marya's laugh-lines, or even Gran's marks of dignity. They clawed at the Queen's face, and her eyes glared through the cracking paper mask of her skin with utter madness.

Her blue, blue eyes.

The slap rocketed against Cami's face. Her head snapped aside, her neck giving a flare of red agony. She spilled backward onto cold stone, elbows smacking *hard*, her left hand crying out and her ass immediately numb. On her side now, all her breath gone, curling protectively around herself. But she wasn't tiny enough to curl up like a pillbug anymore. The Queen's wooden sandal caught her just under the ribs, and the black spots became huge blossoming flowers as she struggled to get a breath in.

"*Bitch!*" the White Queen screamed. "*You bitch! You little bitch! YOU MADE ME OLD!"*

A merciful blankness descended. The real part of her curled up tightly inside her skull, watching while everything outside rocked back and forth, jerking under the force of the blows. It went on forever, and when it stopped, the gray-robed *Biel'y* slid forward and the handcuffs clicked, and it was as if she had never left at all.

THIRTY-ONE

THE DARKNESS WAS A LIVING THING, PRESSING DOWN with chill gritty fur. Stone above her, stone below, the clink of dragging handcuffs oddly muffled as her body twitched every once in a while.

This was familiar, too. It was a penitent's cell, meant to punish those who displeased *her*. In this deep blackness, the black bulge inside Cami's skull relaxed, and it was like drawing aside soft ragged smoky veils. Or like torn blue gauze sliding down from a mirror's unblinking eye, and the reflection beneath coming into focus.

The gray-robed, shaven-headed women cooing as they cosseted and cared for her. They were not allowed to speak—the Queen forbade it. Some of them whispered, though, when the smoke lessened and some focus came back into their eyes. They had sought cessation in the Biel'y, a release from the obligations of Above, and had found it.

Who cared what the price was?

Yet they whispered, and she learned. She was wrapped in discarded pale silk and velvet and played with small things— wooden balls, scrubbed-clean trash brought back by the close-cropped men whose pupils all held pale slivers—for the Queen was all the men saw. They brought the baubles to please Her, and the ones She cast aside the women gathered. The women taught the Nameless to count, and she accepted it as normal. What else did she know?

The voice came filtering through the dark, directionless, a hoarse whisper. It muttered, it teased, it tapped at her ears. What did it say?

She was taken to see the Queen from afar sometimes, and told to love Her. Love pleased the Queen. Heart in mouth, excitement running through her entire body, the Nameless loved the beautiful woman in Her finery, the smoke around Her making all the colors soft and hazy, Her smile meaning all was well with the world. There were other times when the women grew drawn and fearful, and the Nameless understood She was not happy. Those times passed, though, sooner or later, and some of the women disappeared. New ones came.

New ones always came, seeking the drug of forgetting, searching for release.

There were other children, too, but she was not allowed near them. They crept around the edges, scavenging in corners, a feral pack. Sometimes She chose a favorite, and jealousy was rank and rife until the favorite, petted and indulged for a while . . . vanished.

Very familiar. When she moved, pain nipped at her. They had even taken the bandages off, hissing when the fey-charmed cloth spat in their hands. She did not struggle.

And then, a great excitement. The women whispering again— the Nameless was needed. She was called for. She was to be brought.

Scrubbed and dried, her long black hair combed and braided, the women making soft sounds of approval, and then the hall with its mirrors and Her, recumbent on a white-draped bed, the blue of her eyes matching the blue of the Huntsman's. Of all the men, only his pupils held no pale slivers, and he stood to the side as the long pale loveliness stretched, delicately.

"Here is My Nameless," the Queen chirped brightly. "Come to Me, child."

And she did, her heart beating in her throat, her skin alive with joy at the nearness. The incense smoke was thick that day, and the Queen was a haze of beauty, the red-winking gem at Her throat the only color in the world. A white page to be written on, a white bird to nestle in the hand.

The Queen's broad soft hand touched the Nameless's slender girl-chest. "Here it is," She murmured, softly, restfully. "Here is the youth and the living."

"So it is," the other Biel'y chorused, and the Nameless was confused. Was this a Ceremony? Were they supposed to speak?

"Do you love Me?" She leaned close, her face filling the Nameless's world. "Me, and only Me?"

Stunned, the Nameless could only nod.

"Say, yes, Mommy. If you can."

She struggled to shape the words. "Y-yes, M-Mommy." Her tongue wouldn't obey her fully, but She looked pleased.

"Oh, someone has taught you to talk, have they? Well, we will punish for that. But for now . . . " Her hand tensed, and the Nameless could feel the fingernails, lacquered with white paste and sharpened, through fabric. "Give Me your heart, little Nameless. I want your heart. I will eat it, and grow strong."

Horror descended. A terrible draining sensation, as the Queen laughed and her fingers flexed. Casually cruel, a cat playing with a mouse before it loses interest. Her jaw snapped, strong white teeth champing just like the dogs', and the Nameless jerked aside, thrashing and terrified.

Her thin elbow hit something hard and unforgiving, and the gasp of horror passing through the ranks of the Biel'y made the radiance dim. A furious howl arose, for the child, in her struggles, had struck the White Queen in Her lovely, ageless face.

"TAKE IT AWAY!" the Queen screamed. "LOCK IT

UP! TAKE IT AWAY!"

And then the pain began.

She shifted, cold stone bruising-hard under her hip, the chill leaching into her bones. The voice was very far away. It didn't matter. She knew what it was whispering, the same thing it had started whispering after she had done the unforgivable.

"You are nobody," it breathed, hoarsely. "You are nothing."

She lay in the stone-closed darkness, the handcuffs biting her wrists, and listened to her heart's thundering refrain.

I am. I am. I am.

THIRTY-TWO

SHE LAY FOR A LONG TIME IN THE DARK, FLOATING IN and out of her body. The voice kept going, water plinking over stone, wearing away. Her heartbeat was muffled thunder, and the blackness inside her skull was now the softness of a pillow. She could lie still and not think, and everything would be done.

And yet. There was another memory, one that hovered just out of reach. An annoyance, grit in a sandal, the sting of sun on already-burned skin, a poke on an almost-healed bruise.

The Huntsman's big callused hand trembled on the glass knife's twisted, ancient handle. His reflections fought too, the mirrors casting back several images of him as he loomed over the little girl on the altar, her eyes rolling with terror, her thin drugged limbs twitching. The smoke was heavy, full of the resinous drug the Queen exuded, mixed with the spices stolen by the close-cropped men and the glowing, harvested fungus. The feral children were all hustled away, and among them was a boy with messy dark hair, the product of an earlier favorite-husband, and so the only one save the Nameless to be unshorn. He was older, and his heart was fine. The Queen said he would make an Okhotnik for Her, one day.

But now, Her husband-Huntsman stood, and the Queen tensed. She was beside him, Her beauty reflecting in each lovingly polished mirror, the great soughing chanting mass of the Biel'y as yet unaware that something was wrong. They bowed and swayed, some of them falling to the floor and gibbering praises of the loveliness overcrowding the mirrors before them, reflected on every wall of this hall, the heart of Underneath where the Queen was the only light.

The crimson jewel at Her throat flashed. Her red, red lips parted.

"Renew Me. Give Me the heart," she said, and the cry went up.

"The heart! The heart!"

The Huntsman stared at the drugged Nameless. The little girl writhed, twisting on the pale stone of the altar, crusted with the remains of other ceremonies. Unlike the mirrors, the altar was not cleansed until the Great Renewal. The lesser Renewals were left as a reminder, and atop the water-clear mirrors the small skulls grinned down on the ceremony, a few larger ones sprinkled among them. Set in the walls with cement made from the ground-up light-giving fungus, they wept thin trickles of bleaching-clear fluid that must not be allowed to mar the mirrorshine.

The Nameless's eyes were open a fraction. Blue eyes, so blue. The knife lifted.

"Give Me the heart." It was unheard-of, for the Queen to have to ask twice, and the first thread of unease went through the ecstatic writhing crowd.

"The heart, the heart!" they cried.

The Huntsman's lips moved. Why did he hesitate? This one, he seemed to say, but the screams and moans overpowered whatever he would have uttered.

And the drugged girl, sudden desperate strength in her bony bruised and wasted limbs, committed the ultimate sin.

The Nameless rolled free of the altar. She landed on a heap of picked-clean bones, and the gasps and cries of horror began. She scrambled, darting-quick as a cockroach, for a dark gap between two mirrors, and slithered her skinny body through it as the Queen's fury shook the world.

And later, in the tunnels, as the Nameless wandered sick and shaking, the Huntsman had arrived out of the darkness. "She will have a heart," he muttered, and pushed her. "That way, go. Run. Run. She will have a heart. RUN!"

And she had run, through a jumble of confusion and terror, the drug working through her and her entire world shattered, to end fallen and limp in the snow while dogs howled elsewhere.

Whose heart had the Queen eaten that night? It was not a Great Renewal, but She had to have eaten something. Dark blood *dripping down her white chin, her eyes closed . . . whose heart had She eaten?*

And had She thought it was Her daughter's, until age began to crease Her soft blank skin, and wooden hardness spread over the Huntsman's skin?

Light, searing her eyes. The murmur went on, a queer atonal chant, and she finally understood it was *them*, the *Biel'y*, mouthing their ritual response just like the girls at St. Juno's murmured *Mithrus the Sunlord, watch over us all* during chapel every school day.

You are nobody. You are nothing.

Hands on her, she was dragged out limp and bruised and filthy. It smelled horrible. *She* smelled horrible.

How long was I—

She couldn't even finish the thought. Smoke billowed. The hall was cramped and dark, cell doors flung open. The coffin-cubes of stone were empty toothsockets, leering as her head lolled and she blinked, weakly. Her heart kept going, her lungs did too, and their hands pinched and poked before they lifted her and bore her on a gray-robed wave. Thirty of them, maybe more, and others in the hall. But the great mass of whispering and movement she remembered from before was absent.

Underneath was curiously small now, and the *Biel'y* were fewer.

Carried through the twisting corridors, the smoke was so thick she could barely see. The past kept looping over into the present, why did she even keep fighting?

Tor. He'll live, I guess. Marya, though she won't miss me for long. Rube and Ellie, poor Ellie. They'll be okay. Ruby will take care of it. Nico . . . he'll be fine. They'll all be fine, really.

She sagged in their hands. The *Biel'y* began to chant more loudly, a slow ancient tune with the edges of the words rubbed away. Once their choir would have shaken the tunnels with its swelling. Now it was an attenuated cricket-chorus, barely stirring the swirling smoke.

Their hands were cold. Not the bruising chill of the stone, just cold in a different way. Uncaring flesh, forgetting itself. Cami hung, jostled from side to side as the human wave below her marched on bare feet, kicking aside detritus until they came to a more-traveled hall, the fungus dripping clear water as its glow turned to a low punky dimness.

She's tired. She had to bring me here, she's eaten too many of them. Her . . . followers. And the hunters have probably been bringing others down here for her to feed on, but not enough. It was like thinking through mud. *That's why she needs me.*

Nico needs me too, a small voice piped up inside her. *So does Ruby. And Ellie. They all need me.*

And yet she'd been nothing but a problem since she'd run out in front of Papa's car. An extra puzzle piece, a snarl in the yarn, a break in the pattern. Something foreign, alien, forcing its way into other lives.

We are foreigners, Papa's voice whispered in her memory. *Always, we are strangers in all lands.*

Finally, she was hazily glad he had transitioned. He wasn't here to see this. Had he known what she was?

My bambina. It is arranged.

Had Papa known? And if he had, had it mattered to him?

It doesn't matter. He's gone, and I'm . . . here. She twisted fretfully, took a deep lungful of the smoke. Would it hurt when the glass knife flashed down? Or would she just feel a spike of pain, and then the deep relief of oblivion?

The doors to the mirrored hall were black iron, their surfaces powdered with dried ghost-moss. They creaked and screamed as the *Biel'y* pushed against them, each groan and wheeze echoed faithfully through the bars of their song, an eerie mock-grieving. Did she imagine the tremors in their upstretched arms, the drunken swaying as if her weight was too much for them?

Your fat ass, Ellie said, softly, and Ruby giggled in her memory, false-summer sunlight golden over them both.

Missing them was a stone in her throat. The knife would flash down, and they would go on without her being the third wheel . . . but the missing-them was all hers.

Even the Queen couldn't take that. *She* couldn't take the memory of Papa, either, or of Marya's hugs and scolding, or

Trigger carefully showing her how to tie a neat knot, or Nico in all his different moods. Scowling or smiling, angry or relaxed, and yes, even the face he showed when the hunting frenzy had him and she was reminded of just what *Family* and *blood* meant.

The Queen couldn't even take Stevens, or Sister Mary Brefoil conjugating verbs, or Sister Frances Grace-Abiding chiding the girls to lift their knees during calisthenics. Or the cold of snow and the sight of Tor's scars, just like the Nameless's own.

The mirrors ran with light. It was not the silvery blaze she remembered. This struggling corpseglow was not magnified by the polished glass. Instead, it fell into the mirrors and vanished. The skulls above were still weeping, and streaks had been allowed to pit the smooth glass surfaces. Cracks and dust showed, and the ceiling was black behind its pall of smoke.

The *Biel'y* circled the white stone altar, and little things crunched on its surface as they laid her down. It was crusted with layers of filth and dried fluids best not thought about, carapaces of beetles crackling; little things scuttled away from the touch and weight of her flesh. She squirmed, but two of the *Biel'y* came forward with a long rectangular black velvet box, and when they clasped the silver necklace with its flat not-quite-round medallion around her filthy throat the will to move drained from her. She felt it go, swirling from her toes, the silver stinging as it lay against her vulnerable pulse.

I am, I am, her heart kept saying. Idiot thing. What did it know?

She didn't even have a *name*.

They began to sing a little louder, the *Biel'y*, but it was not the massive thundering sound it had been before. Still, the mirrors caught and reflected it, and the incense smoke darkened.

The Great Renewal of the Queen was ten years late. But now, finally . . .

. . . the hour had come.

THIRTY-THREE

"OUR QUEEN," THEY MOANED. "GIVE US OUR QUEEN, our light, our *life! Give us our Queen! Our Queen!*"

Tip-tapping footsteps, mincing, She appeared from behind the largest mirror, the frame of black iron skulls and bones dusty now. Cobwebs had crept between eyeholes and thighcurves that would have never been allowed before.

She lifted her arms, and the sleeves of Her pale silken robes fell back. The skin flopped loosely around Her wasted biceps, and Her fingers were claws. The paste dried on the claw-tips had chipped, and Her face, under a thick screen of bone-white powder, was even more cracked and runneled. Blue eyes blazed, and the red jewel at her throat flashed, stuttering.

"My children!"

The *Biel'y* moaned, swaying back and forth. They packed into the hall but could not fill it. There simply weren't enough of them. Maybe fifty, maybe a few more. Without the Great

Renewal, they would all slowly fade.

"My children," the Queen repeated, and they shrieked in response. Her hands spread, She caught the sound and drank at it, Her reedy voice strengthening. "The Great Renewal is upon us!"

"*Renew, renew!*"

"There shall be a sacrifice!"

"*Sacrifice, sacrifice!*" Shaven skulls under tight-drawn pallid skin bobbed on scrawny necks.

"My new *Okhotnik*, My husband-to-be, went Above, and he brought Me a heart!"

"*A heart, a heart!*"

Tor, she thought, dimly. Everything was very far away. *Bringing me presents. Were they really from her? Or did he steal them, thinking she wouldn't notice? Or did she send them out into the world, into Above, and he was just the way they chose to get to what she wanted?*

Did it matter? Everything was falling away, drying up. The things the Queen couldn't take would go with the Nameless into darkness, and maybe the space in the world Above would be filled by something else. Someone else.

Another thought rose through layers of smoky sponge. *How did she find me?*

The mirror, maybe. Or, like any charmer, through blood. Had the wooden man been looking for her too? Had he whispered in the Queen's ear, *she's alive, I saw her?* Had he regretted giving his heart in the Nameless's stead?

It wasn't like it mattered now.

"A fine heart. A fiery heart. And he will give it to Me!"

"*Give it, give it!*"

Behind her, Tor stumbled out of the dark hole. He looked even worse, if that were possible—bruised all over, one of his eyes almost puffed shut. He was in leather, like the wooden man, but it didn't fit him. The fringe quivered as he moved, his soft glove-shoes scraping, and his black eyes were wide and wild.

A faint faraway anger pressed through the girl's dry-trickling veins. *I thought she would leave Tor alone!*

Something inside her dilated. Just as she'd seen the Strep beating on Ellie, she caught a glimpse of Torin struggling against the Queen's control—and the consequences. He had fought, and fought *hard*.

And the Nameless was suddenly very sure he hadn't known the pin and the shawl were the Queen's poisoned gifts. He had tried to escape, just like she had.

It's all right, she wanted to tell him. *We couldn't get away. But She can't take everything. She* can't *eat everything.*

In his left hand, the glass knife glittered. Wicked-sharp and curving, its twisted hilt patterned on a horn of a creature long extinct before the Age of Iron, a thread of crimson pulsing in its heart.

The Nameless's anger fluttered away, a bird's heart. Maybe

more was needed to make the Queen leave everyone alone. To make Her happy, to make everyone happy.

I hope it won't hurt much. Her entire body was numb, and cold. *Book. Candle. Nico.* The old charm, worn and threadbare, soothed the last remaining ache inside her. At least, once this was over, she wouldn't have any scars.

The White Queen's arms dropped. The *Biel'y* chanted and shuffled, their chorus exhausted, as they gasped through the smoke.

"Now." Her teeth gritted, Her fingers flexing, the old woman in her motheaten white, her parchment hair falling and unraveling, fixed Tor with a piercing blue gaze. "Cut out the nameless heart. Renew Me."

Tor stepped forward. He blinked, his jaw working. The mirror beside him held his reflection and hers, and the Queen's, another shape rippling behind the shrinking old woman. *She* was fading fast, impatient, Her power recklessly spent to bring Her victim here, to force this new *Okhotnik* to Her ancient, hungry will. The new shape would be slender and tall and young, heartbreakingly lovely, and the *Biel'y* would resurge, calling those who wished dark surcease down into the tunnels and dripping darkness.

On the altar, the Nameless stared at her own reflection. Long tangled black hair, her eyes half-lidded, her bruised face slack and peaceful, Tor's trembling evident even in the mirror.

I thought he wouldn't be hurt anymore. The thought rose, slow as bubbles in the sticky caramel Marya made every Dead Harvest to dip apples into. Red, crunching, juicy apples, and the nuts she would roll them in too, golden and luscious. The smell of the sugar, and Marya smoothing her hair.

My little sidhe, Marya breathed in her memory, and the girl's heart gave a leap.

The new *Okhotnik*'s mouth opened. He cried a word that had lost all meaning, and the *Biel'y* screamed.

"*CAMI!*"

The glass knife flashed. It sliced, and there was a shattering of glass and a wail.

The world exploded.

THIRTY-FOUR

LOUD BOOMING NOISES. YELLS. FAMILIAR, SOME OF them—Nico, hoarsely screaming one word over and over, Ruby swearing as if they were in gym class and running the fourmile again, Ellie chanting low and sonorous, Trig's familiar drill-the-security-team tone sharply slicing the chaos, *close it up, take them down, find our girl!*

She lay, her eyelids heavy, strangely peaceful. The mirror heaved, great cracks spidering across its surface, Tor stumbling back with a horrified cry.

He had driven the knife straight into the mirror, pinning the Queen's reflection like a butterfly.

The White Queen screamed again, a dry wall of noise impossible from such a small throat. Runnels of decay crawled through her reflection, each echoed by a streak of darkness on the staggering old woman herself. The small skulls atop the mirrors exploding in puffs of white sighing powder, each a small weeping voice lost in the storm, the other glass shattering over and over as the warcries of enraged Family bravos and the chatter of gunfire swallowed the Queen's cry.

The White Queen went to her knees, her painted claws grasping at empty air, then swiping a stripe of fire across the girl's thigh. The drugged body on the altar twitched before the black-haired boy grabbed her, yanking her free of the cracking, heaving stone. The crone hauled herself up, scrabbling across the crusted filthy obscenity as it split, its edges grinding. They fell, girl and boy tangled with each other, rolling down the sharp steps away from the thrashing monster as it broke into shards of bleached bone grinding itself finer and finer into caustic dust.

The *Biel'y* fought, but they were unarmed and weak, and the death of the brooding hungry goddess who had promised them an end to living's pain made them witless. It was Ellen Sinder and Ruby de Varre who reached the foot of the dais first, Ruby snarling, her coppery hair full of dark dust, Ellen's chant fading as the charm-chain looped around her slim fingers tugged sharply downward, indicating it had found what she sought. Potential flashed, and Underneath rumbled.

The Family boys, led by Nico Vultusino and a gaunt fierce Trigger Vane with a heavily bandaged head, pushed forward to the dais, the last of the *Biel'y* shrieking as they found a different oblivion than the one they were promised. They closed around the girls and the wounded boy, and the last thing the

drugged nameless girl heard as she spiraled down into the dark
was nothing but a dead collection of syllables, repeated over and
over from different throats.

Cami? Cami, wake up! Camille, say something! Get her out of
here—Cami, can you hear me?

It is comforting. There are soft beeps and boops as machines
monitor respiration and heart rate, a cold weight on her throat.
Her pulse is sluggish, murmuring instead of thundering. Slow
and sleepy, a healing whisper.

I am. I am.

"What do they say?" Ruby, hushed and subdued.

"The drugs, maybe." Nico. He sounded awful—hoarse, and
flatly furious. As if something had gone wrong but he couldn't
fix it, the dull rage of unwanted helplessness. "We don't know
what they dosed her with. Nobody left to ask, either—the
Family's scouring the city, but they can't find *him*. How's Ellie?"

"Dealing, I guess. Her stepmother's evil."

"Well, I tried." Nico sighed. There was a faint noise—was
he scrubbing his hands through his hair?

I am, her heart said, slowly. But she was cold, and she couldn't
move. *Who am I?*

"Yeah, well." Ruby, restraining herself mightily. She
sounded awful tired. "Thanks for, well. You know. Fixing
things."

"It's the only thing I'm any good at." Was he giving her that toothy, dangerous smile? "I just wish she'd wake up."

"Me too. Do you think . . . " But whatever Ruby was going to ask went unsaid. An electric brush touched numb skin, and the girl on the bed strained to wake, to move a finger, to *say* something.

Her body lay, inert, only the heart slowly pounding itself along and her lungs rising and falling.

Something changed in the air of the room. Two more breathing presences.

A low growl. "What. Is. *He*. Doing. Here?"

Ellen, deathly tired as well. "Leave him alone, Vultusino. He saved her."

"I told you, I'll—"

"I said leave him alone. You really want to piss me off? You've seen me work, *Family boy*. I'll charm your guts outside your skin and leave you screaming. Back *off.*"

Wow. The thought came swimming through syrup. *Ellie's pissed. Better not mess with her.*

"I think she means it," Ruby piped up, not very helpfully. But then, expecting *helpful* from Ruby was a couple steps too far.

"I—" A cough. A familiar voice. Male, and low. "I'm sorry."

"Oh, *sorry*." Nico outright snarled. "Sorry isn't *enough*, maggot. You lied your way into my house, you—"

"*I thought I was an orphan!*" Tor yelled, and her skin tingled with electricity again. Sounds—a thud, sliding against the floor, and Ellie's sharp shout.

"*Cut it the fuck out!* This is *not* going to help . . . wait. Wait just a second."

Silence.

"Ell?" Ruby, tentative as she never was. "What are you thinking?"

"What's that?"

Tor choked. "That's . . . what . . . I . . . came . . . for. To . . . take it . . . *off.*"

A snap. A sparking. A sting of pain, a numbness ripped away as a chain broke and the silver medallion, not quite round, a not-quite-star of apple pips carved onto its surface, tore free of her skin.

She screamed, thrashing wildly. It was Ruby who flung herself on top of the bed, her arms locking around her friend with preternatural strength. Ellen tossed the necklace aside with a cry of disgust and clambered on the bed too, the machines going crazy with whistles and beeps and sirens. The two girls held the third as she shook and sobbed and screamed, the cries taking shape as they burst free and raced around the room like white birds.

"*Mommy no Mommy no Mommy please Mommy noooooooo—*"

THIRTY-FIVE

THE THAW CAME EARLY, ALMOST-FREEZING RAIN SOAK-
ing into packed snow until roofs all over New Haven groaned
under the weight. Finally, the melt began in earnest, the bay and
the storm drains swollen. Some of Simmerside flooded and the
core birthed three minotaurs in a week.

The hospital kept her on an IV drip, bandaged and full of
antibiotics, charmers visiting every afternoon as well as nurses
and a doctor like a ferret, quick and sleek and deathly afraid of
the Vultusino name. Trig, his head bandaged, was often just outside the door; if he wasn't, another member of the security team
was. When she tried to apologize, he just shook his head, the
white gauze glaring. *It happens, Cami-girl. Don't fret. Get better.*

She slept a lot. When she woke, sometimes Ruby was there,
humming as she leafed through a magazine. Ellie was in Strep
Durance Vile, but Rube reported that the Strep wasn't hitting
her for the moment, since Nico had probably scared the stuffing

314

out of the woman. *I hear he threatened to get her Sigil yanked. She probably doesn't know if he can or can't, but why take the chance and piss off a Family? Here, look at this—they say it's the new fashion from the Continent. Ruffles. Can you believe it?*

And that was all Ruby would say. Fashion, school gossip, and brushing aside her apologies as well. *Don't be ridiculous. Listen, if I bring my French homework, you think you could give a girl a little help? Sister Mary B is really biting my ass.*

Other times, she would wake up knowing she had just missed Nico. She could sense his presence burning in the room's still-shivering air, as if he'd scorched it in passing. But he didn't wait for her to wake up.

He was busy, maybe.

Or angry.

The room was pretty, or at least inoffensive, a private hospital suite in pink and cream. Pills to swallow, dark restful sleep to fall into, watching the slant of light through the windows as it lengthened every day.

She was finally allowed to get up. Ruby brought her clothes—jeans that were a little too big, a T-shirt that hung on her like a scarecrow's jacket, socks and everything but shoes. "Left them in the car, dammit," Rube cheerfully announced, and tripped out the door to fetch them. The guard—a lanky young mere-human who looked like Trig—glanced in, dropped his gaze. He actually blushed whenever he had to speak to her.

"Ma'am? I gotta visit the little boy's."

She tried not to grin. Ruby found this *endlessly* hilarious. "Go ahead."

When the door opened again, she turned away from the window, her question and any amusement forgotten when she saw . . . him.

Tor hunched his shoulders. The bruises had faded, but their yellowgreen shadows lingered. His hair, shaken down over his face, was still defiantly messy and coal-black. He'd lost some weight, and his cheekbones stood out startlingly.

Just like hers. Just like his eyes, no longer black but bright starving blue.

"Your eyes," she blurted, and could have kicked herself. *Way to go. That's nice.*

He sucked his lips in for a moment, nodded. "Yeah. Surprised me too."

They regarded each other. The air was suddenly full of sharp surfaces, pressing against her skin. Each scar on her twitched, and she wondered if his were doing the same.

"I came to apologi—" he began, at the same moment she said, "I'm sorry, I—"

The silence returned.

He wet his lips with a quick nervous flicker of his tongue. "I came to apologize. I stole those presents for you, I didn't know. You've got to believe me. I wanted you to notice. I wanted you to . . . " He ran out of words, stared at her.

"I wondered about that." The words came easily now. Still, she used them slowly, carefully, since they could turn at any moment and knot up.

"I was eight when I ran away. I don't remember a lot, I was too busy staying alive. But she was sending little things Above, trying to find you. I stole the pin from a Twist pawner in Simmerside, and things started happening. I got hired. I saw you. It was like . . . " A helpless shrug, his hands spreading. "I can't say what it was like. Then . . . *she* . . . " He spread his hands. "She called me down there. Into the dark." The scuffed, battered leather jacket creaked a little as he moved. "I'm sorry."

"Okay." It probably wasn't the most helpful thing to say. "You . . . the mirror. You broke it." *You stabbed our mother in the mirror.* She couldn't bring herself to say it. If the Queen hadn't switched favorite-husbands, Cami might never have been *born.* And there was no way to know how their fathers came Below, what they had run from, who they had been.

"It was the only thing I could think of. Look, princess—"

"It's *Cami.*" It burst out, surprising her. As if she really owned the name. She crossed her arms, defensively. Healing scrapes were rough under her fingertips, and the scars were easily visible. It probably didn't matter—his were at least as bad as hers. Still, she felt the old prickle. "Don't call me princess, okay? It's insulting."

A ghost of a grin flashing under the healing bruises and scrapes. "No stutter."

So you noticed. Big deal. "So what are we gonna do? You, and me."

He nodded, like she'd just said something profound. "You're safe here. I've got to go. That's also why I came. I've got to . . . I killed a Queen. They won't let me live."

"There are others?" She went cold all over. *God, couldn't this just be over?*

"Stands to reason, doesn't it? She had to come from somewhere."

"*We* had to come from s-s-somewhere." *Dammit.*

"I just got a feeling. Plus, with your boyfriend around, it's not too safe here."

"Boyfriend?" *He means Nico.* "He's not . . . it's complicated. I don't even know if he's going to want me around. Ruby's grandmother, she said she could send me to another city. Maybe." *Ruby won't talk about it, but if I can get out to Woodsdowne, well, we'll see, won't we?* If Cami could walk halfway across the city with the White Queen's hounds searching for her, what else could she do?

What else would she *want*? Now that she was alive. It was a puzzle, and one she didn't know how to even *begin* piecing together.

"We c-could go together," she offered, tentatively. "You.

And me."

Tor grimaced slightly. "He'll want you around, princ—ah, Cami. Trust me on that." He took a step back, glanced at the door. "I should go."

Don't. If he left, would she ever find him again? Her scars ran with pain, and she saw his answering flinch.

He knew what it felt like, because his scars were hers too. "Tor—"

"I don't belong here, Cami. Not like you do. I wish . . . " But whatever he wished was left unsaid. He shook his hair down, the glower closing over his face like a mask. Who else would see the fear behind it?

Maybe nobody but her now.

"You b-belong." Her tongue tried to knot up, but Cami swallowed hard, and all of a sudden the words tumbled out. "You have *me*. We're the same." *We have the same scars.*

Is it enough? It is.

It has to be.

The silence between them was a thin ringing, but it was no longer stretched over a black abyss. Instead, it was a fragile, delicate thing, like a thin crystal wineglass tapping her teeth. Gentle, and careful, and something inside that quiet stretched between them. A hair-thin line, unbreakable and humming with force.

Blood always tells.

"Family." Very slowly and clearly, so he couldn't possibly

misunderstand. "Us. You have *m-me*."

Torin's scowl turned into a fleeting grin, and he winked, one blue, blue eye twitching closed for a half-second. "Likewise. Take care of yourself." And with that, he was gone out the door, his hair flicked back with an impatient toss of his head.

When Ruby came back, a pair of trainers dangling from their laces in one crimson-fingernailed hand, she sniffed deeply and gave Cami an odd look. But she didn't say anything, and Cami didn't volunteer.

It was, she reminded herself, a Personal Choice to speak, or not.

The distance inside her, where there used to be a huge black fear, was now just . . . silent.

Empty. A hiding place.

So some things had to stay secret. Even now.

The last of the ice had washed away on a flood of spring rain, and the trees were budding green. Every window on the house was painted gold with late-afternoon sunlight, and the limo pulled to a smooth stop. Trig and two of his scrubbed-clean new security boys were in a black car right behind them, a small fish swimming after the sleek black shark Chauncey piloted.

"Home, Miss Cami," he said, through the pane of lowered bulletproof glass. "And glad you're here, if I may say so."

Me too. She ducked her head, the habit of hiding a blush hard to shake. "Thanks."

It was Stevens, gaunt as ever, his hair threaded with rivers instead of trickles of gray now, who came down the stairs one by one and opened her door.

"Miss Cami," he said, and his hand was dry and warm, hard as a stick. "Welcome home."

She swallowed, hard. *Was* this home? Or were the dripping tunnels—flooded now, but cleansed by the Family, Trig had informed Ruby in a low tone when he thought Cami couldn't hear—really home? Would she be shipped off to a boarding school now, sent through the Waste on a sealed train, or—

"*Naughty!*" Marya shrilled, and Cami was enfolded in a bruising-hard hug, right there on the steps. The feywoman's cameo dug into her collarbone, and Cami realized with a start that she was taller now. "*Naughty* little thing! Worrying us to *death*, naughty little wandering thing, bad little *sidhe*! And so thin!"

"M-Marya!" It wasn't the stutter. Instead, it was half a sob, caught in her throat. The dam broke, and she was shaking as the feywoman bustled her into the house past a solemn assemblage of servants all gathered, scrubbed and shining, some of them looking uncomfortable, others looking relieved. The foyer was full, and the stairs too. The maids curtsied, some of them blushing and giggling, and Marya kept scolding Cami, calling her "naughty little *sidhe*" in between hugs so hard they threatened to steal what little breath she had left. She also produced a blinding-white handkerchief and wiped Cami's nose as if she was seven and messy again.

Marya all but hauled her up the stairs, since Cami's legs weren't quite functioning right. "I have a good dinner for you. All your favorites, and apple tart too."

It was hard work to suppress a shiver. "That sounds good," she said, carefully, and blinked away the tears.

The door to the white room had been repaired. So had the hole in the wall where Trig had hit. The broken mirror was gone. Her clothes hung in the closet, and it smelled of fresh lumber and a little bit of paint under the dust-scorch crackle of cleaning charms in an unoccupied room. The window seat was wide and white, and earlier rain still glimmered on the window, throwing little jewels of rainbow reflection onto the carpet.

Nico, straight and dark, sat on her bed. He stared at the wall, as if he just happened to be in here, no big deal, oh well. Absolutely rigid, and the tension boiling off him was a physical weight, colorless but heavy.

THIRTY-SIX

MARYA'S ARMS FELL AWAY. "I GO TO FINISH DINNER," she announced, rescuing the sodden handkerchief from Cami's limp fingers. "*You*, naughty little *sidhe*, do not run away again. Old Marya will come find you!"

I wish you had. "Okay, Marya. I p-promise."

Maybe the stutter wasn't *quite* gone. Or maybe her heart was just working so hard it shook the words up on their way out.

The feywoman retreated, muttering. Cami stood on nerveless legs. She counted to ten. Then counted again.

He didn't move. His hands lay on his knees, tense and cupped.

Finally, she set out across the pale carpet. Weaving a little, unsteady, but the doctor had said she was fine, and she'd wanted to get out of there. It smelled like antiseptic and pain, it was uncomfortable, and she'd wanted to be . . .

Well, *home.* And wherever they sent her, she would call this house *home*, if only inside her head.

"*Say* something." He almost *spat* it, still staring at the wall. His shoulders were shaking, his black T-shirt stretched tight against tense muscle.

She sank down next to him with a sigh. If he didn't want her there, he could move.

He doesn't look the same. Cami examined his profile, trying to figure out the difference. She dug for words, found them. "H–hi. I'm sorry."

That earned her a single, sidelong, sharp glance. "You? What the hell do *you* have to be sorry about? Mithrus *Christ*, Cami, why didn't you *tell* me? We were hunting them already. I would have gone down there with the boys, we would have washed all those stinking tunnels clean and scraped them with fire for good measure. How did you find out? Why did *you* try to fix it?"

Well, at least he's talking. She smoothed her jeans against her knees. The scabs were falling off, leaving fresh pink marks. The scars would fade into white. They always did. "I didn't know what was h–happening. To me. I thought . . . I thought I b–belonged *there*. Not here. I'm n–not . . . " Saying it now didn't seem quite so difficult. "I'm not Family, Nico."

"The *hell*." He leaned forward, inch by inch. It took a few seconds for her to realize he was curling up, defensively, and there were tear-tracks on his sharp, handsome face. "The *hell* you're not. I never wanted to hurt you. I never want you *scared*."

She slid her arm over his shoulder and he leaned into her. Her other arm came up, and she held him. Silent, the wracking shook him. He didn't let a single sound out, turning to iron as she stroked his hair. The lump in her throat made talking impossible.

That's what looks different. She finally figured it out.

The anger was gone. And without it, he was . . . this. She could almost wish him furious as usual, instead of hurt. Tor used a scowl to cover his scars; Nico used the anger to cover up the hurts on the inside.

And me? I can't cover anything up. Which way's worse? They're all bad. "It's okay," she whispered, finally. "It's all right." Over and over again, as if it would help.

Her arms ached after a while, and they ended up lying crosswise over her bed, tossed like shipwreck survivors. Slowly, so slowly, he turned back into flesh instead of cold metal and stone. Her head on his chest, she listened to the thumping under his ribs and the sough of his breath.

I am. I am. I am.

Everyone's heart, she realized, made the same sound. Except maybe the Queen's.

Is that why she had to eat everyone else's? A shudder slid through her, drained away. If there were other *Biel'y* . . .

The sunlight dimmed. Evening was rising. "Listen to me,"

he whispered, finally. "Are you listening?"

She nodded, her cheek moving against his T-shirt. *I am*, his heart murmured. *I am*, hers replied.

"I went to the Unbreathing." He stared at the ceiling. "I told them what to do. I'm the Vultusino now, and I told them if they didn't want a war, they would give me what I needed." His left hand came up. There was a red gleam trapped in it, and the fear was a sharp spike passing through her. Then it faded, and there was a dull red stone nestled in his palm. Smooth and lit with its own inner glow, nestling with a soft tremble like feathers against a Family hand. "Do you know what this is?"

Her breath caught in her throat. "N-Nico . . . "

"It's a heartstone. *My* heartstone, now. There's a price—when I go into Unbreathing you'll go too. And for the rest of our life, you'll have to Borrow, but only from me. It's . . . Cami . . . "

She reached up. Her trembling fingertip touched warm stone. It pulsed, sensing living, unFamily flesh.

I am. I am.

He took a deep breath. As if she could snatch the stone away from him. Or maybe she could take away something else. Something invisible that had been there between them since the first time she'd screamed *You're mean!* Or something that had built up, bit by bit, every time they shared their own private world, their country of two.

"You don't have to take it. You're Vultusino either way."

More words, spilling out haltingly as if he was the one who couldn't speak. "But it's yours. If you want it . . . Christ, Cami, I'm sorry. I'm a fuckup, I've always been, I know, I just—"

"Shhh." She covered his mouth. *A heartstone. A real heartstone.* His breath warmed her palm. After a moment, she took her hand away. "Book."

A long pause. Then, "Book." The word shook. Maybe his pulse was jolting everything he wanted to say around inside him, too.

"Candle." Clear and strong, no trace of hesitation or stutter.

"Candle," he whispered.

"Nico."

"Cami," he breathed.

Night filled the window with indigo, fresh rain rolling down, tapping and fingering the walls and roof. When Marya climbed the stairs to call them to dinner, the feywoman found them sleeping like children, her black hair spread in a wave and his profile calm and relaxed. Her bare arms were striped with fading scars, the marks vanishing slowly but surely.

Their linked hands rested against the girl's chest, Nico Vultusino curled into Cami's side, and between their interlaced fingers came a strong pulsing that winked out as Marya stepped into the room, the heartstone finishing its slow absorption into Camille Vultusino's flesh.

A heartstone is nothing but a heart freely given, a heart shared.

The light filled the room for a bare moment as another soul joined the Family. It was a clear glow, and it dyed the whiteness red.

Red as blood.

finis